THE AWAKENING

D1599846

The Awakening

DANA CLAIRE

Chamberlain Publishing House

To my father, this book is dedicated to you. From the moment I heard you say, "Okay, when is book two coming out" to the moment I wrote "The End," I knew I typed this story at the intense pace I did because of your encouragement and constant reminders you needed to know what happened to Bea and Cash. Thank you for loving my characters as much as I do. And thank you for loving me!

Chapter One

Beatrice

The government called me a weapon, a masterfully planned defense to save Earth. What they didn't plan was for me to question my existence. I was a Blood-Light. The first of my kind. Born without a source. Kidnapped by my own mother, who had placed an alien energy source inside my chest cavity. I would be responsible for billions of human lives. My purpose was to connect to my opposing energy source, my current alien bodyguard-boyfriend, Cash Kingston. Our opposing energy sources were the answer to preventing the extinction of two planets—both Earth and Ferro.

The government called me a weapon. My mother called me a gift. I called it a forced fate.

The metal elevator doors closed. An unnervingly quiet Cash stared in the wake of the foyer lights. I slid closer to him. My fingertips teased the pulse of energy formed by the opposing energy sources running between us as they grazed his palm. Inside, it was cold and brightly lit. The metal doors were lined with bolts like stitching on the hem of a shirt. Instead of going up, we descended.

Cash threaded his hand in mine and gave it a gentle squeeze. My heart raced in response. In the last week, Cash had shown more affection and attention than his typical brooding self would normally express. My kidnapping—yeah, people were after me, hence the bodyguard—had scared us both. We might not have vocally acknowledged there was an "us," but it wasn't something I questioned anymore, either.

"I wish you would tell me who we are going to see," I breathed. I had asked several times in the car on the way to New Jersey from Cartwright, Pennsylvania. Cash had conveniently ignored my question and continued to hum to the car radio. The rest of our newly established "save the planet" team—Tasha, Sammie, Mark, Paul, and my dad—had flown to California yesterday. But Cash insisted we would meet them there, declaring we had something to do together. Alone. Everyone, including my dad, opposed splitting up. Cash had brushed off their disapproval. While I was still in the hospital for minor injuries, he packed a suitcase for me with who-knows-what and threw us both into the yellow Charger Hellcat. The car had belonged to Kathleen Butler, an innocent human killed for being in the wrong place at the wrong time, and with my poor car out of commission, it would have to do.

Being in that car only reminded me of what we had all gone through. The loss. The pain. The sadness. In the last several months, I had learned more than anyone could be prepared to learn in a lifetime, let alone the span of a few weeks. My mother and father had worked for the DOAA—the Department of Alien Affairs—a worldwide organization of secret agents. Surprising even her husband—the man who had raised me, the man I called

Dad—my mother had carried on an affair with a Ferroean that had resulted in my planned birth. Then, when I was seventeen years old, she not only implanted an alien energy source inside me but also erased my memories of my last week with her. It took making physical contact with the energy source that opposed mine to release those memories, revealing to us all that my birth father was Gabe Sayor, leader of the Ferroean Rebellion, of all things. I even remembered my last moments with Seraphina Laylan, the alien whose source I now held inside my chest before she fell into a deathlike coma.

Now I was wanted by the DOAA and the Ferro Council, and I was on the run with Cash and his team of Ferroean Guardians, on our way to bring Seraphina back to consciousness with some kind of procedure called an "Awakening." It's all pretty heavy stuff to handle. Especially for a high school senior whose biggest obstacle six months ago had been beating my latest run time in track. I pushed away the emotions bubbling inside my throat like soda when I drank it too fast and focused back on Cash.

"I assume this isn't a friendly visit then. Should I be worried?" I squeezed his hand, hoping for a response.

Cash wouldn't even glance my way. Instead, his thumb idly ran over my knuckles. I huffed in frustration. So maybe he was more touchy-feely than normal, but he was still the same Cash: stubborn and tight-lipped as hell.

The elevator shook as it went from "L" for lobby to eleven with no numbers listed in between. I reached for the walls to keep my balance as we hit the bottom floor with a little too much momentum. Cash steadied me, countering my sway with a pull toward him. There's something about an elevator that starts on the top floor and goes down that was just unnerving.

The doors opened and I immediately felt a wave of familiarity. I couldn't pinpoint it, but its presence was palpable. We stepped inside in unison. It was a one-floor studio apartment designed like a New York City loft, with brick walls, high ceilings, exposed lighting infrastructure, and modern furniture—*real* modern. Everything was white: chairs, tables, countertops, floor. Even the bed to the far-off right side was all white. And it was floating. Okay, weird. The entrance and white-and-grey-marbled breakfast nook were illuminated with recessed track lighting, but the rest of the place was dim, no windows or natural lighting. It smelled of cedarwood and sage, evoking something strangely familiar, like a distant memory nagging at my senses.

Out of the darkness, a tall, handsome man walked toward us. His caramel-brown hair was laced with strawberry-blond strands. It was flawlessly styled, flowing in a wave like a movie star. His jeans fit perfectly to his body and his white button-down and cognac dress shoes looked like he jumped out of a J.Crew catalog. Unlike a professional model, his face was pale and chalky, and his navy-blue eyes were outlined with dark circles. The combination produced a tired face that looked unnatural to his seemingly well-put-together look. His shoulders were broad and sculpted, reminding me of Cash's, but his torso was longer. In fact, there were definite similarities between the two that couldn't be ignored, particularly in his high cheekbones and chiseled jaw.

Movie Star's eyes narrowed in Cash's direction. It was like I didn't even exist.

"I'm not surprised to see you," he said. The tips of his lips slightly curled at the end of his words. "What took so long?"

I tilted my head— the stranger had expected us, well, at least Cash.

"Options in allies these days are slim," Cash responded, his voice void of emotion. He squeezed my hand silently, letting me know it was ok, and then stepped a foot closer to the man in front of us. I moved a half a step with him. "I'm not saying I believe you, but I don't trust anyone outside of my team anymore."

The man threw his head back and laughed. "You trust me?"

Cash guffawed mockingly. "I'll never trust you." His jaw tightened. Heat radiated off his body, yet a chill ran up my spine. Nothing about their banter was settling. "Is that clear?"

"Crystal." The man rolled his eyes. "Can't wait to hear what happened. Learn anything new, anything interesting?" He rubbed his hands together eagerly, still ignoring my presence. "Do tell. Don't leave anything out. I love a good story, especially one that ends with you at my doorstep. Begging for help, no less."

"I'm not here begging," Cash said, releasing some of his facial tension but still holding onto our threaded fingers.

"Feels like you're begging. Or maybe you're groveling. Can I get a written grovel? Is that even a human thing?" He gazed up to the right as if he was contemplating his own idea.

"I'd beg for you to let me speak at this point." Cash growled. A slight giggle slipped through my lips.

Palm facing the ceiling, the stranger waved his hand for Cash to continue.

"Gertrude is dead. Grouper is dead. Jon and Phil, also dead," Cash deadpanned.

"Jon and Phil don't surprise me, and they had it coming to them, such little weasels playing sides whenever it suited them. They are on Team Ferro, they aren't on Team Ferro. It's like the flower humans pull petals off of. She loves me, she loves me not, she loves me...I mean, how can a flower really tell you that? Humans are very odd."

Cash looked back at me, shaking his head. Sharing his thoughts into my mind, he spoke, *The only thing odd is him. Is this as painful for you as me?* My smile reached my ears, hearing Cash's teasing voice in my head. I couldn't tell if *I* liked this strange guy or if he was annoying, but I'm confident Cash felt the latter.

"Can you focus?" Cash burst out, turning his attention back around. The man pretended to zipper his lips and throw away the key. "If it was only that simple," Cash mumbled. "As I was saying, Gertrude kidnapped Beatrice and was going to kill her. Grouper tried to stop her. She killed him. And I killed her for even thinking about killing Beatrice and taking her energy source."

The strange man's face tensed. His gaze traveled from Cash and found me for the first time. Examining me from head to toe, he stopped for a brief moment on my hand interlocked with Cash's. In that second, everything changed. His initial playfulness turned cold and stifled. His irises started swirling with color. I'd seen this before in Cash when he'd struggled with intense emotions. Ferroeans' source fluctuated with power they couldn't always control, and their eyes were always a window to what was going on inside of them.

"Ashton?" Cash questioned, saying his name for the first time. Ashton's lips thinned and his shoulders rose. Noticing the change in demeanor as well, Cash asked again, "Ashton, what's wrong?"

It all happened so fast. His right hand slid behind his back and then whipped out in front, cradling a pistol. He aimed it at Cash, his pointer finger resting on the trigger. But his gaze never left me. His eyes were wild, more active than I've ever seen a Ferroean's before. Purples, reds, greens, and oranges swirled like a coiled-up snake.

Ashton sighed, loudly. "You'll never understand what I know, and why I have done the things I have done, and perhaps you never will." His bizarre words were directed at Cash, but his eyes stayed glued on me.

My breath hitched in my throat. Why was he using a gun against Cash? A bullet would be a mild inconvenience to a fellow Ferroean, at best. Some of my mother's last words echoed in my head, unbidden: *Four cuts, each wrist and ankle. That's how you kill them.* Only a thermo dagger made from the ferrous metals of their home planet could fatally pierce his alien skin. Didn't he know Cash was a Ferroean? Didn't he know a gun wasn't lethal against an alien? Questions barreled through my panicked mind.

"Has this place gotten to your head? This is ridiculous," Cash thundered. It was another important question. He shook his head as if this was a giant waste of time, echoing my own thoughts. "Shoot me a hundred times. It won't even wound me, you idiot!" Despite his bravado, his grip on my hand grew tighter, sprouting a sliver of concern. Did Ashton know something we didn't?

Ashton ignored the admonishments and glared at me with a wild expression. It reminded me of the day I first met

Cash and couldn't understand his cold, hard stare. Did this stranger realize I possessed the unique source that opposed the one in Cash, the way Cash himself did during our first encounter? Or did this look mean something else?

"Cash." I breathed the word with a hint of warning, my eyes never leaving the barrel of the gun. Something felt wrong. Very wrong. I sidled closer to him, and our shoulders touched. The heat was radiating off him like steam from a kettle. Our sources reacted instantly from the proximity and a shock coursed through my chest.

"You're being dramatic, Ash," Cash said, pulling me ever so slightly behind him. "And you are scaring her to death"—he nodded to me—"for no reason."

"I'm not going to shoot you, Cash." Slowly, Ashton lowered his arm, the gun pointed downward to the ground. I exhaled a deep breath I didn't even realize I was holding back. I could visibly see Cash's shoulders begin to loosen from its initial stiff posture. As he slowly turned back toward me to check on my state of being, the unimaginable happened. The gun's barrel shifted. I could see right down the opening. The loud rupture of the bullet rang in my ear. Not a beat later, it ripped through my shirt and tore my skin apart. I felt the soul-piercing sting in my chest as the bullet pierced my ribcage. Before I could scream, I crashed to the floor, taking Cash down with me.

This stranger hadn't shot Cash. He had shot me.

Chapter Two

Beatrice

The bones in my ribcage splintered as the bullet rocketed through my upper body. The pain erupted like a fire in my core, and then everything went numb as my knees gave out. I slumped to the floor, a gargled scream escaping my throat. The ringing in my ears muffled the thunderous roars of Cash spewing threats at my unexpected would-be assassin. I tasted copper as my mouth filled with warm blood.

I felt pressure against my chest, and was vaguely aware of Cash kneeling beside me, desperately trying to stop the flood of red blood and yellow ichor. The viscous liquids mixed and pooled in between his fingers and ran down onto the pristine tiled floor. I coughed weakly as I tried to swallow away the metallic tang that coated my throat, and I heard myself whimper, but the pain felt far away. *I must be in shock.*

"I swear to the Council, I'm going to kill you, Ashton." Cash's voice lowered to a derisive growl as he glared at the stranger. To me, Cash's voice rang gently in my head, *You'll be ok, I've got you.* One hand stayed pressed into my chest as the other reached back to pull his thermo dagger from his ankle sheath. I could already feel an increase in heat from the slight pressure of his fingertips as they glowed with his kind's healing white light. He released the pressure from the gaping wound for only a split second, but with it a new wave of agony shook me to the core. Ripped from my numb haven of shock, I cried out as the blood flooded faster and faster through my human veins, adrenalin spiking like fireworks. Through the spots dotting my vision, I saw Cash slice his wrist with the blade of the Ferroean dagger. The room was doused with bright white light while yellow ichor dripped from his arm. He held his wrist to my mouth.

"Feed." His command echoed both in my ears and my mind.

Without hesitation, I pressed my lips to his wrist and drank in the vital energy of his opposing source. It was the first time I had ever fed, but I'd heard of the technique used between Ferroeans when one was severely injured. Cash had told me that the method wasn't used often because of its crippling effect on the donor. For most injuries, Ferroeans could simply use their healing touch to restore the wound.

The sticky substance dripped down the back of my throat and warmed my cooling insides. Heat radiated off Cash's skin, warming my face as I pulled against his pulse with my lips. Although tasteless, it reminded me of thick syrup. The source that flowed through Cash's veins in place of blood stuck to my tongue and the top of my mouth. I swallowed feverishly to get as much healing power as I could. My body craved the strength; a strange yet addicting feeling washed over me, reminding me of all the campy vampire shows Darla and I used to binge-watch on my days off from track practice. The thought of my best friend and my favorite sport pulled at my heart. Cash retracted his arm, snapping my focus back to the present and leaving me with a sense of loss. He dabbed at the cut with the end of his shirt, cleaning up the residue left from my lips. My clothing still felt warm and wet as it clung to me, but the fountains of blood and ichor from my chest were stanched. My vision cleared along with the pain, but my head swam with a jumble of confusing thoughts. Why the hell did this stranger shoot me? Nothing about him appeared to be dangerous, and yet the second he scanned my body, I knew something was terribly wrong.

"Why? Why would he shoot me?" My breathing normalized as the source mended my wounds, healing the trauma to my heart and lungs. My gaze traveled to the stranger across the room. He appeared callous and unfazed as he took a seat in a chair with wheels, rolling back and forth. The plastic groaned against the tiles.

"I had to be sure," he replied nonchalantly. "You're definitely her. Hello, Blood-Light. Hello, prophecy." His voice had a singsong quality. "Hello, planet-saving time." And with that he pushed his feet against the floor, sending him into a spin on his chair. I nearly expected him to scream out *weeeee* as he continued around and around.

The absurdity of our situation mounted, and a hot line of anger sliced through my senses. "Who is he?" I whispered to Cash, my confusion written across my face. He seemed unhinged and nothing but trouble. "Any chance I can shoot him back?"

Cash was mad—furious this guy had shot me—but somehow, he managed to chuckled slightly at my comment. Whoever this stranger was, he had a couple of screws loose, that's for sure, but Cash's reaction to him was conflicted.

I couldn't imagine what kind of help he could offer but I knew Cash. If we were here, this guy must be important. Somehow.

The source I'd consumed from Cash continued to heal my body even after I stopped feeding. It was an odd sensation. My strength came back stronger than ever, like I had a double-shot espresso injected directly into my bloodstream. I felt restless. I didn't want to sit still. I was on a high from the burst of energy and if this hadn't been such a strange situation, I'd have had a lot of questions for Cash about what I was feeling.

Instead, I looked up at my bodyguard-slash-boyfriend as he lifted me into his arms. His facial muscles seemed strained from the effort, which normally would have been an easy action with his innate superior strength. My head rested against his chest, and the gentle rhythm of his familiar source soothed me and radiated energy between us. My feet dangled in the air as he took me over to the couch and cautiously lowered me onto the sofa. My butt sank into the space between the white fluffy cushions.

How do you know him? I mentally projected the question to Cash as I pushed myself into an upright position, using one of the decorative pillows to elevate my head.

"He's my brother," Cash growled aloud, giving the other man a sidelong glare. He ran his hand through his hair in frustration, then looked back down to me, his eyes gentle as they met mine. Ignoring the statement he just made, he answered my mental questions from earlier. "Feeding will heal your body faster than any other method of treatment. It's normal to have a strange surge of energy after digesting someone else's source." He swept the little hairs that had stuck to my forehead off to the side with his fingers and pressed his lips to my skin in their wake. "I couldn't take the chance that the source inside of you would be enough to heal your human side on its own. You may feel funny for a while, but it'll wear off." His eyes narrowed as he looked me over. Concern in his voice, he asked, "Is the pain better?"

Feeling like I was in shock all over again, I looked up at Cash in confusion. Grouper had once told me Cash had a brother, but I hadn't believed him. Not until now. *Cash had a brother.* I opened my mouth to voice the question, but I was too late. Cash had already turned, launching himself at the stranger he'd called Ashton.

Chapter Three

Cash

Three seconds. That's all it took for me to register Bea was going to be okay before I turned on Ashton. I was going to do damage. It took everything I had to let myself come here for help. Out of everyone, I turned to Ashton—to my brother. He was the one whose betrayal cut deepest, but I came here anyway, hoping he'd be helpful. Then within moments of being in his presence, he proved himself once again as a traitor.

"By the Council, I'm gonna kill you." I was already in the air when I growled at Ashton, closing the distance between us with a lunge. He ducked his head forward and drove himself into my body. Having no time to avoid him, we tumbled to the ground, taking one of his barstools from the kitchen nook down with us. The white wooden legs broke and scattered splinters across the floor tiles. I rolled on top of him, using the weight of my body to pin him down. I may not have had a weight advantage on my brother, but I was denser and better trained. My elbow drew back past my ear, but before I could launch my intended punch straight into that asshat's face, he caught my fist in the palm of his hand. The shifting force took me by surprise, throwing me backward. I knew I was weak from allowing Beatrice to feed from my energy source, but his strength surpassed what I remembered. When we were young and practiced sparring in the Guard's Program back on Ferro, Ashton and I were usually well-matched blow for blow.

Then I grew up. The elders, in their wisdom, started training me exclusively with Sera, my opposing energy source and, at the time, my girlfriend. As our powers started to develop, I grew too formidable to safely spar with anyone but her, so the program leads restricted my practice to defensive fighting only. Harnessing the power of our opposing energy sources pretty much made me invincible. The year before we went to Earth, I took over the Guard's Program and was expected to resume that position after we came back. Then we found Beatrice. As a Blood-Light holding what had once been Sera's energy source inside of her, her unique genetic makeup made her not only my ultimate weakness, but a danger to all Ferroeans. She was a weapon.

Distracted by my own thoughts, Ashton managed to get on top of me, straddling my midsection as he swung his fists into my face. I twisted my head to the side to avoid his left hand, but he followed with his right, landing a solid blow against my jaw with an unsettling crack. My jaw may have been dislocated, but disbelief hit me harder than his fist. He shouldn't have even come close to striking me. I grabbed him by the throat and tossed him off to the side. I stood, popping my lower jaw back in place as I cracked my neck from side to side. "Learn some new tricks," I sneered as he jumped up to match my combat stance.

"Stop it!" Bea protested in the background. I couldn't see her behind me but I'm sure her face had that cute pout in full effect. She had a way of glaring at me that I found rather adorable, but I was never going to admit that.

"Ah, you're intrigued with my newfound prison strength, huh?" Ashton winked as we circled one another. "What can I say? I've been eating spinach just like that disproportioned human with the anchor tattoo and pipe. Kinda shocked a cartoon has a man smoking tobacco. Say no to drugs, kids." His strength may have changed, but he was still full of obnoxious asides.

We each kept our guard up, circling and keeping our distance from one another. "Do you even know what you are talking about? Or are you just talking?" I opened and closed my mouth. The dislocation had been painful, but no permanent damage. "I guess since you've had nothing but time, you decided to research idiotic Earth television between workout sessions. That makes sense since you've been locked up for almost—how many years was it? Oh right. Four years." I spat, accentuating the number with derision.

"Four?" Ashton questioned, cocking his head to one side in confusion. Time on Earth and Ferro functioned rather differently. I never fully understood it the way our sister did, but for every year spent on Earth, four years passed on Ferro. The time dilation was theorized to be due to the proximity of Ferro to a black hole, as well as a number of other factors like differences in gravity and planet rotation. However it worked, hiding Ashton on Earth helped us keep him hidden. Four Ferroean years had passed since his treason on Ferro, while he experienced only a year of isolation in this safehouse on Earth. The thing was, we'd always kept the location of Ashton's prison a secret, even from him. All he knew was it would be a clandestine location where I could contact King Zane and never be tracked or recorded. It was how I told Zane about Beatrice Walker, the human who possessed the opposing source that was once Sera's.

Using his query as an opening, I swung a roundhouse kick to his dumbfounded face. Ashton stumbled backward into the other cheap barstool, falling to the ground on top of its shattered frame. The floor around us was covered in cheap, white-painted wood.

"Cash, I'm serious. Stop it," Bea begged from her position on the couch behind me. "Why don't we all sit down and talk about this? You're, umm... family?" Her voice lifted into a question on the last word, and I could hear the unease beneath it. I never told Bea Tasha, my twin sister, and I had a brother. Technically, my sister didn't even know he was still alive, and shame was enough to keep her silent on the matter. Both she and our mother believed Ashton was killed for treason against the King of Ferro—our father. My mother hadn't spoken to my father, or me, for that matter, since Ashton's judgment day. And although my sister never held me responsible, she never truly understood why I didn't fight more to save him.

My father came home after Ashton's hearing and cornered me in my bedroom, where I was far off in my head about my brother's pending death. When he told me he would spare Ashton's life but in order to do this we had to never tell a soul he was still alive, I leaped at the chance to save him without ever thinking about the consequences or the details of that secret. Father's exact words: "For his safety, Captain Cash, it must be done. He must forever be concealed. You must pledge your source to this classified information." I couldn't kill my big brother or let another Council member do it behind my father's back, so I murdered my honesty instead and lied to my family as per my father instruction, per the king's request, and sent my brother to a different type of fatality, a prison of isolation.

"Sounds like your girlfriend's scared I might beat you up," Ashton joked, bringing me back to the present. I was caught off guard. The last person I'd called my girlfriend was Seraphina, and she was lying on a cold metal table at the DOAA, barely existing because of my actions. Beatrice and I hadn't named what was going on between us, but I wasn't worthy of granting someone that title again. And yet, here I was having so many stupid emotions for a Blood-Light. A Blood-Light that I wanted to kiss on an hourly basis.

"She's not my girlfriend." I sounded like a petulant child, and I hated it.

"Oh," Ashton said, raising one brow to his stupid perfect hairline. He glanced at Beatrice. "Have you told her that? I didn't realize you haven't had the 'talk.' I mean I shot her to prove..." That's all I had to hear to be reminded he shot Beatrice and the rage inside of me took over. I dashed forward, grabbed his head in my hands and thrust it down into my knee. Beatrice screamed at the shocking display of violence, but I ignored her. He tried to kill Beatrice. He broke up our family. He chose the Rebellion over the Council. I would never forgive him. I repeated the brutal action two more times until I heard the human crack of bones in his nose. Wetness coated my jeans as I saw the blood cascade toward the floor.

Impossible.

I stepped back, shaken to the core. How could my Ferroean brother break his nose? Sure, we could bleed slightly on Earth due to the assimilation process needed to live among humans, but this much blood? Shattered bone? Not possible. Ferroeans may be similar to humans in many ways, but our "flesh and blood" is a combination of liquid metal alloy and our energy source that we call plasma. Plasma is mutable and can harden when needed, but we have no skeletal structure. There are no bones to break in anyone born on Ferro.

Ashton dropped to a sitting position on the ground. He wiped his face with his sleeve and gave a smile I could almost describe as sympathetic. "Surprise."

Chapter Four

Ashton

The pinched skin on my brother's face was exactly what I had been afraid of all these years. I wasn't exactly who Cash thought I was. I had never intended to lie to him, but Father had other plans—he always had other plans, and those were never in line with the truth.

"How did your nose break?" Cash asked. His hands balled into fists. I hoped his curiosity outweighed his desire to slug me again. "How?" he roared. His voice shook the brick walls and the lights flickered in my kitchenette. Okay, not a great sign. I could see the anger swirling in his Ferroean eyes. Blues and greens churned around his pupils. His biceps danced as he clenched and unclenched his knuckles by his sides. The muscles along his forearm pulsed.

"Cash." The brown-haired girl from the couch was now standing. Her voice held warning for my brother. Looked like she knew his temper well. "Do not attack him again," she said with more force than I expected. The pink in her cheeks had returned.

Beatrice Walker, Sayor's daughter, was real. The elder's prophecy was true, at least the part about her anyway:

Someday a Blood-Light born without a source will empower an opposing source and save Earth.

The other stuff was still up in the air as far as I was concerned, but this Blood-Light born without a Ferroean energy source was the real deal. Her chest cavity melted the bullet in half the time it should have. Even with the help of Cash's powers healing her, she bounced back quicker than I expected. The only sign she was even shot was her blood-soaked t-shirt. My eyes dropped to her Ferroean necklace on her chest and a wave of embarrassment hit me as her body reacted to the cold, wet cloth. I looked back up and into her slitted hazel eyes. She was pissed. Okay, not my best first impression but hopefully she could forgive me one day.

Cash caught the interaction and moved toward her. He puffed his chest out like some kind of Earth primate, partially blocking her from me. "Explain," he growled as he threaded his hand in hers.

I waved at them, motioning to their locked fingers. "I should say the same about you two. We are a couple, they hold hands. We aren't a couple, they aren't holding hands. We are a couple but haven't had the talk, let me try and hold her hand again." I paused, watching my brother's face turn from pleasantly pink to fire engine red. Well, at least I was having fun. "Want to indulge me with an explanation? I'm still your older brother. What are your intentions with this Blood-Light, young man?"

Beatrice dropped Cash's hand. Oh, dear brother, the she's-not-my-girlfriend comment just landed you in the doghouse. But how could this girl not see, Cash was already in love with...and that's when it hit me. Cash loved Beatrice. I didn't realize what I saw when I originally saw it. Sure,

I was angry when I saw their interlocked hands but not because they were holding hands but because I saw my brother trusting her before I knew she was the real thing. My brother's been used all these years by my father, and I wasn't going to let another do the same. I hadn't realized...Oh my Council. When he found out the truth, my brother would be devastated. I would not tell him she and I were destined to—

Cash broke my internal thought and with arms crossed against his chest, he said, "I don't have to explain myself, but the alien brother who should have the source running through his veins and mysteriously started to bleed and break like a human because I kneed him in the face multiple times might want to explain how that is possible."

I walked over to the kitchen and grabbed a towel. I held it under the sink, letting cold water soak the fibers as I started to explain "Beatrice isn't the only Blood-Light in this dreadful prison right now." I watched as my baby bro's face filled with emotion: anger, sadness, distrust, pain...it was all there. I wrung the towel out and held it to my face, cleaning the blood off from our spat. "I'm still your brother." I hoped he knew that. I loved him. I always would, no matter how he felt about me.

"Are you?" His tone was sharp and pointed.

I took a deep breath in, clenched my nose. As I exhaled, I snapped my nose back into place. I winced from the mild pain. "You know I look just like Mom. All the Council members used to say we were twins. Totally pissed Tasha off when they did," I reminded him. Aside from the obvious, my mother and I had every facial feature in common. We had the same flowy hair and perfect lip-to-teeth-ratio smile. I was what Earth called a "pretty boy," or so I've been told.

"I was born with a source, but my dad was human. Just like Beatrice's mother was."

Cash advanced toward me, violence swirling in his eyes, but Beatrice tugged on his arm. I heard her speak in a low voice. "Let him finish. I want to hear this."

I wiped my chin and neck, feeling the blood peel off like paint. I threw the soiled towel onto the kitchen table, a white snowball covered in candy apple red. Or was it fire engine red? Was there a difference? "Mom, well, she was kinda a wild child before she got all uptight and stuffy. I'm pretty sure Dad had a lot to do with that behavior shift." I rolled my eyes at the mention of the great and powerful King of Ferro. Our mother was quiet, played by the rules, and never spoke out of turn. She was very much like Tasha, but unlike Tasha she was also manipulative, conniving, and phony. She hadn't always been like that. I wish I had the pleasure of meeting who she used to be. She sounded like someone I would have liked. "Mom and Dad had their marriage pre-arranged by our grandparents as children. Neither of them had a choice in their futures." I unbuttoned my ruined shirt and tossed it next to the towel.

I turned toward the closet by the elevator doors and slid one side open. The wood groaned against the metal slider. I grabbed another white button-down. I have over a hundred of them. Jeans were a luxury my mother and father let me keep. Sometimes for our birthdays we would receive Earth gifts. My request was always blue jeans.

I continued. "Mom traveled with our grandparents to Earth for a mission and had a one-night stand with a human. Dad said he thinks it was an act of rebellion against her parents. It's not like Mom ever told me the story—like she'd fess up to doing the nasty with a *human*." I rolled my eyes, dismissing the notion. "What a hypocrite that woman was! Apparently, she didn't realize she was pregnant until she was back on Ferro. Mom and Dad were married two months later. The woman didn't even have the mettle to admit I wasn't Dad's kid, but he's no dummy. He figured out the math." I shook my head at the old frustration. "He knew the whole time and never called her out on her crap."

"You're telling me King Zane let our mother get away with that kind of betrayal? I call bullshit," Cash barked. His eyes burned with derision, but what else was new.

I glared back at my brother. He was still such a fool when it came to the King. "And you're telling me you think your father would ever admit he'd been cheated on? That his firstborn wasn't even his, let alone half human? What would the Council think? His peers and retainers?" I challenged Cash, trying to get through his thick head. "Come on, brother. You are smarter than that. Far too smart to have such blind faith in a despot like Zane. He'd rather hide me and protect our mother's lie than look weak or like some kind of wounded victim."

For a moment, I thought Cash might consider my words, but then his temper returned. "Why did Dad even tell YOU then?"

"Great question. So glad you asked, brother! I was just getting to that part. It's like you can read minds." I laughed at my own joke. My brother wasn't as amused. "Did you know there are Blood-Lights roaming Ferro that don't even know they are Blood-Lights? Probably hundreds of us, maybe thousands!" I crossed my arms over my chest, needling him with the truth.

Cash shook his head. His lips pursed and his voice lowered to a cold calm. "How is that even possible?"

"It's very easily understood, actually. Most Blood-Lights, or half Ferroean, half human"—I made eye contact with the girl, as if to clarify for her—"were born with their own source, just like anyone else on Ferro. And when we live on Ferro, we are strong enough for our powers to work just like any full-blooded individual. It makes it incredibly hard to detect our humanity. But place a Blood-Light in other ecosystems—ones without the iron-rich core of Ferro, like Earth here—and our human side becomes dominant and weakens our source. I can feel an immediate shift in my body, but I don't need any Earth scientist to assimilate me to fit in. My veins fill with blood as I enter this atmosphere and some of my Ferroean alloy hardens into human bone. I basically grow a skeletal structure at the expense of some of my source. There's a reason Dad never let me go to Earth, but when I traveled with him for a planetary conference that he couldn't get me out of, I couldn't help but realize something was different about me. Stuck, he told me the truth. He had no choice. I couldn't be assimilated."

I watched Beatrice watching me. Her eyes traveled back and forth and up and down as if she was examining every inch to see if we had any similarities. I felt their heat as if she were touching me. Beatrice's eyes met mine and her cheeks blushed deep pink.

"Anything you like?" I asked as I cocked my head to the side and gave her a wink.

Cash's gaze toggled between us, his eyes narrowing. "Knock it off," he snapped. "She has no interest in you. You just shot her, for Council's sake."

"I hear she's single," I quipped. Okay, so maybe that was too far of a tease at my brother's expense but watching Cash squirm was still my favorite form of entertainment.

Cash leaned forward and his body tensed. He looked like he was about to come at me again. Instead, Beatrice jumped in front of him, her hand pressed firmly to his chest. "Seriously. That's enough, knock it off." She pushed him back, this time with two hands, and moved him several inches backward until his calves were against the couch.

Impressive Blood-Light!

She continued, pointedly ignoring me. "I may not be your girlfriend, but I'm not some silly kid either. We don't need a title to define us. What we need is answers. Isn't that why we came here? Or did you really come here so I could get shot, prove I'm a Blood-Light, find out I'm not the only Blood-Light you know"—she turned around and glared at me now—"and then continue to roll around on the floor with your brother? Until what?" Cash attempted to roll his eyes but stopped when Beatrice grabbed his face with both hands. "You thought he could help. We need help. We don't have time for your family drama, or you won't have any family left to argue with, including me. We will all be dead. Put a cork in the anger and tell him why we're here."

Wow. This Blood-Light was crushing it with logic. Move over, Tasha, there's a new equalizer in town. I walked over to my dresser drawer and pulled out a stark white t-shirt. It was the softest one I had, worn by me for years on cold nights when it was too chilly to go shirtless. "Would you like a change of clothes?" I offered it to Beatrice, holding up my shirt for her to see. I hoped she would take the genuine peace offering.

She and Cash spoke at the same time, her "Yes, thank you," drowned out by Cash's, "No, she wouldn't."

THE AWAKENING ~ 27

My gaze toggled back and forth, landing on Beatrice. I threw her the shirt and was glad to see her catch it before Cash could intercept.

"You are not wearing that," Cash sulked, his arms crossed over his chest.

Beatrice threw her hands into the sky, the shirt waving like a flag as she swung her hands in exaggerated distress. "Here we go again, telling me what I can and can't wear. It's like you are stuck in the 1950s or something. I'm an independent woman and if I want to wear your brother's clothes every day, all day, I will." She pivoted on her heels, walked to the bathroom door, and slammed it both on my brother and the conversation.

"Wow. I think she and Sera would get along nicely." Her name slipped out of my mouth before I could think better of it. I completely forgot about her. If Beatrice was the Blood-Light with Cash's opposing source and she was wearing Sera's source-monitoring necklace, what happened to Sera's shell? What happened to Sera? "Is she really...dead?"

Cash ground his teeth so hard, I thought he'd have broken a tooth. Through gritted tusks, he said, "She's alive. She needs an Awakening."

Chapter Five

Beatrice

We thought the safe house would be booby-trapped but all it needed was Cash's thumbprint to get us into the elevator and out the front door. We exited the lobby, waiting for it to blow up from an explosion or errant trip wire, but nothing happened. Poor Ashton could have been released months ago, back when Cash visited in order to elicit his father's help through the safe house's communication wall. But that would have required Cash giving his brother a chance.

Brother. The information seemed so shocking just a few moments ago. Now, compared to everything else I've learned in the last few months, I'd easily assimilated the information as fact.

Cash loaded Ashton's things in the trunk and then motioned for him to take the back seat. Ashton jumped in like a puppy, a rather large golden retriever-like puppy, and didn't even flinch when Cash locked the doors. His face was planted up against the window, watching the birds and the clouds, lost in thought.

I started to walk to the passenger's side when Cash reached for my hand and pulled me back, drawing my body flush to his. His hand stretched around my waist and held onto my lower back. The touch sent shivers up my spine, reaching both my source and my heart. Electricity pulsed to my core.

"Are you ok?" He tilted his head, touching his forehead to mine. The buzz in my chest returned like a radio frequency picking up a signal.

"I'm fine," I lied.

"I'm sorry," he said. His eyes bright blue, like the ocean, said more than his words; no confused overwhelming emotions were present. He was genuinely apologetic. Something that was rare and challenging for Cash.

"For what?" I glared at him coolly. I knew why he was apologizing but he better have the guts to say it out loud. He nuzzled his nose against my ear and kissed my neck. Moisture dampened my skin and my anger started to dissipate. The source running through our veins leaped at the opportunity to be close, calling for us to evoke our connection. I pushed down the words the source repeated: *Connect. Be one. Join flesh. Flesh becomes flesh.*

"I realize we haven't really spoken about, ya know, *us*," he said as his lips trailed up from my neck and nibbled on my ear. The source increased its inner voice, making it hard for me to concentrate.

I pushed away, giving Cash and my body a little more space, which would hopefully help clear my mind and get my source to settle the hell down. It was an annoying little thought that didn't have an off button or even make much sense when it called to me. Kinda reminded me of Grouper, the way everything he said always sounded like a riddle. The mere thought of Grouper made my shoulders slump and my heart heavy. I hadn't known my newfound uncle long, but whenever I'd ask him a question, he'd always reply with a vague, long-winded thought that never actually resolved the question. I had once asked him, "Do you know why my mother would implant an energy source in me?" And he responded with, "I have my theories, but they would just create more questions, a string of useless queries that none alive could answer. And the pain those questions would cause would outweigh the truth of why she did what she did." I remember thinking he could have just answered "no" or "I'm not sure," like a normal person. And it certainly wasn't because he was an alien—all the rest of the Ferroeans I'd gotten to know didn't have the same cryptic nature.

Coming back to the conversation, I had to agree. "No, we haven't talked about *us* at all. There's been a lot of things going on." A sigh slipped out of my mouth as the words I'd been repeating in my head over and over again since the day my memories came back rose to the forefront of my brain. "We are on our way to wake up your girlfriend from her source coma. I can't help but think things will change, and how there's a choice you might not be acknowledging that you will have to make..." I paused, looking down at my nails. The pink paint had started to chip, a pale mirror to the damage my heart was starting to feel. "You'll have to choose. Do you want to be with Sera, or do you want to be with me?"

There—I said it. All the fears inside I've been having since the moment I remembered Sera. We had met. I'd never forget that day. It was the last day I saw my mother alive and it had been a memory that only resurfaced after Cash and

I connected in my hospital room and after Gertrude, Sera's mother, tried to kill me and take back Sera's energy source. It was Sera, barely breathing, who told my mother the opposing source needed to be taken from her and implanted into me. Sera confirmed my mother's suspicions. I was prophesized to lead The Reprisal, the war on our survival. She passed out right after she told my mother to have Cash perform an Awakening on her so that she could further help me learn about my destiny. I had no ill will for Sera. I just needed to know her role in Cash's life. I lifted my head back up, my eyes meeting his. As I did, I saw the light finally flicker alive in his head. As I'd suspected, he hadn't thought about the greater implications of what we were about to do. Sera was still alive somewhere in California, and she was waiting for us to find her and perform an Awakening to bring her back to consciousness. In all his excitement to learn Sera was not dead, he never considered that there was indeed a decision to be made: would he return to the love of his life, Sera, or stay with me, the new "shell" for her source?

I backed away even farther. "Well?" My voice grew with impatience to his silence.

"I don't..." Cash stuttered. He ran his hand through his dark hair, pulling a little more forcefully than normal Cash frustration.

"Fine." I crossed my arms over my chest. Irritation bubbled in my veins, reaching my source. A feeling similar to indigestion plagued my chest. "Let's just go." I rounded the car and jumped into the passenger side to find Ashton in my personal space. His elbows rested on the center console. His hot breath grazed my left shoulder. Yup, definitely a golden retriever.

"This is exciting, huh? Road trip!" He smacked his hands together and flung himself back into his seat. "Should we play some fun human car games? How about Ghost or the license plate game? What if we sing? I'm really into singing now. Or car dancing. I hear that's a thing. Not sure how it works, though—the space is pretty tight. What do you think?"

Already exhausted by his energy, both Cash and I answered in unison, "No!"

"You two are literally no fun." Despite his sulk, I could still hear the smile in his words. It was going to be a long trip.

Chapter Six

Cash

Somewhere near Des Moines, Iowa, we pulled into a motel around midnight the next day. I was tired. The entire ride had been over twenty-four hours of Beatrice pointedly refusing to talk to me from the passenger seat, and Ashton wanting to talk about everything from the back. He remarked on the trees, the sun, the stars, the gas stations we passed. I think he even asked about the color of the car. He wouldn't shut up. And every time I would tell him to stop talking, Beatrice would chime in with a cheerful defense. "I can't imagine what it was like for you being stuck in that prison for so long," she'd chirp. "Don't worry about him—you keep acknowledging and appreciating the world. I think it's beautiful." I wanted to smack the crap out of him for appealing to her softer side.

I checked in with the front desk manager, asking for two rooms, just as Beatrice had requested more than once between bouts of silence. She rounded the corner of the miniscule lobby carrying a bottle of water and a bag of gummy bears. Her lips thinned into a straight line when her eyes met mine. Clearly, still pissed. Not that I could blame her. I can't imagine what a nutjob I'd be if Bea had another love interest. I'd hang him on a flagpole upside down for just having an ounce of her attention. Hell, I wanted to strangle my brother for offering her his spare shirt. Which, by the way, she still had on.

The shaggy-haired manager with the crooked name tag that read *Jerrick* typed into his keyboard. His nose crinkled, causing his long nose hairs to dance. "I'm sorry, sir, we only have one room left but it does have double queen-sized beds. Does that work?"

Before I could answer, Beatrice chimed in. "No, it does not. Do you know where the closest hotel or motel from here is?" She threw a handful of gummy bears into her mouth and chewed, her stare even more deadly now that she had candy.

"Well, we are the last one for about..." The guy scratched his head, obviously at a loss. "I think until you cross the state line?"

Beatrice rolled her eyes and turned to me. She swallowed and cleared her throat. "We can take turns driving. You shouldn't be at the wheel for so long anyway—it's dangerous. We need two rooms." Her arms crossed over her chest and my eyes trailed down to Ashton's t-shirt. I'd stay at this motel just to have a place she could take that thing off.

"Is it really a big deal?" I asked, exhausted from all the driving, the emotional overload from my apparently part-human brother coupled with the belated revelation that I was about to bring my ex-girlfriend back to life to meet whatever the hell Beatrice was to me. Sleep would be really helpful right now.

Oh, and hell no if she thought I was letting her drive the Charger. I saw the way she treated Ol' Betsey before Grouper sent it to the junkyard. That car was already on its last leg, and while I'd never say it to Beatrice, I think Grouper did us all a favor when he fried it. Obviously, Ashton never needed to know how to drive a car, let alone have a license, so he wasn't an option either. That left me and only me to get us the rest of the way.

Ashton walked in, his mouth full of popcorn. He tossed me a green and white bag of sour cream and onion chips. They'd always been my favorite. I caught it midair and nodded in appreciation.

"What's the dealio, kids? We get a room or not?" Ashton asked while tossing a kernel in the air and catching it in his mouth.

"Beatrice doesn't want to share a room with us," I sneered. "Says you smell." I opened the bag and popped a chip in my mouth.

"I did not," Beatrice groaned. She looked between Ashton and me and then back at Jerrick. "Fine. Whatever. We'll take the room." She threw her hands up. "Let's sleep and leave first thing in the morning. The faster we get to California, the faster this all can be over with."

I'm not sure I knew what she meant by that comment but when I tried to tap into her mind and read her thoughts, she blocked me. I thought back to the day we were at Cartwright High School and I heard her speak to me in her mind for the first time. She said *I hate you*. It was then I taught her how to prevent her mind from being read. I told her to think the word "blank," imagine a white or black canvas, or hum a tune inside her head. These mind tricks will keep your feelings blocked from any Ferroean.

She was purposefully blocking me from her thoughts. I didn't know whether to be proud of her for honing her shields like I instructed or annoyed because it was now at the expense of my advantage. Maybe she was alluding to my decision between Sera and her, or maybe the imminent threat on our two worlds? I smacked my head into my hand. Regardless of her intent, it was going to be a long trip to California.

The three of us gathered our things from the car and followed the directions from the manager to our room on the second floor. We passed a small pool where a crowd of teenagers sat around playing music off their phones and dancing in between lounge chairs that had stained, sunbleached cushions. Beach towels were scattered on the concrete and draped over the white metal fence. One of the guys grabbed one and playfully used it to whip his friends. The girls avoiding the towel giggled in response as they dodged out of its way, a few jumping into the pool for safety. Must be nice living with such ignorance during the apocalypse.

We opened the door and walked in. Ashton threw his things on the first bed closest to the entrance and flung himself backward onto the mattress, kicking up his heels and crossing his arms behind his head.

"It's not the Ritz-Carlton but it's not so bad." He gazed to the bed two feet from his.

"How do you even know what the Ritz-Carlton is?" I asked, wanting to smack him. He was having the time of his life on this trip while I was swimming in all the upcoming decisions and crossroads we would have to bear.

"I love the travel channel," Ashton admitted. He gazed between Bea and me and continued. "And although I love the travel channel, I'm not a big romcom fan so if you two could keep the smooches to a minimum tonight, I'd really appreciate it." He kicked his shoes off, letting them volley into the air and land onto the small couch on the other side of the room.

"You don't have to worry about that because Cash is sleeping with you," Beatrice said as she sauntered into the bathroom. The bags I was carrying dropped to the floor with more force than necessary as I reacted to her comment. "Umm, no, I'm not. I'm sleeping next to you," I countered. She peeked her head out from the bathroom door and smiled. The smile was unusual and threw me a little off guard.

"If I sleep next to you, I can't promise I won't kill you in your sleep." And with that she slammed the door. The three pictures of farm life—a pig, a cow, and a goat—that hung on the adjacent wall fell and crashed to the floor. The frames snapped and the glass cracked. She was still getting used to her growing powers and by the sound of the windows tingling from the force of vibration, I was nervous she really would kill me in her sleep.

"Definitely not worried about the kissing noises now but I am worried you might not make it through the night. She doesn't own a thermo dagger, does she?" When I didn't respond, Ashton continued. "Not out of the doghouse, I see? Maybe it's time for the talk." Ashton gazed over at me.

"Shut up," I snapped at my brother, throwing a pillow from the other bed at him.

He ducked. "I mean, to be honest I don't blame her, and I sure as hell wouldn't want to be her, but hell—I wouldn't want to be you either," Ashton sighed. "I'm not sure what I would do."

I was surprised to find myself curious. I slumped on the bed and asked, "What do you mean?"

Ashton sat up and swiveled to face me, sitting on the edge of the bed. He crossed his shin over his thigh. "Well, let me see if I have this straight. She's pissed because you guys have never really defined what's going on between you, clearly." He waved his hands between the door and me. "There are some intense feelings for each. And now, as an undefined couple, you are about to go to California to wake up your girlfriend of, like, five years, with whom you appeared to have comparatively equally strong feelings for. Then when Sera wakes up, she will have no idea you've fallen in love with someone else, let alone the Blood-Light she'd given her source to. So, no matter what her reaction, or who you choose to be with, you will unavoidably break one of their hearts, if not both, and your own in the process." His characteristically flippant expression melted into sympathy as he looked toward the other side of the room and then back to me. "And the soon-to-be-broken heart could be in the bathroom right now."

I didn't know what to say because Ashton was right. No matter who I chose, what I felt, someone would end up getting hurt because of me. And even if I chose one, I would desperately miss the other and I too would be broken. It was an impossible situation to be in.

Beatrice opened the door. Her eyes were bloodshot and a little puffy, as if she had been crying. I wanted to gather her into my arms and hug her, tell her I never wanted to hurt her, but I wouldn't. I didn't know if I could keep that promise. Since we met, I had never lied to Beatrice Walker and I had no intention of starting now.

She strode over to the bed, opened the tightly tucked floral comforter, and slipped in between the sheets. I noticed she was still in Ashton's shirt and my anger exceeded my empathy.

"Don't you want to change into your own clothes to sleep in?" I growled. My patience with her for refusing to remove Ashton's shirt was thinning.

"You didn't pack me any," she responded flatly, pulling the blankets up to her chin.

"Oh." I'm a jackass. I threw her things together so fast when we were leaving, I didn't even think of nighttime attire. I asked the girls, Tasha and Sammie, to get her unmentionables, but I guess no one thought of pjs.

"Cool if we watch TV?" Ashton asked as he unbuttoned his shirt and hung it in the closet.

I nodded. I couldn't care less. He removed his jeans, folded them, and placed them back into his suitcase. He grabbed a pair of basketball shorts and stepped in them. I was just about to do the same when Beatrice reached out for my arm, pausing my movement.

"Can you keep your clothes on?" she asked.

I rolled my eyes. "Are you kidding?"

She sat up and gave me that cute glare I loved so much.

"No, I am not. I know you have to sleep in bed with me. You brother is a giant, so I'm fine with sleeping next to you"—she held up one finger—"if you keep your pants on."

I ripped my t-shirt off my body and flung it across the room. Then I kicked my shoes off and let them hit the wall, releasing a flustered, "Fine." I plopped into bed next to her and huffed so loudly I was surprised the ceiling light didn't move.

Ashton fell asleep within minutes of the TV blaring while Beatrice and I were awkwardly awake. I rolled on my side and faced her. She smelled like strawberries and cream.

It had quickly become my favorite fragrance. I was thankful I at least packed the right shampoo. I took a deep breath, inhaling her scent. I whispered, "How do you feel? How are the headaches? Better?"

Before Beatrice and I fully connected, flesh to flesh, she was getting what can only be described as migraines—or as she once told me, an axe being driven into her skull.

"I'm better. Ever since you've been regularly feeding, they've gone away." She was on her back, staring up at the ceiling.

"That's good." I wanted to alleviate this awkward tension, but I wasn't sure I could give her the answers she needed. "I know you're mad. I get it. I would be mad too. In fact, I wouldn't be handling it with as much maturity as you. I'd probably be breaking something."

Beatrice mumbled, "Or someone."

I released a halfhearted chuckle. I ran my hands through my hair, pulling at the ends before releasing. "True. I don't know what I can say, what I can do to make you feel better."

She rolled on her side using her arm as a pillow and faced me, our lips mere inches apart. Our breaths mingled together. Her hazel eyes were highlighted by the night's moon. They glowed. "I'm just confused about how you feel about me."

"I'm not," I said, shocking even myself. It's true I was confused about what would happen and what we were, but I wasn't confused about how I felt. "Listen, I can't promise you anything because a lot can happen in the next couple of days, weeks, and I don't have all the answers. But I'm not confused about caring for you. I desperately want to kiss you, like hourly, and the thought—"

"Wait! What?" she interrupted me. Her nose twitched as she asked, "You want to kiss me?"

"Yes," I admitted, suddenly feeling uncharacteristically sheepish at my honesty.

"Not feed, right?" She clarified the question.

"No." I took a breath, realizing I may have spoken too soon. "Although now that you mention it, I really should feed. It would be good for both of us. After healing you today and fighting with asshat over there, I am extremely vulnerable."

"How vulnerable?" she asked. The angles of her lips rose, bringing heat to all my limbs.

"Well, any Blood-Light could definitely take advantage of me, that's how vulnerable." I scooted closer to her. My source hummed its own unique tune.

She leaned in, closing the distance, and kissed the tip of my nose, causing the rhythm inside to hasten into a thunderous beat. "Then you better watch out for Ashton. He could get tempted." She flipped over onto her other side, away from me, and faced toward the bathroom.

I grabbed her and tossed her onto her back, positioning myself on top of her. Her lips tipped up to the sides of the room as she started giggling. "You think you're funny, don't you?" I asked.

She nodded feverishly, her eyes now playful. "Sure do!"

I slowly lowered myself, spreading her legs apart and pressing my hips into hers. Her smile immediately faded and was replaced by the heat in her eyes. I dropped to my right forearm to bear some of my weight. Using my left hand, I brushed away her fallen hairs.

"This is how I love seeing you," I admitted.

"Oh, and how's that?" she whispered. "Under you, completely defenseless?"

I traced her lips with my fingertips, pulling her bottom lip apart from her top. Her moisture clung to my skin. "Well, now that you mention it, yes, but..." I leaned down and pressed my lips to the gentle curve of her jaw. I trailed those kisses up to her cheek and then pulled away a millimeter from her lips. "More importantly, I love seeing you smile."

The tips of her lips rose incredibly high. I lowered my face. My bottom lip brushed her top lip and just like the first time she kissed me, she lifted her head from the pillow and pressed her lips against mine. I caught her bottom lip and breathed in ethereal energy. I took and took, filling up with both power and pleasure. Our kiss deepened as my hand gripped the back of her neck and my fingers threaded through her hair. We rolled together until Beatrice was on top of me. Her legs weaved through mine. Her mouth devouring me with purpose, as if trying to prove with every heartbeat that we were meant to be together. My hands trailed down her back over her butt and grabbed the back of her thighs. Light flowed out of her and through me. The source pushed into me, harder and harder, as her body moved over me. I tightened my hold around her. My hands trailed back up her body, along the neckline, and pulled her hair. She whimpered and moaned as I exposed her neck. Her pulse throbbed. My eyes caught the gleam of the moonlight in her necklace, and I stilled.

Breathlessly, she gasped, "What? What is it? Why'd you stop?"

"Your necklace. It's purple. It's *only* purple."

Chapter Seven

Ashton

Morning came. It appeared as if the two lovebirds made up. I even saw a stolen kiss between them as Cash packed up his bag. He hit the TV off button, shutting down a cartoon talking dog patrolling the neighborhood. And humans thought aliens were weird. Cash sat at the small table in the corner. The cracked picture frame that Beatrice had destroyed the previous night was laid out by his feet, a chilling emotional display of her growing powers. Shards of glass sprinkled around it, glistening off of the natural sunlight coming in through the windows. My eye lids barely parted. I wasn't used to daylight. Who knew what a different effect it had on me than the artificial lighting that I had been subjected to in my prison for so many years?

Avoiding the glass shrapnel in the carpet, Cash slipped on his shoes and stood. "I need to make a call and touch base with the team. I'll check us out in the lobby while I'm down there," he said in a tone that was surprisingly lighthearted. He zippered up his luggage and gave a kick to the baseboard of the hotel bed I absolutely did not want to leave. "Get up! As soon as I'm done, we need to get on the road."

What time was it? I yawned, stretching my arms over my head. "It's not like fifteen more minutes of beauty sleep is going to affect the end of the world."

Cash threw his bag over his shoulder as well as the words, "The way things have been going, it might!" His glib tone carried unintended weight.

"Can I use the shower?" Beatrice seemed to ask the room, but the question was obviously directed at me since Cash was already out the door before she finished her sentence.

"Sure," I said, swinging my legs over the bed and standing up.

Beatrice paused, tilting her head ever so slightly in response to something I couldn't understand. Her eyes squinted, and I swore she wriggled her nose like she was smelling something.

I walked over toward where she stood with a white terrycloth towel in her hand. She was still in my white shirt and it had me wondering. Could Sayor have been right? I wanted to tell her what her father had told me, but I loved my brother and knew the second he found out I might never get him back. And what if it wasn't true? This was years ago. I hadn't seen Sayor since my judgment day and so much of that day had been tainted in lies. What would one more lie be?

I stood in front of her, so close that when she looked up, I could feel her breath on my chest. Involuntarily, my hand lifted. I traced her chin with my fingers. She was soft like the skin of a peach. But when I breathed her in, she smelled of strawberries. She stilled as I trailed down her shoulders, tracing the bones and muscles that I could feel through the cotton. I stopped at the hem of the sleeve. Her breath hitched as she swallowed hard.

"What are you doing?" she asked in what could only be recognized as a whisper. I felt warm being so close to another person after so long in isolation. "Are you ever going to take this off?" I asked her as I tugged on the sleeve. "Or are you planning on living in my clothes? Not that I am complaining. They look better on you anyway."

Her breathing quickened as her chest expanded and contracted hastily. She didn't answer but she did breathe me in, and this time I was positive she was smelling me. Her face twitched with confusion.

"I knew your father—I knew Gabe Sayor," I admitted, breaking the tension. Hearing Sayor's name out loud twisted my gut. As much as I believed in his vision of a future for Ferro, I couldn't help but feel betrayal by his omissions. He never told me the prophesized champion was his daughter. He only told us about a Blood-Light, one born without a source, that would lead The Reprisal against the ruling Ferroean Council. He never told me Sera would be harmed or possibly killed. All he told me was I needed to prepare myself and be ready to stand at their side when the day came. The intentional exclusion of Bea's identity only reinforced my fear that Sayor never fully trusted me. That no matter what I did or could do for the cause, I would still always be the son of our enemy—the illegitimate child of King Zane.

Beatrice took a step backward. "I don't know my birth father. I only know my dad, Robert. The man you knew abandoned my mother and never bothered to know me." Her eyes were thin, unforgiving slits.

I stepped forward, keeping distance with her small step back. Her caution against me was warranted. "I'm not sure he had much of a choice in that."

"You always have a choice. Cash told me that." Her eyes burned with conviction. "And you know what? I believe in that saying. Nothing is simply set in stone before us. We always have the right to control our own choices."

I returned her accusing glare. "And you don't think Sayor chose what's right? He stood up for what he believed in, whether you can see past your own selfish feelings or not. He stood up for your mother and clearly didn't give a crap what the consequences were. He died for our cause."

As if her eyes could get any smaller, she crinkled her face. "Did you know my mother? Did you know Faye Walker?"

"No, I never met her. I didn't even know her name, but I knew who she was. I know the story of their time together. Do you?" The volume of my voice grew as she questioned me and the cause Sayor believed in. She had no idea what our rebellion had been through. The catalyst for everything was her father's love. But all she was seeing was her own abandonment.

Beatrice took another step backward, propelled by the intensity of my zeal. I continued, undaunted. "Sayor was so in love with your mother. He would have done anything to make what they shared legal, to roam free on Earth. Most Ferroeans think of humans as pets, inferior beings to be used for amusement at best. Sayor fought for something better for our peoples. He believes we are equal, and so do I. When he met your mother, they fell hopelessly in love. He thought his authority as a Council member and the clout of being descended from one of the founding bloodlines would have made a difference. He thought he could change the law."

She backed up another step and I followed forward. As her ignorance grew, so did my anger. "He was wrong. His attempts at change were the perfect excuse my father needed to excommunicate Sayor from the High Council. He used your mother as leverage, convincing the Council your father didn't have the planet's well-being in mind; That he only cared about himself and his human love affair and ruining his credibility."

Beatrice's hazel eyes were wide and swirling with the colorful emotion of her transplanted source. Purples and blues collided as her anger matched mine. "And Cash? Tasha? How did they feel? Did they believe humans and Ferroeans should be together?" she questioned. She crossed her arms at her chest, the towel covering the rapid rise and fall of her rib cage.

"They were young, oblivious to my father and his cruel, selfish behavior. Cash worshiped him until I pledged my allegiance to Sayor. My 'disloyalty' punctured a hole in Cash's perfect family vision. Cash would never go against my father or the Council, but it *did* plant seeds of doubt in his mind."

Her brow furrowed. "And you are proud of that?" She studied my face, and I was glad she was at least trying to understand.

"Yes, and I would do it again." Despite all that had occurred, there was pride in my voice. "To protect my brother, my sister, and my mother, I would do it all over again the same way. I'd follow Sayor to the ends of the earth not just because I believe in his cause but because I want a better world for my siblings. My destiny, although not as planned out as yours, is also tied to the prophecy."

This information seemed to shake her slightly. "How?"

I took a deep breath and released. "The prophecy that a Blood-Light saves Earth is true, yes. But the connection required to save both planets isn't your source to Cash's. It never was. It's your source to mine."

Beatrice took another step. Her back hit the wall hard, but she didn't seem to notice. He brows pinched together. "You're lying!"

I followed her, cocooning her into a corner. I was a good half-foot taller than her, so I hunched down, bringing my body closer to hers as I leaned in. "I'm most certainly not." My hands pressed against the distasteful flowered wallpaper on either side of her, trapping her there. "And whereas my father thinks your mother was Sayor's weakness and I'm fully certain he would think you were my brother's as well; *I* think you are something else. I think you are something more." Her breath, ragged and fierce, blew against me. I dropped my head in line with hers, pressing my lips against Bea's, parting them with my tongue. It had been so long since I felt another's mouth on mine. For a split second, I felt her tongue move in synch with mine, but then she pushed me, hard. The force was enough that I flew across the room, crashing into the wall and causing the drywall to bend and break in my wake. I landed on the remains of her destruction from the previous night, shrapnel of broken glass and wood digging into my skin. My eyes focused on Bea's necklace. The long onyx dagger held by a silver hilt was still black. I had assumed it would change as the prophecy deemed it to turn when our sources connected. I was wrong.

I took a sharp inhale, and, on my exhale, I breathed, "What do you think you are, Beatrice Walker?"

Her voice was bleak, absent of all emotion. "I'm a weapon."

Chapter Eight

Cash

The car ride for the next couple of days was odd. Beatrice wasn't talking to anyone. Ashton was talking to everyone. If we stopped at a gas station, he'd talk to the couple getting gas next to us. If we stopped to get food, he'd talk to the waitress so much he'd distract her from serving other tables. He was like an insistent toddler, asking question after question. For the last hour, he'd even been singing loudly along with the radio. He wasn't kidding, he liked to sing, and he knew all the lyrics to every song. I considered yelling at him at one point, and then realized it was far less stressful letting him entertain himself with music than to hear him prattle on and on the whole ride.

I wondered if he was starting to wear on Beatrice. She hadn't defended him or addressed him since we left the seedy motel the other night. And if it wasn't his annoying social behavior, what was her reason for the sudden disinterest in his antics?

My cell phone rang, Tasha's name lighting up on the screen. I handed it to Beatrice.

I turned down the radio and glared at Ashton through the rearview mirror. He didn't notice the volume shift. "Shut up! It's your sister and she shouldn't have to find out you're alive because she heard you bellowing Taylor Swift lyrics like some preteen human." I looked at the car navigation. "And at the rate we are going, she'll learn that in person soon enough."

Ashton motioned with his fingers a zipped lip and tossed away the pretend key, a gesture he regularly threw at me. "Yeah, yeah, if it was only that easy," I mumbled out of habit. The back seat now quiet, I nodded to Beatrice to answer.

"Hey," she said. "Yeah, we are close, about thirty minutes out." I heard my sister's voice say something on the other end of the line but couldn't make it out. "Lunch does sound good. We can't wait to see everyone, but I think Cash needs to talk to you privately when we get there before we all sit down together." She raised her eyebrows at me, and I could see sympathy swirling in her half-Ferroean hazel eyes. "Umm, not sure why." Beatrice's reply was a little too fast. She didn't like lying to Tasha. I could relate. "Maybe you could wait in his room while everyone else is in the club lounge?" Tasha said something else I couldn't hear, and Beatrice answered. "Yeah, no. He'll need two beds. Room 1530 sounds great." Beatrice stifled a dark laugh. "Speaking of that, can I stay with you?"

For a second my anger flared, and I resisted the urge to snatch the phone and throw it out the window. Realizing her mistake, Beatrice shook her head and mouthed a silent apology to me. "No, no, the extra bed is for me. I was kidding. It's been a long trip." She muttered, clumsily covering her slip.

I whispered, "Hang up!"

Beatrice nodded quickly, obviously wanting to get off the phone as much as I wanted her to. "Miss you too. See you soon." She hit the end button and tossed the phone into the cupholder between us. Her body slumped against the headrest as she let out a frustrated sigh. Ashton poked his head through the space over the center console.

"Bea's a shitty liar," he singsonged in that annoying voice he liked so much. Keeping my eyes on the road ahead, I pushed on his forehead and he sat back into his seat. I caught his reflection in the rearview mirror. His Cheshire smile reached his ears. God, I wanted to rip that smirk off his face.

"Not everyone can be as deceptive as you, especially with the ones they care about," Beatrice barked, spinning around in her seat to face Ashton. The leather groaned under her rapid movement. It was the first time I had heard her speak to my brother in days, and it wasn't like Beatrice to be mean-spirited for no reason. It meant only one thing: It wasn't irritation that had incited her sullen mood. My brother had done something to earn her anger.

Trying not to get distracted as Bea stared daggers at Ashton from the seat beside me, I asked, "What did I miss?" I tried to keep my tone even, but anger rose inside me, fueling my source. Clearly, something had happened between them. It wasn't in Bea's character to ignore someone, especially when she could conspire with my brother to piss me off. And it wasn't like Ashton to get ignored and just let that go. He would have either increased his charm or his pestering, but he wouldn't have accepted it mutely.

She swiveled back in her seat and faced the front. I could feel the heat of her anger rising around her.

"Well go-ahead, Blood-Light, what did my brother miss?" Ashton pressed. "Anything you'd like to tell him?"

My brows furrowed. "Bea?" I questioned. My hand moved to her thigh and I squeezed it, trying to be encouraging.

Beatrice pushed my hand away and crossed her arms over her chest. Her face reddened.

"Beatrice, what is Ashton talking about?" I demanded. Rather than giving a response, her lips pressed into a fine line and she turned her head away from me to the window.

That was it.

I swerved the wheel, and the tires shrieked in protest as they left the pavement and bounded over the dirt of the road's shoulder. I threw the Hellcat into park and angled my body so I could see both Beatrice and my brother.

"Tell me now before my imagination gets the best of me and I lose my mind." I spoke carefully, feeling the source inside of me spark to life. Beatrice could feel it too. I saw her body jerk in response. I was two seconds away from pounding my brother into submission for whatever he did to hurt her. "What the hell has Beatrice so pissed, Ashton?"

"I kissed her," he spat out, his face devoid of his usual humor. Beatrice turned in her seat, red hot with fury at my brother. The colors in her eyes swirled. I waited for her to say something, anything, but she just glared at Ashton. If she had the power to shoot lasers from her eyes, he would be charbroiled.

He didn't look away, but stared right back into Beatrice's eyes, continuing. "In response, she threw me well across the room." He returned his gaze to me, the humor returning to his eyes. "Like through the drywall!" He rubbed his lower back theatrically. "She's kind of a bully. You need to watch yourself. You could be next!"

There was a beat, and then I started to laugh. Hard. I threw my head back into the seat and closed my eyes for a brief moment. Here I was caught in the middle of loving my old girlfriend who was barely alive, loving Beatrice who has yet to be defined in my life, and now my very charming brother decided to insert himself in the mix. If the elders could see us now; even they might be confused.

I shook my head. This I could deal with. "Sounds like you got what you deserved." Crisis averted- I started the car. The engine purred back to life.

Beatrice smacked my arm, stinging me through the fabric of my sleeve. "What was that for?" I asked, rubbing the spot she'd connected with. Her powers were increasing, and she still didn't know her own strength. "Maybe you are a bully."

"Told you," Ashton grumbled.

"Are you serious?" she asked, her eyes like saucers they were so wide. I pressed on the gas and turned the wheel, getting us back on the road.

"What do you want me to say? I'm not shocked Ashton tried to kiss you. He's been looking at you like a hungry lion since we picked his ass up from the safe house—"

"Ahem, *prison*," Ashton interjected.

I shook my head. "Fine. Prison. I don't care what my brother does. You obviously didn't kiss him back and, to boot, you kicked his ass. Couldn't have handled it better myself. Would you rather me be pissed and attack him again?"

All of the color on her face drained, causing me to question her reaction. "No." She paused, her face contorted with optional responses. "It's just an interesting time for you to have matured," she deadpanned.

Tapping into her mind, I tried to hear her thoughts but all I heard was *blank blank blank.* Weird. She was jamming my mind-reading powers. Again. "You are getting exceptionally good at shielding your thoughts. Been practicing?"

She turned her head toward the window, ignoring me both physically and mentally, not even shocked I tried to pry her thoughts from her. The rest of the car ride was silent. Even Ashton was quiet. If she wanted to tell me how she was feeling, she'd have to do it when she wanted to. It wasn't like I was an open book to her all the time, and I had more pressing matters to worry about. Particularly, how my sister was going to react when she found out our brother was still alive and I had been keeping it a secret from her for the last four years. I doubted she'd respond with understanding and appreciation, even if I was part of the reason he was kept alive to begin with.

We pulled into the hotel lot and parked near the main entrance. The sky hummed with low-flying planes as they came and went from the nearby LAX airport. We each grabbed our own bags without speaking, bypassed the lobby, and beelined straight up to the fifteenth floor. As Beatrice had arranged, the crew would be in the club lounge to the left, but Tasha would be waiting in a room to the right.

I turned to Beatrice. "Why don't you go see to the others? Ashton and I should do this alone." She gave a curt nod and immediately headed to the left. She was pissed—that much was obvious—but something about the way she was acting made me think it was more. I shook the thought. Whatever it was, it would have to wait.

"You ready?" I asked Ashton. He was uncharacteristically quiet, an air of tension around him. His face was stoic as he nodded. "Here we go," I said as I knocked on the door. Tasha opened it slowly and with her left hand instead of her right. That was odd. Her face was pale as snow and her eyes heavy. Ashton gave a faint smile. "Hey sis, it's been a while."

Chapter Nine

Ashton

Tasha's face when she opened the door was not what I had envisioned. Yes, she looked shocked to see me, but the way her chest was rapidly moving with breath and the way her right arm dangled lifelessly didn't have anything to do with her disbelief I was still alive. Her eyes were swirling with oranges, reds, and yellows. The lower lids were lined with water. She'd been crying.

"Tash?" Cash and I questioned in unison. I continued, "I know it's a shock, but we can explain. When..." I stopped as my eyes caught the sun glistening off of the floor. Yellow ichor trailed behind Tasha like the wake behind a ship. Her wrist was dripping with it, confirming what I had already assumed. She was injured. Cash leaned in, attempting to grab her, but she yelped. "Don't! Stay back."

Her eyes were wild, thrashing with colors, a Ferroean trait. She slowly walked herself backward, drawing us into the room. Several rogue tears rolled down from her eyes and landed on the floor. As we followed, we saw why Tasha was so distraught and why she was wounded.

Six DOAA agents clad in black suits, grey ties, and white button-downs stepped into view. They all had thermo daggers in their hands and were staggered in fighting form.

"You cut my sister," Cash growled, his gaze traveling from Tasha's hobbled arm back toward her attackers. He raised his palm and pointed to the lamp on the table. It exploded. Pieces flung across the room. Two of the agents ducked; the rest were unphased. Now we knew who the newbies were. "That was your first mistake."

My eyes locked on the remaining agents to find out whose dagger was used. The fourth one, a woman muscular enough to compete in a heavyweight championship, was the culprit. She was tall with broad shoulders, her face expressionless. She had black and blues forming under her right eye. Well, at least Tasha wasn't easy on She-Hulk. I traveled down her arm and locked on the telltale yellow ichor dripping off her dagger. I wanted to take her down right there and murder her for wounding my sister. But I knew Cash would be pissed if I acted rashly and put us all in more danger. Regardless of my brother's temper, he was the most skilled in combat situations. Not to mention, I couldn't heal as easily on Earth. And despite apparently being here for the last four years, I couldn't even be sure what powers I had access to.

"Your second was using her as bait to lure me into your little..." Cash looked around the room. "What is this anyway? An ambush? Six DOAA agents aren't even enough to make me sweat. But I'm happy to kill each and every one of you so the DOAA can have one big memorial. I'm sure they will thank me for saving funeral money." Cash pointed his palm at the sliding doors to the balcony. The glass shattered outward.

"Cash," Tasha warned. Her voice was weak, and it nearly broke me. Cash heard it too. For a quick second, I saw fear.

A large man with silver hair and a burly lower body pushed through the six men and women, knocking She-Hulk from my line of sight. "Enough," he roared. It was Director Dodd.

"This is new. You left your doghouse? I'm honored," Cash growled. Dodd never left the DOAA HQ. "Where are your fifteen bodyguards? Your Ferroean attack dogs?"

Our family was close with Dodd, as close as any Ferroean family could be with a human. He was head of the Department of Alien Affairs and probably the only human who knew what I actually was.

"It's nice to see you again, Captain Kingston." He nodded in Cash's direction. "Ashton, what an unexpected surprise! A pleasurable one at that." He leaned his hip against the hotel room desk and crossed his arms. "I must admit we were hopeful you were still alive but none of our informants could ever figure it out; at least not until recently. Your father hid you well. If you were willing, I'd still greatly appreciate a sample of your blood. There's so much I'd love to learn about you." During the one trip I had to Earth, Director Dodd doctored my paperwork for my required assimilation. Already part human, the surgery wasn't only unnecessary, it was impossible. Director Dodd was fascinated by Blood-Lights. I specifically remember him asking Zane if I would undergo blood tests and a few physical evaluations. More for his own edification than mine, I'm sure; Zane drew the line there.

"You realize how off that sounds, right? Blood, saliva, urine test. Did Superman get this treatment when he came to Earth? I think not!" I tilted my head. "Have you put on some weight? I think a go around the track might do your human heart some good. Even better, when was the last time you sparred?" My brow lifted. "Wanna get a round in? I'd give you blood that way." I'd be happy to test my updated fighting skills on this sanctimonious ass.

Dodd shook his head like a disapproving father. "Oh, the Kingston boys are such hoots. It's interesting Tasha doesn't share your humor." Dodd snapped his fingers and the agent with the long scar across his cheek grabbed her, putting pressure on her injury. Tasha muffled a whimper, but her eyes softened.

Cash and I roared in unison. I put She-Hulk and Scarface on my mental hit lists.

"Oh good, back on track with how serious this is. As long as you give me what I need, Tasha will be fine. We came under no pretense to hurt her." Dodd motioned his chin in Tasha's direction. "However, Tasha had other plans, so we had no choice but to weaken her."

Cash crossed his arms over his chest. "Enough of the chattiness. What do you want?"

"We are here for the Blood-Light girl."

Cash waved his hands around. "Does this room look like a dating service? Go find your own girl," Cash quipped, his smirk not reaching his eyes.

One of the female agents—this one had a long neck so long it seemed inhuman—grabbed Tasha by the hair and threw her on the bed. I leaped forward at Giraffe Guard. Cash grabbed me and pulled me back. I broke out of Cash's hold. "Let go. I'm fine," I told him. I was anything from fine. I know Cash was just protecting me but By the Council, they were hurting Tasha, my baby sister I hadn't seen in years. I wanted to tear their human hearts out.

"Tsk, tsk," Director Dodd reprimanded. "I wouldn't do that, Ashton."

The Giraffe Guard pinned Tasha down at her shoulders while Scarface held her legs. Tasha squirmed and bucked. Anger fueled my source, sending currents of shockwaves through my limbs. My insides felt like they were on fire. The She-Hulk leaned over Tasha and slit her ankle; more of her internal source poured out and pooled on the bed, a touch of red blood mixing with the yellow ichor. Tasha bucked and then settled, showing defeat.

This time it was Cash that lunged forward. I held him back, grabbing his arms. He didn't fight my hold. "What do you want?" I asked the human who held my sister's life in his hands. My fingers pressed into my brother's skin. He too was losing patience.

"I've already made my request. Where is Beatrice Walker?" Director Dodd knew what I knew, what Cash most likely knew, and what Beatrice had confirmed to me herself. She was designed as a weapon of war for the side of Earth, regardless of her kind, human heart. Other than an open wound from a thermo dagger, Beatrice was the only other means to kill our kind. When no one said anything, Director Dodd continued, "She's a great asset to our agency and belongs with us. Let me refresh your memory: She's tall, hazel eyes, long brown hair? Faye Walker and Gabe Sayor's daughter?"

I winced at the sound of Sayor's name on his lips.

"I don't know who you're talking about," Cash answered. "I mean honestly, though, if that's your type, I'm pretty sure you can put that on your dating profile and options should come up."

Director Dodd ignored my brother's smartass answer and nodded to She-Hulk. The DOAA agent grabbed Tasha's open ankle wound and dug her fingers into the fresh cut. Tasha let out a high-pitched shriek I could only hope was heard by the rest of our team.

Cash and I both pressed forward in unison. I could feel my brother's shoulders tense and his source running up and down his body under my grip on his arm.

"Shhhh, Tasha dear. I'd hate to give the rest of your crew a heads up we are coming for them." Dodd's cell phone rang, and he answered. "Good. We have the twins and a surprise guest; code name, Resource. Adhere to protocol 874689."

Code name. I had a code name. Both Cash and I looked at each other, confused by Director Dodd's reference to me. "We are on the fifteenth floor. Send deploy and cleanup."

I'd watched enough human action movies to know deploy was an attack team and cleanup was a team who dealt with the bodies and any witnesses. I guess he lied. Someone *was* dying today.

"Tell me where she is," Director Dodd demanded. "I don't have time for this." He glanced at Tasha. "And neither does she."

"Don't, Cash—don't tell him anything," Tasha gurgled. Thick, yellow fluid dripped from her mouth, impairing her speech.

The Giraffe Guard held the knife over her left ankle while Scarface held the thermo dagger over her left wrist. She had lost too much source. Any more, and Tasha would be dead. Cash would never give up Bea's location, but I could never let anything happen to Tasha either. I had no choice. I had to trust that even if the DOAA captured Bea, they wouldn't harm her because of how valuable she was to them.

"The rest of the team is in the club lounge, on this floor down the hall outside of the main elevators. Beatrice Walker is with them." I released a breath I'd been holding as the knife was released from Tasha's arm.

Cash and Tasha shouted in protest at the same time, Cash roaring an insult as Tasha screamed "No!" from her supine position on the bed.

"Fantastic. You've always been an asset to us, Ashton. I hope when we call on you down the road, you continue to work with us this well. Thank you," Director Dodd said politely. "You four stay here; the rest of us will go to the club lounge with the others." Director Dodd walked toward the door with his two additional DOAA guards in tow. He turned and locked eyes with Tasha. "You've been so very helpful, my dear." And then he nodded at the guards that held her down, slipping out of the room.

Giraffe Guard and Scarface drove their thermo daggers toward the fatal blows to Tasha's ankle and wrist, but Cash was quicker. He barreled into the two agents and took them down. I jumped over the bed Tasha lay on and extended my arms, knocking the two other guards over, one being She-Hulk and the other Tiny Tim—he was short but wide and stout.

Tasha's whimpers were background noise to the groans of the guards I hit. I rolled over She-Hulk, who appeared unconscious from the fall and rolled on top of Tiny Tim, still struggling to get up. I pinned him under me and went blow after blow to his face as if he were a speed bag. Red human blood covered my knuckles and sprayed across his face, blurring eyes, nose, and mouth. I kept punching well after he was likely dead.

"Behind you!" Cash screamed.

She-Hulk had regained consciousness and had snuck up on me. Her forearm circled the front of my body, strangling me at the throat as she pulled me off her fallen teammate. My breath caught, and I heard Tasha shouting for Cash to help me. My brother had problems of his own, though. Normally, two DOAA agents would be nothing against him, but he was staggering against their combined attack. He must have been weaker than he thought from healing Beatrice days before. He needed to feed.

"I know Tasha," Cash said, hearing her sob my name. "I'm working on it." His voice came between winded breaths dealing with Scarface and Giraffe Guard. The corners of my vision were starting to darken from lack of oxygen, but I could clearly hear the cracking and snapping of bone from Cash's direction.

"Please don't let my brother die twice!" she cried.

The blackness increased, and somewhere inside me I knew I was about to pass out from the chokehold. Then relief hit me, the world snapping back into focus. I gasped for precious breath. Cash had my attacker restrained above me in a painful-looking arm lock.

"Hey, brother, want a crack at this one?" Cash said.

I stood. I cracked my neck side to side, glaring at She-Hulk. "Would be my pleasure. *So* kind of you to ask, baby bro." I tipped my lips up to the sky. "How would you like to die, human? I could give you options. I'm generous like that."

The woman in Cash's hand spit in my direction. A bloody fluid stuck to my shoe. My gaze followed the gook. "I really like these shoes. Was that necessary as your last act on Earth?"

"I'd never have killed you. You are too valuable to Earth. I may not like you, but our orders are to take you alive." The human's voice was pained from my brother's tight grip. "But I'd be more than happy to end the lives of your siblings."

Cash and I both tilted our heads. Well, that's a weird thing to say.

"That's not very nice," I said as Cash tightened his hold. "Are you saying you don't like Tasha and Cash? Tasha, how does that make you feel? Sad, rejected, angry—pick a sentiment."

Tasha scooted herself back on the bed. She was in an upright position, but her body was slouched. She needed Cash to heal her. I internally cursed my human side. My nature made it impossible to heal full-blooded Ferroeans on Earth.

"Confused," she breathed as her gaze locked with mine.

"See, now you've confused my sister," I said. "She's very intelligent and that is hard to do." Cash reached down with his free arm, grabbing his thermo dagger from his ankle sheath.

She-Hulk spoke. "She'll be even more puzzled when she finds out you're a Bloo-" With unnatural speed, Cash slit the guard's throat and threw her to the ground. Dark arterial blood flowed like water from the fatal wound and spilled across the front of her dark suit.

Tasha looked at Cash with bewilderment.

"What? She was starting to talk too much," Cash answered with a shrug, but the look he had in his eyes was not so cavalier. Neither of us wanted our sister to learn I was a Blood-Light from a DOAA agent. He was justified in holding that secret a tad bit longer—the mere idea I was still alive was enough of a brain teaser.

Taking advantage of my remaining strength, I moved all four of the guards' dead bodies into the bathroom as Cash tended to my sister. He threaded his hands inside hers, and white light doused the room. An amber glow outlined their hands as they held each other tight. Tasha needed a stronger source once we found safety. I would remind Cash to fuel up with Beatrice tonight.

By the Council. We'd completely forgotten. I soared out of the bathroom, my voice echoing off the thin walls.

"They have Bea!"

Chapter Ten

Beatrice

I don't know why I paced in front of the club lounge doors for so long. I was wearing out the already-thin brown carpet with my shoes. Too many emotions and uncomfortable feelings swam in the pit of my stomach. I knew I should have told Cash I kissed Ashton back or, even more importantly, what he told me about the prophecy and how it was his source—not Cash's—that would create the connection to mine that would save our planets. I couldn't explain why or how that was, though, and I didn't even know if I believed Ashton about any of it. I knew that if I went into the lounge with all of that bottled up, everyone would know something was wrong. Finally making the decision to delay facing the team a little longer, I went back down the elevator to the lobby. I needed to call Darla, my best friend, my confidante, my walking diary and advice hotline.

In the meticulously curated lobby of the hotel, I found an oversized green chair big enough to hold not only the weight of my body but my heart. After I punched in the numbers, the cell phone only rang once before the most excited human I had ever known answered with boisterous mock-accusations.

"Are you kidding me! You waited how many days to call me?" She left no room for me to answer. "I've been dying, *literally dying,* to talk to you for like a week. I know nothing. No briefings on any alien relations. No updates on the fate of the world. How can I help if I am in the dark? Sugar snaps, am I being cut out?" She paused for the first time in so many sentences.

"Hello to you too," I chuckled. I kicked my feet up on a nearby matching ottoman.

Barely skipping a beat, Darla continued, "Do you know what kind of torture this is for me? How's Barbie—I mean Sammie? I kinda miss her. How's hot alien bodyguard-slash-boyfriend doing? How's Tasha? Literally tell me everything! Chris and I miss you so much."

I laughed as Darla finally took a chance to breathe. We had been friends since kindergarten. It took her all of a minute to accept that I was part alien and that my life in the last several months had turned her world upside down as well. She was along for the ride no matter what. Talk about having a ride-or-die friendship.

"It's been...a week," I admitted. The exhalation of breath was more forced than I had intended.

"Why? What happened? Please tell me Gertrude's ghost hasn't come back to haunt you. Devil's Doritos, I knew that woman was awful from the moment she made me do laps in gym class and thought that was my idea of fun. Posing as our gym teacher and having the audacity to make me glisten every Tuesday and Thursday? Pure evil, I tell you."

"Yeah, I mean gym class sucked, but I'm pretty much still pissed she captured me, killed Grouper, and tried to kill

Tasha." I sighed. I didn't have any energy left to make light of recent events.

Darla picked up on my feelings and reigned in some of her enthusiasm. "Yeah, okay, you have a point. She sucked in many ways. And how about the fact that she's your boyfriend's ex's mother? What a plot twist."

I threw my head back into the chair cushion. I couldn't believe that was just a little over a week ago. It felt a lifetime since then. "Well, anyway, yeah, she's still dead, and so far, no ghosts. Thankfully."

"Oh, well, that's good. So...what's with the long voice?" She paused for a half breath then continued. "Is it the fact that your boyfriend's former girlfriend is still alive somewhere and you are bringing her out of her source coma and then they might be together and you might be alone? Because that would put a damper on any party. Like what happens if he chooses her but you both still have to save the world together? That kinda ruins the romance." Before I could answer her rather blunt question, she continued. "Hold on. Yes, can I get a caramel vanilla bean latte with oak milk, heavy on the whip, extra caramel sauce. Do you have a sugar-free option? No? Oh, okay. Oh well, there goes the calories burned from taking the stairs instead of the elevator today." I heard the woman confirm her order in the background. "Okay, I'm back. You were saying?"

I laughed, my cheeks indenting. "I miss you."

"I miss you too," she said. "So, tell me—what has you upset?"

"Well, it's all the things you said but there's also something..." I paused. "Well, *someone* else."

If Darla had gotten her latte already, I'm sure she would have dropped it right to the ground. "Are you kidding?" Her voice echoed in the receiver. "You like someone else? What other hot alien protector-boyfriend did you find in the last week? How does so much happen when I'm not around? This is so unfair. I should have been able to go to California with you. I'm missing everything. And how come no hot alien guys are after me? I mean, come on. I might not be an awesome half-alien babe like you, but I'm a delight!"

I couldn't help but chuckle. "No, it's not like that. Cash has a broth—"

"You like his brother? Oh, Beatrice Walker, when did you start playing with fire? Are you nuts? And how hot is the brother? Eye color? Hair color? Tell me everything!"

"Darla, stop. No, I love Cash. I will always love Cash. It's not like that. I don't feel anything for him romantically. It's weird. It's like we have this weird connection. He feels, actually more like smells, familiar. I don't know. It's the strangest thing."

"Ew. He smells? Like what?"

My eyes lifted to the right as I tried to remember what it was the first time I walked into his apartment and what I smelled in the hotel room. It was so potent that I stopped and intentionally breathed it in before showering. "Like cedarwood and sage."

"That's weird. What is he, a yoga studio?" Darla laughed at her own joke.

I shook my head. "Yeah, I know. It's super odd. And he was talking all this smack, saying I'm not supposed to connect to Cash but that I'm supposed to..." My breath hitched as I suddenly noticed the burning gazes of multiple people swarming the lobby and looking around. They all wore the same black suits, white button-downs, and grey ties as Dominic and Claude, the two DOAA agents that came after

Cash and me several months ago back in Cartwright, Pennsylvania. They were after our opposing sources as well as capturing me for the DOAA.

"Bea, you still there?" Darla's voice, full of concern, rang in my ear. I had almost forgotten about her. Clutching the phone in my hand, my palms sweaty, I slowly turned around, sheltering my face from view.

My voice lowered to a mere whisper. "I have to go." I heard her protests as I clicked the end button. I dialed Cash.

"Bea?" he questioned when he answered. His voice was shaky. "Where are you? Are you okay?" He sounded out of breath. I don't think I'd ever heard him winded before.

"Are you?" I asked. What had I missed while I was on the phone?

"Tasha's injured. It's a long story. I had to heal her. I'm not my usual self right now." Of course. He'd been using his source to heal others a lot lately. He needed a chance to rest and recharge. "Where are you?"

"I'm in the lobby. I just saw..." But before I could finish, he screamed into the phone, his voice hoarse, "Bea, run!"

Chapter Eleven

Cash

Beatrice tried to protest, refusing to abandon the rest of us. With no time for an argument, I compromised and told her to bring the car around. I explained Tasha was badly injured and we had to get her out of the building. She seemed satisfied enough with helping as a getaway driver and thankfully she complied. Before hanging up, Beatrice relayed that as many as fifteen agents were headed our way by elevator and the same number by stairway. We couldn't fight that many with an injured Tasha, an untested Blood-Light, and me with my severely diminished source. And we were too far away from the club lounge to even warn the others of the incoming threat.

"Why is no one answering their cell phones?" I groaned in frustration after having dialed Robert, Sammie, Mark, and Paul in quick succession. Not one of them picked up.

"Because we all thought we were just meeting in the lounge and then going to lunch. I didn't even have my purse on me," Tasha's voice was strained, as if I should know better. Who doesn't bring their cell phones these days? I wanted to make a bigger deal of this, but Tasha was injured and the last thing I wanted to do was pick a fight with my impaired sister.

"How are we getting out of here?" Resentment seeped through Tasha's voice and I wondered when she would allow it to come to the forefront. Tasha had always been logical, so I imagined she was waiting until we were out of the woods to unleash her anger. To find out your older brother was alive while simultaneously undergoing torture probably caused several conflicting feelings.

"We could jump," Ashton suggested, looking outside the balcony down below.

I followed his gaze. Glass shards covered the concrete platform from my powers when I took out the sliding doors. I shook my head. "Tasha's too injured."

"Not if she lands in the pool." Ashton pointed to the large kidney-shaped basin of water fifteen stories down. "It's our only choice. The three of us cannot ward off that many DOAA agents all armed with thermo daggers." Ashton went over and slipped his arm under Tasha's shoulders, cradling her. He dipped the other arm under her knees and lifted her up. Her legs dangled off his forearm as he cradled her like a baby. I heard him tell her in a gentle voice, "I've missed you more than you know. Hold on, okay?"

I ignored Tasha's whimpers and stepped through the hole in the sliding doors to the terrace balcony. I couldn't listen to the pain I had caused her. It would break my source into pieces. Ashton followed with Tasha in tow. While a jump from this height might be suicidal for a human, it was a viable though possibly painful escape route for a Ferroean, even as weak as we all were.

We exchanged nods, and I counted to three, then we all leapt off the balcony in unison. The wind whipped my hair and cheeks back as I adjusted my body into perfect diving form. If there was one superpower I had always wanted, it was flying. I'd guess this is the closest I'd get to that.

The splash of the water around us was like a volcano erupting inward. Water doused the lounge chairs and towels on the side of the pool. Thankfully, the area was empty, and no humans witnessed our miracle dives. Ashton and I had been able to slip headfirst into the water for a smooth landing, but Tasha wasn't able to adjust for the fall. Her dive was messy, and the force of the water against her body dazed her. I swam to the ledge and pushed myself out; my clothes hung on me like a weighted blanket. I helped Ashton lift Tasha from the water. Her limbs were still weak and lifeless. I had only a short time to heal her and it wasn't enough. The trauma to her source points was too great and source plasma was still freely oozing out of the open wounds. With Ashton already a half-human liability, Tasha close to death, and my powers completely diminished, we had to get the three of us out of here and fast.

I looked past the patch of grass to the steel gate enclosing the pool area. The yellow Hellcat was waiting for us on the other side with Beatrice in the driver's seat. Her head swiveled as a tirade of irritated shouts ripped from above. Fifteen floors over us, the DOAA agents saw we had escaped, and they were enraged.

"Move!" I yelled to Ashton. He was holding up Tasha, carrying most of her weight against his side. No response was needed. They darted for the fence, Tasha's arm around Ashton's shoulder for support. I was on their heels, leaping up to catch the fence and lifting myself to the top.

Ashton lifted Tasha up, and I pulled her up and over with Ashton right behind. "Why didn't you melt the fence?" Ashton's voice sounded below me.

"Because then the enemy could walk right through it." I pointed to the handful of agents now on our tail. Tasha's face was pale and drained. I held her in my arms.

"Look at you, getting carried around by your brothers," Ashton said from behind me. "Aren't you the luckiest girl?" I glared at Ashton. I was certain Tasha was not feeling lucky no matter how cute he was trying to be. I gently put her in the back seat of the car and followed her in. I had to heal her. I motioned for Ashton to sit in the front. We watched the agents climbing the fence trying to chase after us. In unison, Ashton and I yelled, "Go!"

Bea didn't need more than that to throw the car into drive, pulling away from the sidewalk and gunning toward the exit. "What the hell is going on?" Bea breathed, keeping her eyes on the road as she raced down the side street.

"Make a right here. Get on the Pacific Coast Highway," I said motioning to the road. "Take this all the way. It runs parallel to the ocean. We need to drive up toward the Palisades." Thankfully, Beatrice didn't argue this time.

Tasha cut in, answering her question. "I was waiting in the hotel room like we discussed. There was a knock at the door. I thought it was you guys. When I opened it, I was attacked by DOAA agents. I fought back and apparently that ticked them off. I gave one a black eye." So that's why She-Hulk had marks over her brows. "They held me down and slit my right wrist with a thermo dagger. It was pretty much silent until about ten mins later when you knocked." She stared up at me. "I expected Beatrice and you. When I saw she wasn't with you, I drew you into the room. I knew they were after her and I'd hope we could give her time to escape or at least get to the others." She motioned with her eyes to our brother in the front seat. "Always surprising me, huh?"

"They didn't say anything?" Ashton asked.

Tasha hesitated. "Director Dodd said, 'I wonder how your brothers will react when they see this.' It didn't make much sense until I saw you both at the door." Tears were starting to well up in her eyes.

I ignored the incoming emotions and fixated on what she had said. "He wasn't surprised you were there. I wonder what he meant about 'until recently.' Who the hell would know you were still alive but Father and me? And no one knew I was coming to get you, especially not Zane. I didn't even tell Beatrice." I took my thermo dagger out and slit my wrist. "Feed. You need to heal faster. Your wounds are too deep."

"You're weak, Cash. This is the weakest I've ever seen you. I won't take any more. I'll feed from Ashton."

Ashton turned in the front seat and gazed back at our sister. "Tasha, I know you've been through a lot today and I really hate to add to that, but I can't heal you. I don't have those powers on Earth."

Tasha's eyes widened. Her irises swirled, blues and greens collided with reds and yellows, a kaleidoscope of colors. "What? What do you mean? Why wouldn't you have those powers on Earth specifically?"

Beatrice caught my eyes in her rearview mirror and mouthed, "Say something." I did the only thing I could. I told Tasha the truth.

"He's a Blood-Light."

Chapter Twelve

Beatrice

One turn after the next, I followed Cash's instructions without comment. In fact, we otherwise rode in relative silence, none really knowing what to say. If anyone had the right to be asking a million questions right now it was Tasha, but she'd allowed herself to slip into a troubled sleep after only taking the smallest amount of healing from Cash. She refused to take more than she needed to close her wounds, demanding they wait until we met up with the rest of the group, where she would feed from someone in a stronger state.

I assumed that was where we were going—some safe house or rendezvous point they'd all previously discussed when I wasn't around. It made sense, but I couldn't help but feel a little chafed at the thought that I was the only one in the dark. I took comfort knowing that at least Ashton was likely right there with me even if his mind was some- where else. He gazed out the window, watching the scenery change from the congestion of the city, to suburban hous- ing developments, to eventually a winding road that took us through tall thin pine trees and hills that eventually made my ears pop from the elevation.

"Keep an eye on your left," Cash said as he peered out the windows. I closed my mouth, held the sides of my nose to close the passageways, and blew air into my nostrils, hoping to alleviate the drowning pressure in my head. "It's coming up soon, the next opening but the turn is easy to miss, Sammie said. It's before the bend in the road." In a lower voice, "And with the way you drive, you're likely to..." He didn't finish that sentence. "There! The opening." He pointed over my shoulder.

I swatted his hand away when I spotted the mailbox. If I hadn't been driving insanely slow, I might have missed it, but with Cash's snide comments about my driving skills, I drove at a snail's pace. I easily turned into a driveway that looked more like a service road than an entrance to a home. A few car lengths farther in, we were stopped by a looming gate of wrought iron, the wall it connected to almost obscured by trees and climbing vines. I looked at Cash, but he was just staring at the closed gate as if waiting for it to open. I looked around, trying to spot a security camera we could wave at, but if there was one it was well hidden.

"What's that?" Ashton asked from the passenger seat, pointing out the driver's side.

"Can you both stop putting your fingers in my face?" I asked, narrowing my eyes at the nearly choked-in-ivy intercom box you see in parking garages. There was a button covered in dust, and what looked like a speaker with twigs sticking out of it. I put the car back in gear and maneuvered it so that I could open my window in front of it. I hit the red button.

"Hello, is this..." I suddenly realized I had no idea where we were or what I was supposed to say. "What do I say?" I asked Cash.

"Your name, unless you've gone mute again." Cash winked at me through the rearview mirror.

"You're funny!" I balked. When Cash and I first met at Cartwright High School, he flustered me so much, my vocal cords paralyzed in his presence. But now, I was not even close to fearing him. "My voice works perfectly well, thank you."

"Thank the Council." Cash's sardonic tone increased as he said, "Maybe there's a password like in your human movies." He peered out his window. I took a breath and then turned back to the box.

"Hello, is this "Dr. X's" home?" I emphasized the strange name I'd been assuming was code, and really hoped this was the right place. No reply came through. Not even static. I tried again with the same result, and then noticed a little slot underneath the speaker. It was just the same size as...

I patted down my pocket, pulling out the key card Cash had given me before we left Cartwright. He had handed me that and a picture of my mom, Dr. X, and me. Told me to keep them safe since they were left by my mother as clues.

"I'm impressed," Cash said, and tugged on my braid from behind me.

I slipped it in, and for a moment felt total dismay as the box whirred to life, and then sucked the entire card in. Before I could curse my stupid idea, there was a soft chime, and then the card was spit back out again. I grabbed it as the gate opened inward, permitting us through.

The pine trees crowded close to the curving dirt road, obscuring whatever might be ahead of us as we climbed at an angle. I was just about to ask where the hell we were when the trees finally opened up just enough to see a large turnaround situated in front of the oddest split-level home I'd ever seen.

The four-story monstrosity was a Frank Lloyd Wright nightmare—all low-pitched roofs at various heights, overhanging geometric eaves, and floor-to-ceiling windows tinted too dark to see through. It sprawled out in front of us, and I could see the hill drop away directly behind, an evergreen valley far below. One of the floors practically hovered over the open space with only minimal support. I felt dizzy just looking at it.

I pulled the car to a stop as close to the front door as I could get and resisted the urge to throw myself out of the car. We'd been cooped up too close and too long. Farther away there was a garage door, currently open to reveal a beat-up-looking black minivan and a dark blue sedan.

"Now what?" I said to Cash.

He checked the position of his thermo dagger at his ankle before swinging open the passenger door. "Now we go in." He looked around. "Unless you'd like to go for a hike or a bike ride, maybe even a—"

I cut him off. "You are literally the most frustrating alien ever!" Ashton waved from the front seat, asking to be added to that list. "Oh my god, you are too! Happy?"

Ashton nodded and twisted in his seat. In a soft voice, he said, "Hey, sis." Tasha had curled up against the door during the ride, her head cradled in her own arms. He leaned over his seat and stroked her hair, his fingers untangling stringy clumps that had stuck together from all the plasma and blood she'd lost in the fight. He didn't seem bothered by it. "Time to get up."

Tasha's eyes fluttered as Cash opened his door, ran around to the other side, and gingerly helped her out of the car seat. She leaned heavily against him, and I could see Cash's knees bend and then recover. He was too weak to even support part of her weight. Ashton must have noticed too, because he quickly climbed out of the front seat to get his arm under his sister.

"I've got her," Cash growled, but his face had paled from either pain or weakness. Maybe both. His teasing charm had vacated our conversations and was replaced with complete exhaustion.

I reached out to him and his shoulder tensed for a moment under my hand, but he met my eyes. "Ashton and I can get her inside. Why don't you go get that door open?" He relented, his eyes resigned. He let me slip into his place, steadying Tasha's other side. She winced as her weight shifted even slightly over her feet, and I remembered the slashes to her ankles. "Ashton..." I didn't have to say anything more. Her brother scooped her up in his arms, and before she could protest, I said, "We don't need you opening up those cuts Cash healed closed, okay? It's just a short distance to the door." Tasha gave me a faint smile, and the three of us followed Cash up the walkway to the front door. He'd barely knocked when it opened inward suddenly. Sammie was in the doorway, radiating a mixture of anger, relief, and concern.

"It's about time! We were starting to..." Her voice trailed off as her eyes turned into slits. The sight of Tasha in Ashton's arms stunned her silent, and she threw open the door. It crashed against the house from the force. "Oh, this is...What happened? Get her inside! Ashton, by the Council, how are you..." She pursed her lips as her eyes narrowed, saying his name, remembering he was supposed to be dead. We ignored that for now and let her usher us inside the huge foyer of the odd house.

The floorplan was open—I could see past the entryway and into the living room ahead, and the dining space and kitchen area sprawled to the left. The huge panoramic windows looked crystal clear from this side, and I could see out over the forest beyond. The floor stretched out to the right into a study—no, a library? Laboratory? Art studio? I shook my head, turning my attention back to Tasha and resolving to understand my surroundings after she was taken care of.

Ashton didn't wait for direction, but instead beelined for the long, fire engine red couch in the center of the living space. He laid Tasha down as Mark and Paul rushed in from the kitchen area. They stopped, their eyes wide as saucers when they saw Ashton.

"Explanations later—one of you needs to heal Tasha, fast, and I don't mean hold her hand. Cut your joint and let her feed," Ashton barked and stepped away. Mark snapped back to reality at Tasha's name and darted to her, kneeling beside her and saying soft comforting things. White light started emanating from his hands as he used his source to finish the healing Cash could only partially start.

I looked to my boyfriend-slash-bodyguard, a small smile of relief on my face that Tasha was going to be okay. But his eyes were glazed over, and before I could reach out his legs went out from under him and he dropped to the floor.

As soon as he fell, Sammie and Paul were at his side. Cash had been worse than he'd let on. He must have been holding on just long enough to get Tasha to safety, but he had nothing left. We carried him down a flight of steps to another sitting room below.

"Come upstairs when he's stable," Sammie said. Her voice sounded clipped, like she wanted to say more. She and Paul left us there alone, and I closed my lips around his, a gentle kiss allowing my source into him. He didn't hesitate and drew the ethereal energy in, taking all that he could. Warmth crept into my chest as the source burned from him, heating my veins and forcing them to flood with energy. He shifted, cupping the back of my head with his hands. I could feel him healing and growing stronger beneath me as I myself felt relief, and after a minute or two I forced myself to pull away. I hadn't realized how much I needed him to feed. We were a balance. "Cash," I breathed, feeling light-headed but calm.

"I'm here," he said quietly, his eyes closed but relaxed. "Thank you. I'm feeling like a rock star again." He kissed my cheek and then my nose. I smiled under his sweet touches. Heat permeated my skin and then cool as he pushed himself away.

I ran a hand through his hair. "Why don't you rest a little? I'll be back down in a bit." He mumbled something in reply, already half asleep. I stood and made my way back upstairs in time for a shouting match.

"What do you MEAN you couldn't heal her!" Sammie was staring Ashton down as Paul loomed next to her. Her hands were on her hips, her nose scrunched high.

"Exactly that," Ashton replied calmly, his hands up in surrender. "I'm special, like Beatrice." Ashton winked at me as he saw me under the framed entranceway. "My powers don't work the same as yours on Earth."

"What? That doesn't make any sense." Paul's face twisted, causing his dimples to appear. "Beatrice was made, like, on purpose."

"So you are saying I'm an oops baby?" Ashton teased. "How rude of you, Paul." He drew out Paul's name like he was tasting it on his tongue.

"By the Council, Ashton, are you saying you're a Blood-Light?" Sammie threw her hands in the air. "And how the hell are you still alive? You are like a damn cat, nine-lives!"

"Meow!" Ashton motioned with claw-like hands.

"Enough!" Mark shouted, his voice uncharacteristically loud and commanding enough that everyone, including Sammie, listened. He was still at Tasha's side, his healing momentarily paused. "Two of our team members are down. I'm sure Cash has an explanation for Ashton, and as our *Captain"*—he emphasized the word, and I realized it was the first time I'd heard the team pull rank on one another—"he will fill us in if and when he is able. He glared at each of them in turn. "Until then, keep your voices down." He examined Ashton. *"And* your heckling." Sammie and Paul gave him a quick nod, snapping into old military habits while Ashton saluted him. I almost giggled but instead breathed a sigh of relief and made a mental note to thank Mark later for his acute sense of priorities. Tasha was still lying on the couch, but color was starting to come back to her complexion.

"Is Cash ok?" Mark asked me, taking in my presence.

"Yeah, he's resting." I looked back at the stairway I had come from, remembering how fast Cash fell asleep. "He needs it, more than I think any of us knew."

I took a chance to absorb the surroundings. The living room furniture was mismatched, but not in a thrift store kind of way. The materials were all expensive and in good shape, but none of them looked like they belonged in the same room. In further contrast, a modern chandelier of geometric glass and shards of silver and gold hung above the seating area, reflecting light through the room with every disturbance of the air. Before I could turn to get a better look at the study-slash-laboratory, I heard someone approach me from behind.

"Tea?" A tall man with white flowing hair, a brightly colored bow tie, and glasses at the tip of his nose walked in. He carried two mugs in his hand, both shaped like some kind of cartoon character. One was held out for me, and I took it on reflex. It was warm and smelled of bitter green tea and tart pomegranate. I held it in my hands more like a prop than anything I planned to drink.

"You must be Dr. X?" I don't remember him from the week my mother kidnapped me, but I recognized him from the time-stamped picture of the three of us together that Cash had given me. He was everything the team had said he would be: composed and socially awkward.

"Technically yes, I am, but I have many names." He sipped his own mug of tea and smiled, his eyes bright and hazel like mine. "Welcome to my humble abode. I'm glad the group arrived mostly intact, if not a little worse for wear. Shall we sit? We have lots to discuss." He didn't wait for a response as he ushered me to a large kitchen island in the middle of the modern kitchen.

I quickly averted my eyes from the far windows. The clarity of the glass made it look like the floor simply dropped out into the valley below. The counter was littered with bowls and plates of snacks, as if he was hosting a small party rather than a house full of fugitive soldiers. The snacks themselves didn't quite seem right, though—there was salsa, but no tortilla chips; a pile of nectarines; a whole cauliflower next to a bowl of some kind of dressing that definitely wasn't ranch—balsamic maybe? And who just has a whole jar of black licorice out for guests? Despite the odd spread, my stomach growled. I hadn't eaten in hours. I eyed the potato chips but grabbed a nectarine instead, craving sugar but not enough to go for the horrid black candy staring back at me.

"Oh, before I forget! Robert wanted me to tell you that he's safe and at the Hive—he'll be there waiting for you after you all take care of Seraphina's Awakening." Dr. X dipped a potato chip into the salsa and popped it into his mouth.

My emotions seesawed—first, relief knowing my father was safe, but then conflicted at the thought of Sera. Cash still hadn't made any sort of choice, and I didn't feel like I had the right to press, either.

"What's the Hive?" I asked to distract myself.

"Ah! It's the cave base for the rebels—you've been there." Dr. X munched on more potato chips and salsa.

I had a vague inkling of a cave from the memories that had only recently been restored. It was where my mother had Sera's source transferred into my chest cavity. "I don't remember much, honestly," I replied. "But we met there, right?" I fidgeted with my hair, wrapping the loose strands from my braid behind my ear.

Dr. X nodded. "We did. Faye brought you there and I performed your source assimilation. You did very well during the procedure."

My hand automatically went to my chest and rubbed the raised diamond-shaped scar under my shirt, the mark from the very surgery Dr. X was talking about.

"The Hive is the major hub for the Ferroean Resistance on this side of the wormholes. It's built right on top of one, in fact." He must have registered my look of complete confusion. "You"—he pointed at me with a potato chip in his fingers—"haven't seen a wormhole, have you?"

I breathed a sigh. There was a lot I hadn't seen, or understood, or needed to know more about if I was going to help save our planets. "No. It's some kind of...portal...right?"

Dr. X snapped his finger, forgetting there was a potato chip there. Salty crumbs took off into the air, but he just shrugged and brushed his fingers off on a napkin. "Correct! But that can mean a lot of things, can't it?" He sat back, his tone adjusted from glib to academic in an instant. "You see, Earth and Ferro have a very long symbiotic relationship. While divided by light years in terms of physical distance, there are a number of interstellar doorways—wormholes—that travel from one to the other. Some theorize that the sheer number of these so-called "portals" distort time, which could be why one year spent on Earth is four years on Ferro, but that could honestly also have something to do with a number of gravitational differences, the black hole near Ferro, or something we haven't even found out about yet."

I listened, trying not to look overwhelmed. "So there are...more than one wormhole?" I asked.

Dr. X smiled proudly, like a teacher to his prize student. "Exactly! Although most of the major openings on Earth travel to one big central wormhole outside of Ferro's capital. The DOAA built their complex over one of the largest. They say it's to protect it, but it also restricts any major movements from the Ferroean Council to Earth. The oldest stable wormhole is in the Scottish moors; people like to say it's the one near Stonehenge, but that one is actually rather unstable. I don't think it's been active for a good couple of centuries, at best. Other somewhat stable wormholes exist on small islands south of Tokyo and off the coast of Bermuda, but those are a little harder to defend or use effectively, given that they are in the middle of an ocean."

I remembered all the stories of the Bermuda Triangle I'd been terrified of as a kid and realized it may not have been so foolish after all. I took a few bites of the nectarine, considering this new information. Just sitting up here had restored some of my energy, and I suddenly felt eager to check on Cash.

"Very good," Dr. X said, reading my mind even though I knew he was human, and that wasn't possible. It felt suspicious. "Here, take these down to him. If I recall, they are his favorite." He handed me the bowl of potato chips. They weren't sour cream and onion, but they'd do in a pinch. I thanked him and stood but then turned. There was a question eating at me since Cash handed me the picture.

"Were you and my mother close?"

Dr. X tilted his head, causing his glasses to fall almost off. He caught the frames, readjusting them on his face. "What do you mean close?"

"How long have you known her?"

Dr. X smiled but it didn't reach his ears. "Since she was born. She was my daughter."

Chapter Thirteen

Ashton

Dr. X sat in the driver's seat of the black minivan as I sat next to him in the passenger bucket seat. The cloth was ripped at the armrests from wear and tear and the headrest was missing. Dust covered the dashboard while bird droppings spotted the windshield. I wondered if this car had been ever cleaned.

Cash was behind me on the van's plastic floor. Beatrice leaned into his side. The others sat opposite each other on makeshift wooden benches screwed into the interior walls, chatting softly. I found myself captivated by the rolling landscape of what the others had called the "State Park of Topanga." Most of what I'd seen of Earth so far had been highways, suburbs, and cities that, while a hell of a lot grimier than Ferro, were still functionally similar. Paved roads. Glass and metal buildings. The occasional patch of curated greenery. Even the suburban homes from human sitcoms were uniform and boxy, even if they were painted garish colors and covered in gaudy decorations. This was different. This was alien to me.

The van picked up a cloud of dust as it bounded over the uneven dirt roads. Everything was dry and shades of yellow and brown. Even the thick vegetation had a dusky cast to it as it spread out around us, thick like short, scraggly forests in some spots, thin and dry in others. Great sandy rock formations jutted from the ground, with no indication that the humans had bothered to minimize or terraform them into something more usable. In fact, I noticed a few had plaques posted up nearby, as if there was something important to say about a hunk of mud or dirt. Humans certainly make strange decisions, but there was something bizarrely beautiful about the chaotic expanse of hills and desert that surrounded us on all sides. It almost made me forget about what we were doing here. It was the calm before the storm. We had an hour to get into the Department of Alien Affairs headquarters, perform the Awakening, and get the hell out of there.

Dr. X had a secret passageway in through a vent that filtered the recycled air. He had created a remote-control app on his phone, allowing him to break into the DOAA's system and paralyze the fans for five minutes. All six of us had to get through it before the automated backup system clicked back on. The front and side perimeters were heavily guarded, but the DOAA believed the back entrance and the vents were impenetrable.

"And why's that?" I asked.

"Because I created the system and I told them so," Dr. X reasoned. Sounded good to me. I just hoped Director Dodd hadn't uncovered the secret by now. When it came to the DOAA, anything was possible, and everything could be expected.

"Wanna tell me the plan again, Doc? I feel like this is too easy. Are we missing something?" I asked, not even looking his way. I was mesmerized by the yellow expanse of grasslands to our right as a pair of birds circled and swooped, landing in the crooked branches of a shrubby tree. "It's quite simple. We park the van in the employee lot on the side. It's the closest to the back where the vent entrance is. My van is parked in the lot all the time—I have a corporate sticker and everything—so no one will question the presence of an employee vehicle." His stomach rumbled. "Did you know they are adding a new restaurant wing in the DOAA? I'm looking forward to there being a sushi option."

I swiveled my head to Dr. X, who was unfazed by his own admission of excitement to a new selection of DOAA cuisine. I'd heard this guy was strange. Remarkably, he was living up to those rumors.

"One of you can melt the hinges. We will all climb in. Once I set the timer, we will have five minutes to crawl through and down the vent to where they are holding Seraphina. Tasha will give me Gertrude's source and we will implant it in Seraphina. Then Cash will zap her and awakened she shall be."

Cash moved in between our two bucket seats. His head tilted toward the doctor. His voice was low and growly like a grizzly bear. "Did you say I will zap Sera? What do you mean by zap her?"

"Yes. You will have to zap her with your source. Her wrists and ankles, to be exact."

The van's metal skeleton started to vibrate as I watched my brother's fists clench into a tight ball. I wondered if Dr. X had a death wish because the next move my brother was about to make was murder. I placed my hand on his shoulder while turning my attention to the doctor. "Hey, Doc, not to sound ignorant but I think Cash here"—I glanced at Cash, whose bristling source caused the metal in the van to clang—"is a little concerned. I know you are human and all, but if we are 'zapped,' as you so delicately put it, on our four joints, we most likely will die." I removed my hand from Cash and grabbed the water bottle at my side. "So I think maybe a lengthier explanation would be beneficial for all of us." I twisted the cap off and sipped, allowing the cool liquid to calm my heated insides. "Especially you, who could lose his life prematurely to the opposing source behind you that you've angered."

Dr. X looked strangely confused. His nose twitched. "I only said getting into the DOAA HQ would be easy. I never claimed an Awakening would be." His glasses started to slip off his face. He pressed his pointer fingers into the bridge to slide them back up to the base. "If an Awakening was simple, don't you think more Ferroeans would have tried it? Why do you think it's done by multiple technicians in the sanatorium center on Ferro? It's a delicate procedure."

Cash was now full-fledged growling. I crossed my calf over my thigh and finished the remnants of fluid, tossing the bottle to the floor. This whole vehicle was a garbage can. I doubted it would be noticed.

"Dr. X, do you think you could explain in detail how Cash can..." Beatrice turned to me and asked, "Is there any other word I can use to replace zap?" I shrugged my shoulders. How the Council was I supposed to know? This was the first time Dr. X had told any of us what an Awakening entailed.

Tasha had moved to the front of the van behind Cash, keenly attuned to our brother's temper flares. "How about charge? I think that would be a correct and less-murderous word."

Beatrice nodded. "Can Cash *charge* Seraphina without accidentally killing her?"

My brain started working overtime as understanding hit me. I rubbed my hands down my jeans. They were starting to sweat. "I really hate to be the one to ask this question, but it would absolutely put a damper on this mission if Sera somehow didn't come out of it alive, so I think I should address the elephant, zombie, or llamas—whatever else a human would notice—in the room." Cash, Beatrice, and Tasha all stared at me as I spoke. Not one of them had thought of it, which gave me more to worry about—our blind faith in Dr. X.

"Has this ever been done before on Earth, an Awakening I mean?" Dr. X continued to look at the road. Part of me was thankful his focus was on driving given this man was behind the wheel. The other part of me was concerned he didn't answer right away.

After a long pause both Dr. X and Cash spoke at the same time, Dr. X's "No, it hasn't" drowned out by Cash's, "Yes, of course it has."

My head thudded into my hands. We were so screwed.

We arrived at the DOAA's vent opening. It was a square metal flap approximately three-and-a-half feet on each side. I stood there watching Cash melt the lock. The heat from his power radiated off him and heated my skin. The lock disengaged and with a loud bang the door swung open and clanged against the adjacent structure. All of us ducked except Dr. X. He stood watching the five of us in crouched positions. "Are you coming?" he asked, ignoring our stances as he crawled in. One by one our crew entered. Cash and I were last. He grabbed me by the arm and pulled me back.

"Whatever happens in there, you make a promise to me, brother." His face was stoic as his fingers pressed into my skin. "You make sure Beatrice gets out alive. You make sure she saves this world. Promise me—now."

I had known my brother my whole life. I had never seen him act so selfless until I saw him with Beatrice. Yes, he put our planet before himself and I always admired that, but he had never put one life in front of it all. And for that I admired him more.

"Promise me?" he asked again. His tone was edged with worry.

I placed my free hand on his shoulder and gave it a squeeze. "I promise, brother. Crede Mihi."

"Crede Mihi," he responded.

We crept into the small space and closed the metal flap. Cash melted the steel closure behind us before we crawled to meet the others.

For a maintenance vent, it was well-lit inside. The corners had pinprick white lights every other panel. The smell of bleach was overwhelming. "Anyone else concerned with why the DOAA vents are so clean?" I whispered.

"It's not the vents. It's the sterilized halls below us. We are above the medical wing of DOAA headquarters. It's the only place they could safely keep Seraphina," Tasha answered in a low voice. Dr. X had his own office in the medical wing. As the scientist assigned to her care, he checked on Seraphina regularly. I'm not sure if that was by design on Dr. X's part or blind luck, but either way I'd take it.

"At the count of three we must move and move fast. Ready?" Dr. X whispered to us. "One. Two. Three. Go."

My knees and shins pressed into the cool metal as we crawled like our feet were on fire. We made it through and down the vent in less than three minutes. There were no guards at the door or security cameras to be wary of.

"Is it me or is the DOAA a little too trusting?" I asked, observing the corridor outside the room Sera was being held in. Cash shook his head. "I think they are just ignorant. She's hooked up to machines keeping her 'fresh.' They know there's no way to get her out of here with her incapacitated."

We rounded the hall to the metal, wood, and glass hospital-looking doors. With a whoosh of Tasha's hands, she commanded the entrance open. We followed her into the room.

Three metal tables lined the wall of the softly lit room, and only the one in the center was occupied. Curling strands of Seraphina's jet-black hair draped over its edge, her supine body covered by a white sheet. Wires and tubes strung from her arms and connected to a multi-armed, spiderlike device towering over her form. It must have been some kind of machine to keep her body preserved as Cash had described.

Sammie sucked in a loud, pained breath, causing the rest of us to turn to see what was wrong. "What? It's not every day I see my best friend look like a DOAA science project. I swear to the Council I'm going to break some agent's limbs if this doesn't work." She flipped her hair over her shoulders, trying to look hardened, but I saw the fear in her eyes. I nodded in agreement with her. It was a disturbing sight, seeing Sera lie on an operating table hooked up to human-made robots keeping her alive. Her chest barely rose.

Cash pulled back the cloth, letting his emotions get the better of him. Energy crackled in the room, affecting the lights above us. Sera looked like she always did, perfect. Skin flawless, lips plump, hair still perfectly curled and free of frizz. Cash cupped her face and whispered something in her ear and then he stood. His face was drained, all emotion replaced with the necessity of what he had to attempt. "Let's get this over with."

Dr. X nodded. He pulled out a chair from behind a desk littered in paperwork. He turned on the computer screen and started to tap away at the keyboard. "Tasha, I assume you have Gertrude's energy source?"

Tasha pulled out a velvet black case from her pocket and untied the closure. She dipped her fingers inside and pulled out a glowing yellow stone: Gertrude's source, extracted by the team when they'd fought her weeks ago.

"Good. You and Cash will perform the Awakening. I need to monitor Seraphina's vitals from this computer. The others need to stand close to the edges of the room so they don't get hit."

"Hit by what?" Paul said, speaking for the first time in hours. I get it. This was not a Council's dream vacation by any means. He and his brother Mark had been extremely quiet.

"The source," Dr. X said as he cleaned his glasses with his shirt and placed them back on his face. "Tasha, you will need to make a small incision in the shape of an 'X' over her assimilation scar and place the source stone on top of it. It may start to sink into her chest cavity, but that's ok."

Tasha sucked in a deep breath as she reached for a long, sharp tool set out on a nearby tray. I think the humans called it a scalpel. She made two crossed slits in the center of the scar, then placed Gertrude's source over Sera's chest.

"Cash, you need to 'charge' "—Dr. X paused and glanced at Beatrice for approval of his new term, and she nodded—"Seraphina's wrists and ankles as fast as you can. If you think it wasn't a large-enough charge, revisit the area and charge again. If you break the skin of her shell, she could die. It needs to be a charge strong enough to ignite the source but careful enough you don't cut or damage the flesh. Got it?"

Cash's eyes turned to narrowed slits as he glared at Dr. X. "Yeah, sounds easy." He turned to our sister. "Go stand with the others. I don't want to blast you."

Tasha walked over to Mark and stood by his side. I backed into the corner and leaned up against it. I guess there were worse ways to die than this.

Cash rolled the sheet up from the bottom so that we could see Seraphina's feet. He repeated a similar motion with her pant legs, rolling them high enough to expose the bare skin around her ankles. He then turned her wrists so that the inside was visible, exposing those points as well.

"Ready?" Cash must have been asking himself rather than us, because he didn't wait for an answer. He held up his palm, releasing four short charges, each perfectly aimed at both of Seraphina's wrists and ankles. Bright white light filled the room for a moment, and then everything went utterly, completely dark. Whatever else Cash did, he had knocked out the power.

Chapter Fourteen

Beatrice

Darkness. We were standing in complete darkness. I'd been holding my breath since the moment Cash had sent out the charges, and now I had no idea if he'd just killed Seraphina, alerted the DOAA to our existence, or even worse, both. But within seconds, the fluorescent lights of the medical examination room flickered back on. And as if timed by something more powerful than us, Seraphina's body tensed once, and then her blue eyes opened, framed by impossibly thick dark lashes. She gasped for air, and I finally took a breath myself. A tear escaped down her blushed cheek as she breathed Cash's name.

He placed his palms against her face, a white light outlining her head in an almost angelic ringlet. He was healing her. His eyes held back moisture. It was such a tender and private moment, I wanted to look away. Their mutual love was obvious, and it nearly broke my human heart. The energy source inside me had simmered as well, vibrating at the lowest decimal. I thought my jealous turmoil would have wreaked havoc on my source or altered its escalation, but it didn't. All its reaction confirmed for me was that I definitely didn't know much about the power inside of my chest, and only Sera could help me learn more.

"You did it," she breathed. Her voice was raspy at first. She swallowed a couple of times, pulsating her throat. "I knew you would come back for me. I knew you would figure out what needed to be done and do it. Thank you." Tasha, Sammie, Mark, and Paul closed in on her bed. Sammie and Tasha had tears running down their cheeks. I took a couple of steps closer but kept my distance. It didn't feel appropriate to crowd her bed with the others.

"Did you think we wouldn't? Come on now." Cash's voice was soft and void of the argumentative quality he normally gave me. Her beautiful pink lips tipped up toward her ears, showcasing her perfect white teeth. Her hands covered Cash's on her face.

"I missed you." She spoke as if no one else was in the room. "Crede Mihi."

Cash leaned down and kissed her forehead and whispered back, "Crede Mihi." He released each of the tentacle-like connections dangling between her arms and the machine that had been keeping her shell alive.

Sammie pushed her brothers out of the way and threw her arms around her best friend, knocking Cash over in the process. Instead of fighting her, he backed up a step and smiled, a rare gesture between the two teammates. "I missed you. Like so much. Can you not do that again? Or at least tell us the plan. I moped around forever mourning you."

Seraphina laughed and wrapped her arms around Sammie. The white sheet around her fell from her upper body down to her waist exposing her black tank top. Her head rested in the crook of Sammie's shoulder. Her eyes closed as she hugged her best friend. The gesture reminded me of Darla and me. I wished she was here right now.

"Missed you, girl. Now tell me, did you keep Cash in line for me while I was gone?" They giggled and released.

"Like I could keep that asshat in any line. He's a freaking roller coaster ride. There wasn't a day that went by I didn't want to stab him with a thermo dagger. He's a royal pain in my—

"Enough about your ass, Sammie. Give Sera some room to breathe." Cash pulled Sammie by the shoulders back in line with him while asking, "Sera, do you need anything? Water?" He turned slightly toward Dr. X, who was still sitting behind the computer at the desk off to the side of her metal bed. "Shouldn't she be weaker or look ill or something? Do we need to get her food?"

"Actually, she's fine. Her body has been resting this whole time. She should feed but not on human food. Feeding directly from someone's source will help strengthen her connection to the source and increase her vitality." Dr. X paused. I cringed, hoping he wouldn't tell her the source was her mother's. I knew the others, especially Cash, wanted to wait to tell her Cash had killed her mom. It would be a hard story to tell. "We need to get her on her feet and moving. Plus, we all need to get out of this building as soon as possible before we alert anyone to our presence." Dr. X looked at the bottom of the screen. "We have exactly nineteen minutes before the guards do their rounds on this floor. Lucky for us no one is ever down here on a Saturday unless they are doing security checks."

The blue light of the computer screen reflected off his glasses, highlighting his hazel eyes. It was rare to see eyes that looked so similar to my mom's and mine. I wondered if anyone else had noticed. I caught myself at moments just staring at the man that was my grandfather. He had no emotional connection to that information, where I was completely dumbfounded by the revelation. I asked him a hundred questions about my mother, my grandmother, but he had very little to offer. He wasn't in my mother's life outside of the DOAA. No holidays, bedtime stories, or sundaes together. They worked jointly at the department since she was a child and then when she was an adult but as far as family, he didn't really value the good stuff, the stuff my mother desperately instilled in me. And now I understood why. She tried to give me what her life lacked.

"I like the purple bow tie, Dr. X. I see you are stepping outside your red- and brown-tie ways. Purple is very classic chic," Sera said, acknowledging Dr. X's style. He nodded in appreciation, then went back to his *tap tap tapping* on the computer keyboard.

I caught Tasha looking back and forth between Cash and Mark. It was such a subtle glance that I almost missed it. Mark stepped in front of Cash, sliding a doctor's chair with wheels over to the bedside. He sat and rolled up his sleeve.

"I guess I'm going to have to heal you to get some attention, huh?" Mark grabbed a thermo dagger from his boot and cut his human shell, exposing his Ferroean vein. Sera smiled and reached for his hand, pressing her lips to his wrist and absorbing the alien plasma.

Paul jumped up from the metal table he was sitting on. "Hey, I would have offered if I knew Sera was handing out attention. All I ever get from this group are jabs about my lack of Ferroean history. Attention would be a nice change."

Sammie growled. "That's because you never pay attention. I literally have no idea why Cash put you on this team. Other than for entertainment."

Cash laughed. "She's got a point there, Paul. If we ever get back to Ferro, I'm throwing your butt back into Guard's training again, and you are taking the written courses with a teacher less interested in your looks." He held his finger up. "But she's right, I do enjoy your sense of humor." Cash winked at Paul, whose right dimple was dancing back and forth as he bowed in acknowledgment of his wit.

"Good to know I'm appreciated. Always at your service, Captain." He teased.

Dr. X motioned for Tasha to come over to the computer. Tasha smiled as she passed in front of me. That small act of kindness was the only reminder I was in the room. I had felt like an intruder from the second Sera opened her eyes.

"Tasha will finish up here. It's set to wipe out all the data from the Awakening in the DOAA computers so no one will be the wiser." His glasses started to slip from his nose. He used his pointer finger to push them back up. "Well anyone with half a brain will already guess what we did but they won't have proof or data. You'll need to stay here until its completed." Dr. X looked down at his watch. "It'll be another twenty minutes or so. I'm headed back to the cave. I'll exit the DOAA as if I had been working here all morning and catch a ride on the corporate bus. Sera knows the way back by van. We must meet there tonight before sunset. Do not be late. Our next steps will be laid out. There's not as much time as you think." Dr. X cautioned. He stood and let Tasha take his seat. He nodded to Sera as he headed to the back door. "And do not get caught on the way out." Then he slipped through the back door and was gone.

Sera finished with Mark, returning her focus back to the crew. "So how much crap did you all give Cash when you thought I was dead?" Sera winked at Cash.

Sammie didn't even let anyone else answer. She crossed her arms over her chest and glared at Cash as she responded. "A ton. Especially since this asshat made us a couple on social media. Like I would ever date his sorry ass." She glared at Cash before turning back to Sera, who was all smiles. "Sorry. I know you are all into him, not that I understand why. But don't worry—it was like for a hot second because then we had to pretend to break up so he could start..." Sammie paused and looked at me. Her eyes went wide, acknowledging for the first time I was still in the room. Seraphina's gazed followed.

"Hey Beatrice," Sera said, startling both Cash and me. Sammie wrapped her hair behind her ears nervously. I waved while switching my weight back and forth from my left to my right foot. Yes, pathetic, but I wasn't exactly sure what else to do. I wasn't a part of the team when Sera had been alive, and it was obvious they all had a good thing before me.

"It's been awhile. How are you feeling? How's the opposing source adjusting to your body? Are you adapting well?" Sera asked. I pointed to my chest. Words were caught in my throat. "Yes, the opposing source in your chest. How did the implanting go? When did your memories come back? What do you recall from them?" She was spewing out questions like she'd been reciting them in her sleep. She pressed into the bed, reaching her hand for Cash to help her sit upright. He wrapped his fingers around her and pulled her cautiously. He combed his hands through her hair, ridding it from her vision. She swung her legs over the metal table and revealed she was in olive cargo pants. Her outfit was the same as the last time I saw her, and she still looked flawless, not even wrinkled. "We need to get to work. I can help you with your connection and understanding your power. I need to know what you know and what you remember."

Words were having a hard time linking to my vocal cords. All I could do was concentrate on Cash's hand holding hers and my mind was mush. It seemed he had already made his choice and my heart, my very human heart, was broken.

Cash chimed in. I'm not sure if he knew I was sad or if he was intentionally trying to help since I was currently mute, but I was thankful for the assist. "She remembers meeting you and you being injured but Faye did a really good job of burying her memories. It took a flesh-to-flesh connection to release them."

"Flesh-to-flesh connection?" Sera tilted her head. It appeared she was confused by what Cash had just said. "That's interesting. What do you guys know about the opposing energy sources?"

"The Blood-Light's source is the one that will save Earth," Paul interjected, standing up straighter.

Sera nodded. "Yep. Exactly. I don't know why they jab at you."

Paul smiled while Sammie rolled her eyes. "Don't go feeding into it, Sera! We all know that."

"Well he is right, and he said it first. But what have you guys been told about the connecting source?"

Tasha, who was still at the computer, looked up from her screen and spoke. "It's Cash's and Bea's source connection that saves both Ferro and Earth." It sounded like a statement but given Tash's furrowed brows, she may have meant it as a question.

Sera shook her head. "Don't you think it's odd that the DOAA wants Cash dead or alive, but they would never harm Beatrice?"

Sammie interjected. "Not really. Cash is kinda an asshat. I want him dead on a regular basis."

Sera chuckled. "Well get in line, honey; Cash's shell is like mine. It's not needed to save both planets. Our sources, opposing energy sources with purple centers, are what's needed." Turning to face me, she continued. "Has your necklace turned purple yet?" Her eyes pointed to the dagger-shaped onyx necklace around my neck. I hadn't taken it off since the day Cash gave it to me.

I nodded.

"Fantastic. What were you doing when it happened and where were you? It'll be good for me to know during training." I gulped as I watched Cash's Adam's apple bob.

"It's happened a couple times, in different places," I paused. Panic flared in the pit of my stomach. How the hell was I going to explain they were all when I was with her boyfriend? "In the hallway at school and once when I was in bed," I said hesitantly.

"That's it?" Sammie asked. She flipped her bouncing blond hair over her shoulders and huffed loudly. "Beatrice has to be asleep to get her full power mojo going? What is this, Sleeping Beauty?"

Sera shook her head at Sammie and pressed me for more information. "Beatrice, anything more? Were your emotions heightened at all?"

My face caught fire as my chin moved up and down. Words were having a hard time formulating on my tongue. I swallowed. "Once when I was upset with Cash, and once when Cash was feeding."

Cash's face went white.

Sera laughed. "Looks like Sammie's not the only skin you've punctured, Cash. It seems as if Beatrice becomes emotionally charged when you're around as well. That's ok. He tends to have an effect on all of us. But we will have to get the necklace to turn purple without Cash as the catalyst. We will work on it."

Cash changed the subject and drew the conversation back to the original question. "So why does the DOAA want me dead?" He turned toward Sammie before she could interject. "Do not keep interrupting with reasons *you'd* like me dead! It's irrelevant and annoying." She huffed and plopped herself down into one of the rolling chairs. She crossed her leg and arms at the same time. "They want my source to be implant into someone else? Another Blood-Light?"

Sera angled her body toward Ashton, who was in a corner leaned up against the wall, quieter than a church mouse this entire time. His gaze was on the floor until Sera addressed him.

"Not necessarily. Ashton, why haven't you told them?"

He looked up and shrugged his shoulders.

"Told us what?" Cash said, grinding each word out through his teeth.

Addressing the whole room, Sera said, "It's not Cash. It's Ashton. He's a Blood-Light and he's the one destined to connect to Beatrice."

Chapter Fifteen

Cash

Understanding hit me harder than a wrecking ball as all the pieces started to fall into place, answering all the questions that had been floating around for days, if not longer: Why Father had kept Ashton alive. Who he was to the DOAA and why when they found us, they didn't want to kill him. Who he was to Sayor. But most importantly, now I knew why he went after Beatrice in the motel. The thought of them being together like she and I had been for the last several months drove me wild, wilder than words could ever explain.

I lunged at Ashton taking him and a surgical tray down with us. The clang of the metal hitting the floor sounded like bells in the distance. "You've been after her this whole time. That's why you kissed her. That's why you look at her like she's Ferroean plasma." I threw a punch connecting to his face. The skin tore open under his eye and his blood dotted my knuckles. "How? How can we ever trust you? How can *I* ever trust you?" I slugged him again. His defense was lame. He barely blocked my assault, which pissed me off even further. "Lie after lie, you come between everyone I love." Ashton rolled me over, pinning me to the ground with his knees.

"I can't write the prophecy, brother. I'm not an elder," he argued. Getting into the fight, he threw a punch. I lifted my head to the side and evaded it, sending his hand into the concrete floor. I wiggled my right leg free, bringing my knee into my chest. I kicked him in the torso, shooting him across the room, where he flipped over an empty metal table and landed on a medical machine, crushing its core. The device's beeping noise that was once a low rhythm, grew like a car alarm, screaming in a constant echo. Ashton wobbled as he tried to stand.

"Stop it," Beatrice screamed from somewhere behind me. Ignoring her plea, I ran at my brother, taking him down a second time and ramming him into a medical cabinet. The glass shattered and sprinkled all over the floor. I threw another punch. This one Ashton blocked with his forearm. He countered with a blow to my chest and actually made contact. Instead of feeling pain, it fueled my anger.

"Ashton, Cash, stop." Tasha's voice sounded over Beatrice's. "I can't take much more of this. Mark, Paul—stop them."

Mark and Paul backed up from the chaos ignoring my sister's request. "It's not our fight," Mark said in a soft voice.

Paul's voice wasn't as quiet. "Serious family issues those Kingstons have!"

"Shut up!" Sammie shouted. "You're not helping."

Ashton pinned me for the second time. "I'd say I'm sorry, but I can't. I'm not sorry and yes, I did act on it. If we are to connect, there has to be a closeness. I was testing the waters but there wasn't—"

I didn't let him finish. I threw a right hook and caught his nose. Blood flung across the room, streaking the floor and covering the shards of glass. Ashton pinned the arm that just clocked him.

"I know I have hurt you over and over again, and I know I've disappointed you countless times, and, yes, Paul is right. We have some serious family issues but I *do* love you."

Love was not something I was sure my brother was capable of. He shared that with my father, even if they weren't biologically related. With my free hand, I pushed him off me and rolled on top of him. Ashton's face was covered in blood with purple and blue hues laced underneath. He looked exhausted but he continued.

"You have a lot of nerve being this angry. I'd think someone in your position would think twice before lecturing me. You can't have your cake and eat it too. Isn't that the human saying for you cannot have whatever you want, brother?"

My anger grew hot and wild. I lifted my head and, with all my fury, head-butted Ashton so hard I broke his nose for the second time this week. Blood gushed everywhere as he bowled to the side.

The room looked like a tornado had come through it. Mark was holding Tasha, who was now crying while he spoke. "You both are idiots. You're lucky it's a damn Saturday! That could have alerted the DOAA we were down here. Was it really worth the risk?"

I was still sitting on the ground looking up at wreckage. Ashton pushed himself to stand. Paul had his arms crossed over his chest and shook his head. Sammie looked like she wanted to claw me. Nothing new there. Beatrice was paralyzed in the middle of the room, staring directly at me with a wild expression. Her eyes were swirling with one color, yellow—pure Ferroean source. But it was her necklace color that had me speechless. It was flashing solid purple. Sera took one look at Beatrice and then at me. Her gaze continued to volley until complete understanding washed over her.

"You two fell in love."

Chapter Sixteen

Beatrice

The room was eerie quiet in the wake of Cash and Ashton's brawl. No one moved. Tasha's face paled while Sammie's was fire engine red. Mark and Paul looked like disappointed parents. Ashton was at the small half-sized sink, cleaning up his nose with paper towels and cotton swabs. Cash remained frozen in his solemn standing position. His lips thinned into a straight line as he observed the room. Without a word, he turned on his heels. His hand reached for the main exit door but before he could command them open, Sera spoke.

"Stop! Right now, Cash Kingston." Cash stopped dead in his tracks but didn't turn around. His shoulder muscles bunched under his shirt. Sera took a deep breath in. "This is not at all what I imagined my Awakening to be like"—she paused as if to compose herself—"but I swear to the Council I didn't almost die to come back and sit here crying because the man I love fell in love with someone else when he thought I was dead."

Wow! Ok so not the mature response I would have imagined. And it certainly was not the response I'd be capable of.

"Emotions are high. Ashton is right. Well, sort of right. We do not have time to sit here and judge anyone for their actions. We have two planets teetering on extinction and the one thing we don't have is time." She turned to face me. Her swirling Ferroean eyes seared into mine. It was the first time since her Awakening her source was shown. "And although the girl inside of me, the girl who is still very much in love with Cash, is upset that this happened. I'm not totally surprised."

Well I was—first, by her level-headed response and second, her lack of surprise.

"When you are the shell of an opposing source you are innately attracted to your opposite source and both of you had just experienced similar tragedies. Cash lost me, or so he thought, and Beatrice lost Faye, her mother." She sighed. "We will have to deal with our personal emotions later."

Cash's shoulders relaxed slightly as he retreated. His steps were slow and careful. He turned, angling his body toward Sera. He wasn't denying his feelings for me but he wasn't yelling "I choose Beatrice," either.

Sera's eyes narrowed in. "Can we focus on what needs to be done to save these planets and deal with how the three of us—" Ashton interrupted from over by the sink littered with red soaked towels. "Make that four, please!"—Sera rolled her eyes— "the four of us feel later? Can we put our personal relationships aside?" Her gaze followed those she questioned. "Cash?" He nodded refusing to look at me. "Ashton?" Sera's tone was pointed. Ashton huffed, blowing air out and up, reaching the hairs on his head before agreeing. "Beatrice?" The tension around Sera's mouth softened. "Can we not let how we feel for Cash be a focus? Because I need you and you need me. I can't do that if we are going to have underlying issues."

I liked this girl so much so, it made it hard to be jealous of her. I also respected her and her morally high ground question. "Yes," I responded.

She took a deep inhale and released all the oxygen from her chest. "I was starting to explain everything before Cash attacked Ashton, and there is a lot to explain. Are you even the slightest bit curious as to how I'm not shocked Ashton is alive and how I know Ashton's role in all of this?"

Cash crossed his arms over his chest. His muscles flexed and bunched under his blood-stained grey t-shirt. "Now I am," he growled.

"Me too," Sammie chimed in. The group focused on Sera like she was telling a bedtime story and lingered on every word she said.

"When I called Faye and asked her to come to the cave it was because I got a call from Gabe Sayor. I assume you know that is your father?" She directed her question to me.

"My biological father, yes, and I thought he was dead," I clarified for her. Robert would always be my dad. She nodded as if she understood.

"Wait, Gabe is alive? How?" Cash asked. "It's a known fact, Zane had him killed."

"Yes, he's very much alive and he had help with his escape. I don't know how it was kept a secret for so long. Sayor has built an army of rebels made up of humans and Ferroeans. Some live on Earth, some on Ferro. His following reaches the thousands, maybe more, who want our kind and humans to coexist as one community and be accepted by each other. The way it should be. The way it always should have been."

"Don't you think it would have been nice of him to tell his daughter he was alive?" Cash all but spit. His anger emitted from his words with each accusatory tone.

Sera ignored him and continued. "I was told there was a Ferroean meeting for me to attend in a clandestine cave. Sayor was the one who warned me it was a trap. Someone had planned on killing me and taking my source." She gazed at me. "They were taking it for you."

My eyes widened. If that was true, why did she let them?

"I let them because they were right." Damn, she read my mind. "I don't know exactly who is behind all of this, but I believe they wanted you to save Earth. I also believe they may not want to save it for the right reasons."

Tasha shifted out of Mark's embrace and moved closer to Sera. "Gertrude warned us. She said, 'Beatrice Walker was a plan. A very well-thought-out plan.' But she also said there was no prophecy and that the Council wanted to rule Earth."

"My mother was right in some respects. Beatrice was a well-thought-out plan by both the Council and Earth. Scientist couldn't figure out how to save both planets until the elders prophesied the Blood-Light theory. Hence, Beatrice and Ashton."

"Earth and Ferro are working together?" Tasha asked.

"Doubtful," Ashton said with cotton balls up his nose, making his words sound deeper and muffled.

"No. From Sayor's understanding, Ferro was acting like they were working with Earth but never had intentions to stay on that path. Beatrice's power isn't only to stop both asteroids. It's also a way for Earth to..." Sera stopped. "Sayor wants to speak with Beatrice first. I gave him my word I'd let him tell her before I told the team. Tonight, at the cave, he will explain everything. For now, all you need to know is that DOAA and Ferro are no longer working together. We need to protect Beatrice, train her, and blast these damn asteroids out of the universe before both planets are destroyed. Then we will tackle the poorly managed governments and rectify these worlds."

"How can you be so sure Sayor is telling you the truth?" Mark asked. His brows wrinkled so intensely it looked like a unibrow.

"What are the two prophecies we've been told since we were kids?" Seraphina asked. Cash rolled his eyes. "Humor me," she continued.

"Two sources are born when there's an eminent threat," he grumbled like it was a waste of time for him to repeat.

"Yes. And that's an organic occurrence. We cannot control it, correct?" Her eyes lit up with her words like Tasha's do when she's reciting Ferroean history.

"Yeah, so what?" Cash asked.

"And what's the second one we've been told?" She nodded motioning for Cash to continue.

"You must save both worlds because if one falls so will the other."

"Yes, and that too is true but not maybe the way you think. The way any of us think. This is what my mother meant. She went to see an elder and they told her that their premonitions are not nature, which is fact; they are speculative, which is subjective. Elders are given their premonitions by the Orb on Ferro. We need to go to it. We need to figure out what it meant when it told the Elders the second premonition."

Cash ran his hand through his hair, and I swear he might have a bald spot after this he tugged so hard. "The Orb?"

"I am not going back to Ferro," Ashton spat. "That's Sayor's big idea? Going back to the planet that will surely put me right back into a prison?" He didn't even let Sera finish.

"This is bullshit. Elders, Sayor, Dodd, Zane. They are all full of it." And with that Ashton walked out of the room and into the hall where we heard a swift kick to the wall.

Chapter Seventeen

Beatrice

I ran out the door and followed Ashton down the brightly lit DOAA hallways. "Hey, wait up," I yelled. Ashton ignored me and kept walking. His hands were in his pockets and his head was tilted down. "Come on. I just want to talk. You didn't even let Sera finish. She didn't say she was sending you back to Ferro." He kept on his path. "You shouldn't tilt your head down. Your nose will bleed more."

Ashton pivoted; his playful demeanor gone.

"I know you don't want to hurt anyone. I know you don't want to hurt Cash." My lip corners pulled down.

He shrugged his shoulders. "It's all I ever do no matter what my intentions are. But I'll be damned if this big plan of Sayor's is to take me back to Ferro. Forget it. I'll roam Earth on my own until we all perish."

He'd had a lifetime of letting people down that I wasn't there for, but the man who stood before me wasn't about to give up. The more I thought of why he reacted so strongly to Sera, the more I understood. It was the memories of his planet, all filled with sadness and pain, and the thought of having to go back to the origin of that pain was too much for him to bear.

"I know you don't mean that," I said, moving closer to him. "Saving Ferro means something to you and so does saving Earth."

"Does it? I mean I think I'd make a great vagabond," he said with less anger. I crossed my arms over my chest and tapped my foot against the floor, waiting for a real response. "Fine. I care but I'm not going back to Ferro."

Changing gears, I asked him something I've wanted to ask since the day in the motel room. "What did Sayor tell you about me?" Knowing my biological father was alive threw me for a loop. When I thought he was dead, I could hate him for leaving me. But now, knowing he orchestrated the source inside of me and that he was breathing, my traitorous heart was curious about him.

"You as his daughter or you as the prophetic savior?" I tilted my head. I hadn't realized there was a difference. Seeing my confusion, Ashton continued. "Beatrice, Sayor never told me his daughter was the Blood-Light. I'm sorry. He never told any of us." My heart sunk into my chest. "He told us of your power. You were designed as a weapon for Earth to use. The little secret Sera didn't tell the team back in there was that you have the power to kill our kind like a thermo dagger. You are the only being with that power and that makes you very dangerous to Ferro but a hell of an ally to Earth."

My mouth dropped. "Excuse me?" I must have heard him wrong. "I know I'm a weapon. I'm supposed to connect to Cash," I paused. "Or you and kill the asteroids, right? I'm not intended to kill Ferroeans! I won't!"

"You may have to." The voice behind me sent goose-bumps to my skin and an involuntary electric jolt to my core. Cash. "You are the only being powerful enough to kill a Ferroean other than thermo daggers or an expired source."

"But how?"

Cash sighed. "An opposing source's power can kill our kind because of their strength. It's how the opposing sources will destroy the asteroids. However, the opposing sources usually need each other to alter time and manipulate metal as dense as a Ferroean to the point of combustion. But you don't need me to activate the necklace. You're able to turn it purple without me touching you."

"But I still need you. It only happens when you are around."

Ashton cleared his throat. "You need intense emotion. You get all hot and bothered when Cashy-poo here is near." Cash growled at Ashton. "It's true, baby bro. She's all fiery when you are around her."

"Regardless, when the necklace is purple, you'd be able to strike one of us. A hit to both wrists and ankles and we would perish. You are a gift to Earth, but you are an executioner to Ferro. It's a mystery why Zane even wanted you to exist."

"I would never kill someone, alien or human. I wouldn't!" I placed my hands on my hips. Before I could dispute my destiny in more detail, our luck had run out. A man in a dark-grey jumpsuit with the letters DOAA on his chest rounded the bend. Cash looked down at his watch and muttered *crap* under his breath.

"Who are you? What are you doing down here?" the man said, moving closer to our position. He reached for his gun strapped to his belt and held it in the air, pointing it straight at us.

"Just your friendly aliens," Cash said, standing in front of us. "You're an early bird, you know. According to my watch, we still had three minutes before you were supposed to patrol."

The guard, still holding his gun with one hand, grabbed his walkie-talkie with the other. "We have intruders in the secondary basement hospital floor. Send backup now!"

"Was that necessary!" Cash grumbled. He held his hand up and moved his fingers to the right and left several times. The gun danced in the guard's hand until he lost his grip and it crashed onto the floor. With a flick of Cash's wrist, the gun flew to Cash's feet. He picked it up and pointed at the guard.

"If I were you, I'd run." The guard took one look at Cash and the lethal human weapon he held and ran in the other direction, but it was too late. An alarm sounded. It rang so loud, reminding me of Cartwright's fire drills. But instead of excitement I'd feel to be freed of the school lecture, terror shook me to the bones. We were in the belly of the beast outnumbered by hundreds of DOAA agents. We would never make it out of here.

A swarm of agents, all dressed in their black suits with white button-downs, skinny grey ties, and black shiny shoes, flooded the hallways behind Cash. Panic and fear crawled their way into my stomach. The fluorescent lights above us flickered like strobe lights while red Solo Cup-looking lights positioned every other white light blinked rapidly.

"Grab my hand," Cash yelled.

"What? Why?" I said, looking around like he lost his mind. Now was definitely not the time to hold hands. "Just do it," he said. His voice elevated. He held out his palm and I threaded my fingers through his. He held our interlocked hands up high. I could feel the source between us ignite. A burst of crackling white light glowed from our fingertips. My source snapped and pulled like a cord of power, spreading from my chest to my extremities.

The agents were frozen at the end of the hallway midrun, weapons immobilized in the air. The alarm noise was muffled, still there but not blaring.

The crew ran out of the room and toward us and the open vent.

"Go, get up there. Melt the fan belts and crawl through. We will hold them off," Cash ordered. Sammie, Mark, Paul, Tasha, and even Sera didn't think, didn't argue. They obeyed and ran to the vent, climbing in one after the other.

Cash's eyes locked onto mine. "Remember the first day we met at Robert's house and then when we were at Kathleen Butler's house and we froze the people around us?" I nodded. I remembered, but I had no idea it was Cash and me who did that. I thought it was a power he had. I do remember Grouper saying something like, "a power you must be happy to have back." But I had no idea it had anything to do with me. Reading my mind, Cash said aloud, "No, it's a power I only have with my opposing source, and it's how we will slow the asteroids and have time to blast them."

"Oh wow!" Realization hit me. "We'd have a way out." Cash shook his head, but it was Ashton that answered.

"You can't be moving fast, small movements only. The second you start to fail or run, it's too much kinetic energy and can affect time. You haven't necessarily frozen them.

You've slowed them down to an inconceivably decelerated pace. And it's taking even more energy for your connection to allow our team to not be affected. That's what Seraphina has to teach you. Right now, your connection isn't strong enough to hold them off for long or allow for others to not be impacted. In fact, Cash, how long do we have?"

"Less than a minute." Cash's eyes went over my head connecting to Ashton. "When I release her hand, you run and get her the hell out of here. I'll hold them off." He tossed the gun to Ashton. "Use it on them if you have to."

A frisson of fear shot through me. "No. No, we won't let you," I screamed-begged. My stomach dipped and rolled with the thought of losing Cash. Thankfully, there were no contents in my stomach to expel.

"You will! Because you have to, Beatrice. You have to," Cash commanded.

I violently shook my head. Ashton chimed in. "We are running out of time."

"Beatrice, I need you to promise me you will go with Ashton. I need you to trust me. I can handle myself."

I searched Cash's eyes for understanding, for him to change his mind, but there was nothing. He was steadfast in his decision. "They will take you dead or alive. They don't care about saving your shell. But they do mine. Let me sacrifice myself and you leave. They won't hurt me if I'm their weapon."

He shook his head slightly. His thick lashes lowered. "I am not giving them the key to killing my people. I'd be playing into their hands. I will be fine. I promise you. You need to go. Now. You need to trust us."

He was referring to Ashton and him. It was the first time I saw him put faith into his brother. Not that this was the moment I wanted him to believe in Ashton. I wanted Cash to run with us. I wanted him to be safe.

"You have to go." He looked at Ashton. "Go to the cave. Save our planets. And take care of her." Ashton nodded. "Don't mess this up, brother."

"I won't."

Cash was already pulling his hand away from mine. My eyes fluttered as I felt the connection fade. The tingling sensations on my skin began to dull while the alarm's blare increased in volume. Tears wetted my cheeks. I tried to hold on, but the burst of power left me. Cash turned to me, genuine adoration and trust reflected in his eyes. Despite the warm tears that ran down my cheeks, I could make out the movement of his lips as he mouthed the following words while echoing them in my mind and making them permanently ingrained in my memory: "I choose you. It's always been you. I love you!" And with that he broke our embrace and ran toward the agents.

"No!" My chest rose and fell rapidly. I watched Cash take two agents down with a roundhouse kick before they could get their weapons to fire, but the slew of agents in their wake had enough time. Shot after shot struck Cash's chest, sending him stumbling backward. I knew the bullets wouldn't kill him, but they would impair his fighting abilities, giving the DOAA agents time to slash him with thermo daggers.

Ashton grabbed my hand and yanked me in the opposite direction. "We've got to go." I tried to resist. I dug my heels down using all my weight to counter his pull. "He'll be ok. Stop fighting me. You're wasting time. We cannot get captured." He yanked on me again. My cries sounded. Cash turned his head slightly, hearing my screams, and an agent sliced his chest with a Ferroean knife. Cash faltered, taking a knee. More rounds of ammunition were fired into him. His torso jerked with each blow. His eyes pleaded with me to leave. I spoke words into his head for him to hear: *I love you.* I turned toward Ashton and allowed his hand to swallow up mine and lead me out the vent exit.

My eyes squeezed as tears rained down my cheeks. My breath caught in my throat. My source and heart pounded as I moved as fast as I could through the cubed tunnel with Ashton. We hit the end of the road, nothing but a metal wall. Ashton held the palm of his hand up and it burst open. A bright light shone through, the sun's rays blinding me. I squinted as we stepped through the opening. A black van skidded around the corner. Smoke emitted from the wheels as if they were on fire. The sliding doors opened. Mark and Paul were on the other side. Ashton picked me up mid-run and threw me. Mark and Tasha caught me and set me down in the van. Sammie was driving. Sera was in the passenger seat. Paul reached out his hand and clasped onto Ashton's forearm as he ran parallel to the vehicle. He flung him into the van and shut the door with so much force the van shook. Sera's eyes volleyed back and forth, looking between Ashton and me. The tense pinch to her brow confirmed her fears. "Where is Cash?"

"They have him."

Chapter Eighteen

Cash

Waking up was like walking through a wind tunnel. Each time I tried to open my eyes they were pressed back down by something stronger than my will. My body couldn't fight the weighted feeling; it succumbed to a deep, dark sleep. Dreams collided with reality and reality felt like a nightmare. The last thing I remembered was leaving Beatrice, having no idea if telling her I would be ok was the truth. Her hazel eyes pleaded with me to stay as I returned a plea for her to go. And even now, I couldn't differentiate what was real and what was delusion. The low, muted hum and steady vibrations felt like a needle car beneath me, but I hadn't been in one of the Ferroean transports since I left home. The air smelled too clean, too antiseptic, but in a way unlike human hospitals and their endless cleaning chemicals. The purity of it, free of smog and other pollutants, assaulted my unaccustomed senses. In between feverish thoughts, my vision drifted out of the window and I saw flashes of sharp angles, glass, and metal. A sea of white and silver surrounded me, except for the occasional slash of deep jade green, like the perfectly straight razor trees my mother had always liked so much. The images came at me from every angle. It was like I was falling and yet never hit the ground.

When I finally had the energy to pry my eyes open, I winced against the brightness of the room. Turning my head slightly, I took in my surroundings. I must be dreaming. I was in a square bedroom that resembled mine, not mine on Earth but in Ferro. It had the same white walls outlined in florescent lights. But how? If this was my room, then my commands would work.

"Latmon, water?" I called into the abyss.

I pushed up on my hands and looked down at my attire as I tried to sit up. What the hell? I had on white cotton pants with a thick, cream-colored drawstring and no shirt, Ferroean-issued sleepwear. I pushed the white fluffy covers to the end of the bed and stood, fighting back a wave of dizziness. My hand rested on the edge of the mattress, catching myself before I fell. I looked down and the bed was floating just like my bed at home.

The door opened. "Captain, you called for water?" Latmon said, holding a pitcher filled with water. The tray was brightly lit with a blue ringlet. I swayed back and forth. I must be hallucinating.

"On the contrary, Captain. You are most certainly not dreaming. Welcome home." I placed my hands above my ears and pressed. My head throbbed and pulled with dull pains as his voice reached my eardrums. "How?" I croaked.

"I believe your father would like to answer that question himself. Both your mother and he are waiting for you in the crystal garden. It's a pleasure having you back with us." He snapped his fingers and a metal floating table appeared. He placed the water on the tray and with a flick of his wrist it soared through the air and landed in front of me. "Your water, as you wish, Captain." He nodded and with that slipped out through the automated door. My shaky body sunk into the plushness of the mattress as I sat back down in bed. I grabbed the glass of water and chugged. The cold liquid cascaded down my throat and settled in my empty belly. It gurgled from the sudden intake, causing me to feel ill.

"This cannot be good," I mumbled into the vacant room after taking my last sip. I licked my chapped bottom lip with the welcome moisture.

I stood and called out. "Day attire." Latmon came back into the room and handed me a white linen button-down shirt and white dress pants. "Cognac or black belt, matching shoes?"

"Cognac and, yes, matching would be fine." I reached out and grabbed the accessories. "How is the King?" I asked as if Latmon would ever sing anything but high praise. If I was really home, I'd know by his response.

His brow dipped. "I'm sure he is pleased his son is home." I shook my head, having no idea why I even asked. Latmon walked toward the door, but before slipping out he turned, his eyes void of emotions. "You should know your mother and he mended things. I would be cautious of how you respond to their situation."

Before I could question him, he was gone. I could summon him back. As the royal valet, it was his duty to respond. But what he'd just said contained more information than Latmon has provided me in all my years of existence. I'd take what little info I could and go from there.

I slipped into day attire and several paragraphs of fluorescent blue words appeared, floating in the air in front of me.

Daily Ferroean News Alert:

All private citizen thermo daggers must be turned into security outside of the Observatory. Warning! If any Ferroean does not comply you will be sentenced to one ferrocade without personal source. Repeat: All thermo daggers must be relinquished by the end of the day today.

I swiped the holo-bulletin away, having no idea what that was about, and stepped out of the room. I headed into the maze of brightly lit corridors. The curved ceilings were lit with white and sky-blue fluorescent strips. My eyes were still adjusting to the new environment as they fought to remain open. Did the DOAA drug me? And if so, how did they manage it? The only sedative that could knock out our kind was ferrophene, and it was made exclusively by the elders.

The corridor of the residence wing was all too familiar from my youth. After my room came Tasha's. The name plaque she had meticulously designed and had printed in acrylic plastic was still firmly attached to the door at around the five-foot mark—her height at the time. I was sure if I opened the door not a speck would be out of place. That was Tasha for you. Next would have been Ashton's room. I hadn't stuck around much after his judgment day. I reached out to the fingerpad lock, curious if the room still contained any of his things. The perimeter of light around the pad flashed dark blue once. It was locked. So much for that distraction.

As I neared the end of hallway, two armed men in white and black Guard uniforms snapped to attention. "Captain," they both said, nodding respectfully. I nodded back as I willed the glass doors open with my hands. A guard stood in my path. "New protocol, Captain." He held a portable scanner up to my chest. The muscles in my face strained as I crossed my arms over my source.

"Protocol? I'm the Captain of the Guards. What new procedure is this?"

"Security measures before entering the King's premises. All sources must be scanned and verified."

I stepped back, a small smile peeling at my lips. "The King is that concerned for his safety?"

The younger Guard spoke. "No. The King is mighty and smart. These measures are in place for the safety of the people." He leaned in and in a quieter voice spoke. "There have been rumors that sources have been stolen and placed in other chest cavities. Can you believe that, Captain? Think of all the chaos that could cause if the wrong source got into someone else's hands."

The older Guard, several years his senior—I could tell by the pinch of his skin around the eyes and forehead—gently pulled his partner back in line with him and out of my face.

"Don't mind the kid, Captain. The youth and their insatiable imagination." He took the scanner and held it to my chest. I uncrossed my arms and let him proceed. He held it at my source while I watch the thin illuminated light scan my chest cavity. A small ding sounded which I guessed confirmed my authentication.

"Do you think I'd let someone take my source, an opposing source, from my chest cavity? If you had trained in my Guard program, you'd have known that would not be possible."

"Yes, sir. My apologies. Sometimes I speak too much," the younger Guard admitted.

"Your name?" I asked. He spoke too much indeed, but he also could be valuable to me one day. If he heard rumors of sources being stolen and implanted in other Ferroeans, he might be able to tell me something useful in the future.

"Samptim. It's Samptim, sir, but my Earth name is Tim."
He stood up straighter.

I shook my head. "Have you been to Earth, Samptim?"

Samptim's excitement was stanched. His shoulders slumped with his response. "Well, no, Captain. But I'd like to go."

"Until you do, your name is Samptim."

"Yes, Captain."

Chapter Nineteen

Beatrice

The car ride to the cave was quiet. No one spoke a word. I sat on the floor in the same spot I'd been in on our way to the DOAA, but now Cash's spot was empty. As if out of respect, no one sat there. My arms wrapped around my bent knees, my mind lost in thought. I had no idea what the agents would do to him, but I couldn't fight off the fear that I'd never see the man I loved again.

Tasha put her arm around me and leaned in. The warmth of her body comforted me. She spoke softly into my ear. "I believe Cash is the strongest being on any planet. I refuse to allow you to even think of him as gone." She kept her arm around me but said in a louder voice for the whole group to hear. "My brother didn't sacrifice himself for any of us to mope! Let's do the job we are supposed to do and save these worlds." Her voice broke the heavy silence that had settled on us like a weighted blanket.

Sammie wiped her nose with her sleeve as she balanced the steering wheel with one hand. Her voice was gruff. "I'm sure he'll annoy them all to death and meet us at the cave very soon."

Sera, sitting in the passenger seat, placed her hand on her friend's shoulder. "I believe we will see him again. I really do." There was a confidence in Sera's voice that made her assurances seem almost possible. It was Ashton's lack of speech that scared me the most. He sat at the end of the van in complete silence and vacant gaze as if he was somewhere else completely.

Sammie pulled into the state park lot and we all jumped out. Mark and Paul tapped into their sources, melting the van down into a barely recognizable pool. Sera led the way along a well-worn trail, passing an old log cabin bathhouse meant for hikers. It was flanked by a park welcome sign with several rows of cartoon tree clusters.

"It's a bit of a journey." She motioned to a trail off to the left, looking back at me. "Do you remember that path, Beatrice?"

I focused on the surroundings. There was a hint of recall pulling at the back of my memories, some half-formed image that was only now coming into focus. "That's the trail my mother and I hiked the day she died."

"Exactly. And it's also how we get to the cave." Sera's smile didn't quite reach her eyes, but it was confident nonetheless. She started down the path, taking the lead in Cash's place.

"On foot?" Paul groaned. Sammie pushed him from behind, causing him to stumble, and then ran past him up the hill. Not to be outdone, he chased after her and they made the climb together.

Three miles later, we arrived at a landing halfway up the steep incline of the mountain. The path continued upward toward the summit, but Sera stopped us. She raised her palm at a dusty wall of yellowed dirt, and as if by magic it fell away, evaporating into the earth. A pristine set of metal double doors appeared in front of us, far too well kept and untarnished to have existed here long. With the flick of her wrist, the doors opened on their own.

One by one, we entered the corridor. "This is the exit I ran out of while my mother fought those Ferroeans," I breathed, taking in my surroundings. My hands brushed against the sides of the tunnel as I walked farther, remembering the panic and fear I felt the last time I had been in this spot.

The dark space was illuminated by thin strips of light built into the floor, but the walls around us appeared organic and imperfect. If it had been human-made it was certainly not new. But unlike the baked, dusty rock native to the rest of Topanga, the walls were unusually cold, damp, and hard to the touch. I knew it didn't belong here. "What is this?" I asked, looking back at Sera.

Sera paused a moment, reverently running her hand along the wall at her side. "It's the ferrous earth native to our home world. It contains iron and just being in proximity of it strengthens our source. There are places where you can find it on Earth, special places where parts of our planet have spilled into yours and where such natural materials are dominant."

"Special places?" I asked, taking my pointer finger and outlining a heart in the rock. My finger left a faint trace behind in the moisture.

"Add a CK and it's like you carved his name in a tree." Ashton came up behind me and whispered in my ear.

"Shut it," Tasha said, acutely aware of her brother's ability to provoke me—or anyone else, for that matter.

Sera continued. "Yes. There aren't many of them, but these places are special because they connect our worlds to one another. These doorways—we call them worm-holes—allow us to travel nearly instantaneously from our world to yours, and your world to ours. The only difference is the openings to Ferro are guarded where those to Earth are not. Many humans have accidentally fallen through. We use influence and send them right on back." Sera chuckled.

Tasha chimed in, and I remembered she was the historian among us. "It's said there used to be more of them, partic-ularly in Northern Europe, which is why so many of our old family names sound somewhat British or Irish. Ferro has long been fascinated by Earth culture. We are much older than Earth but when your planet came into existence, we were immediately drawn to it as if the universe knew a high purpose for our two worlds."

Sera nodded. "The natural materials on either side of the wormholes end up a mix of both Earth and Ferro. It takes some serious training in ecology and botany, but you can learn to spot these places if you want to. More exist than we can actually use—the anomaly has to be of a certain size to be utilized reliably, and it's around these large, stable worm-holes that the DOAA has mostly built their headquarters. One of the largest we know about is hidden beneath the headquarters we were just in, purportedly far underground the facility. I've never seen it myself, but it makes sense."

The strange tunnel narrowed, bringing us to two huge doors made of the same odd material as the first one.

"Need a little help with this one guys," Sera said. Tasha and Sammie flanked her. The three girls lifted their hands, aiming their palms at the seam. Their combined energy and force willed the monstrous doors open, and I felt a blast of cool air from inside.

A rather loud, incredibly familiar voice could be heard immediately. "Seriously, I thought these accommodations would have hair dryers. How am I supposed to avoid frizz? Do you think these curls are natural? I am not showering until we are out of here, and that's on all of you. Do not tell me this awful damp mud or whatever it is, is good for our skin, either. I'll be puckered up like a raisin by the time you let us out of this tropical grotto. It's like Florida without the sun and nobody visits Florida for the humidity."

Sammie and I looked at each other and whispered at the same time, "Darla?"

As the doors fully opened, hitting the adjacent walls with a thud, an entire underground world appeared. The cavern was as vast and deep as an aircraft hangar, and balls of light hovered far above us, illuminating the floor below. The space itself was filled with stations and equipment that reminded me of those emergency field stations they set up outside disaster zones, except that all of the machinery, the temporary partitions, the tables, and the shelving units were made of a pristine white metallic material. Even from afar, I could tell it wasn't painted white. The metal itself was matte and almost porcelain-like. The more I looked, the more I saw familiar bits and pieces—a few laptops, some familiar brands of snack food. There was even a colorful clothing line on the other side of the cavern hung with a variety of shirts. A honeycomb of doorways lay beyond.

My eyes snapped back, and there she was. My best friend in the entire world was right in front of us, yelling at our other friend Chris and some hapless older man I'd never seen before. "You say I'm in danger, but the only person in danger is you, my friend, if I cannot blow-dry my hair!"

Sharing a smile, Sammie and I bolted toward the pair. Sammie tackled Chris as I barreled into Darla, and the four of us hugged and embraced, swaying back and forth. I never wanted to let go. Eventually we released each other, and I grabbed Darla by the shoulders and shook her whole body. I had to make sure she was real. "What are you guys doing here? How did you get here?"

"Well, this man"—Darla pointed to the gentleman in his late forties if I had to guess—"scooped us up one day after school. Said we were easy targets since we were your best friends. Gave us a whole thirty minutes to pack for a trip he told us nothing about. And he clearly left out some very important details, like electrical capabilities and sleeping arrangements. Don't even think about your hair in this place. I've only been here one night. If this place has a *Yelp* page, I'm leaving a bad review."

My belly rumbled with a laugh so hearty my whole body shook. Darla was sunshine in your cup of coffee and Chris was a woodburning fire with marshmallows to roast. Chris threw his arm around me. "I missed you. Getting into trouble, I presume?" He leaned in to kiss my cheek, but as soon as his lips touched my skin, they were torn away.

"Get yourself a new girl. This one is taken," Ashton growled. He had Chris by his polo shirt. I smacked his hand.

"Ow!" Ashton exclaimed in pretend pain. It was like *deja*-freaking-*vu*. If Cash could see Ashton now, he'd be proud. I couldn't count the number of times Cash had freaked out about Chris showing the smallest amount of affection, and now his brother was doing the same thing. The sudden thought of Cash pricked at my heart. He'd be okay. He had to be.

"Ca—Wait, who are you?" Chris asked, his voice rising in surprise. His eyes volleyed back and forth between Ashton and me. "Where's Cash? Oh no, should I be watching social media again? Is this the new guy?"

Ashton tilted his head. "I have no idea what this has to do with socialized media, but the last thing my brother would want to see is your damn lips on his girl."

The last time I surprised Chris with my relationship with Cash, I made a social media joke that had Cash confused as well. These brothers had more in common than either would ever admit.

"Brother?" Chris mouthed to me.

"Yes. Ashton is Cash and Tasha's older brother," I grumbled. "It's a long story."

"Well, I'd love to hear about it," the older gentleman that Darla had been yelling at interjected. He was handsome for his age, tall and broad-chested. He had really fluffy hair that reminded me of my own, lots of volume that would likely do just as badly in this damp air as Darla suggested. His nose was shaped a lot like mine as well, small and button-like but fitting for his face. "I hope Sera's Awakening went well and you are unharmed, Beatrice."

Ashton was at my side before the man made another move.

"Ashton," the gentleman said. His voice was polite but also cautious.

Ashton crossed his arms over his chest. "Sayor." My mouth dropped. The handsome man was my biological father.

Chapter Twenty

Cash

As I walked through my mother's meticulously maintained royal garden, a gentle breeze played against the crystalline leaves of the quartz willows and through the tangles of climbing stone roses, filling the space with a chime-like music. I'd forgotten how fresh and clean the air on Ferro was compared to that of Earth, and I let it blow through my hair, closing my eyes. Rays of golden sunshine filtered through the branches above, casting mottled green and amber shadows along the pathway. This spot was an oasis in the bustling capital, and while needles flew by with their passengers far overhead, I'd have to strain to hear them through the gentle noises around me.

I thought about what the overly eager young Guard had said about rumors of sources being stolen and transplanted into other Ferroreans. Or was it into humans? He didn't say, now that I thought about it. Regardless, it didn't make sense. There are specific reasons why a source might be transplanted, but it was not the sort of thing done lightly. Unless sources were being stolen and transported back to

Earth. If that were the case, could the Rebellion be the reason?

The winding path turned a corner, opening up into a small courtyard with a delicate glass fountain at its center. Perfectly clear, cold water rose and fell against the hand-blown spires of spun glass twice my height, the largest no thicker than my pinky finger. I saw my mother first, peacefully reclining in one of the few lounge chairs bordering the space. She was exceptionally beautiful. Her long, white dress was threaded with gold filaments, its train spilling over the deep green grass beneath her. A small circular tabletop floated beside her, a simple white disk that carried one of the few Ferroean fermented juices that I actually found palatable since discovering real food on Earth. Her greying silver hair was pulled up and held by an intricate gold brooch that matched the high-heeled sandals on her feet. Luminescent words dangled in the air before her. She was reading a book, probably something she found in the Earth libraries.

As distracted as I was by the welcome sight of my mother, I was equally anxious to report to my father. Zane was sitting at his mobile desk, a hovering white tabletop equipped with a secure digital screen and communication relay. It was covered in shade. He had two guards on either side of him.

As I approached my parents, the guards retreated into the recesses of the foliage, the small jingle of leaves accompanying them in their wake. It was a known fact my father didn't have personal discussions around even his most trusted guards. My return was certain to start a variety of rumors, so it made complete sense that they would already know to keep their distance.

"King. Mother." I inclined my head respectfully to each in turn. I never called her Queen—no one did. That was an Earth word. She was referred to by our people as Subaltern, but it was an archaic term used sparingly.

"Casheous," she said as she swiped the words in the air away. I stifled a wince. I hated being called my birth name. Traveling to Earth was a rite of passage. Once you did, you could decide to go by your assimilation name. Not all of the older generations respected that.

Latmon appeared out of thin air and startled me. The Ferroean servant had been well trained to remain unnoticed until needed. "Your lunch, Captain." He presented me with a small silver tray. A glass of purified water sat beside a large mint-green pill.

"I'm not hungry," I growled, waving it away. I hadn't been awake for more than an hour yet, and I already missed grape soda and potato chips. Ferro provided nutritional sustenance, not empty calories. We had powered drinks, pills, and a few sad imitations of Earth's more interesting protein bars. The only recreational consumption was fermented beverages, and even they could vary greatly in quality and flavor.

Latmon's nose pinched. "I wouldn't imagine you were, Captain. It's still your lunch pill."

"Oh Casheous, just take it. Why must you cause angst to anyone who speaks to you?" my mother complained as if I had interrupted her day.

"It's Cash," I corrected her. I took the pill and threw it down the hatch. I waved off the water and Latmon left as fast as he arrived.

Latmon's appearance was only a reminder of my sudden and unwanted return to Ferro. I had no interest in small talk or formality. "Why am I here, Your Highness? And why did the DOAA spare my life?"

Zane waved away the computer screens hanging in the sky. "It wasn't an easy task considering all the recent trouble you have caused me, but I bartered with them for your safe passageway home. A price I was willing to pay." I opened my mouth to say what they'd done to Tasha, but he silenced me with his palm. "You freed Ashton out of his post without even consulting me, you broke into DOAA headquarters, you stole a Ferroean due back for transit next month for proper burial, and you and your brother killed how many agents in that hotel room?"

My eyes immediately found my mother, but the surprise wasn't hers; it was all mine. She didn't even flinch. My hands balled into fists. I could feel the sizzle of my source burn as it rushed through my Ferroean veins. "You knew Ashton was alive?"

She held up her finger. "Not at the time you left for Earth. But yes, I am aware now." As if that mattered. I know I didn't keep in touch myself, but she never reached out to Tasha or me when she learned this world-shattering news? Fire ignited inside my core. I wanted to blast my mother off her chair. "Since you are all-knowing all of a sudden, are you aware Zane knows Ashton isn't his son? That he's a Blood-Light?"

Her lips thinned into a perfectly painted red line. "Yes. I am aware. Is there anything else, son, you would like to question me about?" Wavering with evident anger, she swiveled in her seat, rotating her legs over the side of her chair. Her gold heel caught the sunlight as she stood. "Do you think you have the right to judge me, to judge your father? Do you think you know everything?" she asked, a sudden dramatic crescendo in her voice. "Casheous, you were always my troubled son. And yet you were always the one who showed the most potential. Do not go down a road you cannot come back from with your condemnatory tone. You'll never understand what I know, and why I have done the things I have done, and perhaps you never will."

She repeated the same words my brother said to me when he shot Beatrice. For a quick moment, I glanced around as if Ashton would pop up and yell surprise. Before I could make mention of her comment, she turned away, heading down an opposite footpath flanked by two guards. The floating tray carried her drink behind her as she disappeared around a jadeite topiary.

I returned my focus to my father. "That was a fun reunion. Do you share my mother's good will?"

"Sit," he commanded, waving my mother's relinquished chair closer to me. I sat sideways rather than recline uncomfortably, crossing my shin over my thigh.

"You shall return to the Guard's program and continue training the new recruits. They are currently in ULT and will be ready for your leadership tomorrow."

I shook my head, trying desperately to make sense of all of this. Zane wanted me to start training the Guards in Unit Level Training and abandon my team on Earth. One thought flared in my brain. I had to get back to Beatrice. "Your Highness, I must return to Earth. I have to connect my source to the Blood-Light, Beatrice Walker. We have to save Ferro and Earth as per the Orb's prophecy."

"Ashton and Beatrice will handle the asteroids. You are lucky to be alive and you are lucky I am a forgiving father. If it was anyone else, what you did by freeing your brother would have resulted in the removal of your source for two ferrocades. You will manage the Guard Program." I opened my mouth to protest, only to receive that silent look of reproach from my father, who inherently does not want to be cut off mid-sentence. "There is much you do not know and much to prepare for. The asteroids are nothing compared to what's coming long-term and I need you here to help us prepare. I need you to build my army."

My face twisted. "Army?" I questioned. The word tasted sour on my tongue. Why did King Zane need a larger army? "King, I do not mean any disrespect, but I will be going back to Earth. I'm not leaving my team until I know they are safe."

King Zane's eyebrow rose incredibly high as the tip of his lip tilted down. "Don't you mean until you know Beatrice Walker is safe?"

I crossed my arms over my chest. He knew. Zane Kingston was a lot of things, but a fool was not one of them.

"If Seraphina could see you now. She would be extremely disappointed in your favoring another."

And that's when I realized he had no idea of the Awakening. He didn't know Sera was alive. I nodded. The fact that she was alive, and he was unaware, told me the Rebellion was stronger than I imagined. And maybe he did have something to fear after all.

He continued. "I do not have time to fight you and I am well aware of how trained you are, so let's make this easy on both of us. If you try and run back to Earth, I will have Beatrice killed. If you try and contact her or anyone else on your team, I will have Beatrice killed. If you do not follow my direct orders, I will have—"

My teeth grinded against one another as I cut him off. "Let me guess...Have Beatrice killed? Wouldn't that cause both worlds to destruct?"

"I'd find another way. I am very resourceful." He smiled cruelly and I believed him. Zane always had a backup plan.

"How would you even get to her? You know she's protected by the enemy now," I asked, knowing the Rebellion would protect her with their lives.

"Very easily. Because my reach goes further than you know. My reach is inside the Rebellion."

Chapter Twenty-One

Ashton

I stared at Sayor. Part of me wanted to punch him. The other part of me, the one I'd probably call the logical part if it existed, wanted to hug him. He was alive and still leading the Rebellion. His survival meant the survival of our cause. It meant our mission still stood a chance.

"You look good for a dead guy," I said, releasing some of the tension in my facial muscles. The three rebels carrying stacks of clean, folded practice uniforms in the background smirked as they passed by. I'm sure they had a similar moment with Sayor upon learning he was not, in fact, dead.

Sayor nodded. "I understand if you are upset with me. I might feel the same if our positions were reversed." He extended his hand while he spoke. "You'll never understand what I know, and why I have done the things I have done, and perhaps you never will."

My heart sunk with those words. When you took an oath to join the Rebellion, these were the first words you spoke. They were a pledge, a pledge acknowledging your commitment to a cause and placing your ego behind your purpose.

These were the words spoken to Sayor directly from the Orb.

I extended my hand and shook his. "Two worlds as one, this oath I take: to Ferro, to Earth, to the Rebellion." He pulled me into a hug. My eyes welled with moisture. I forgot what we were fighting for and made it about myself. And for that, I was ashamed.

"It's good to see you, my friend," Sayor said as he threw his arm around my shoulder, pulling me into his side. Even though I was at least six inches taller than him, I felt small.

Bea look at us like we had eight heads. "Bea, this is Sayor. Your old man," I introduced.

"I'm not that old," Sayor said. A small smile grazed his lips briefly until he refocused on Bea.

Beatrice crossed her arms over her chest as her brows dipped together, but it was the other girl that spoke first. "Seriously, this guy is your dad? Shouldn't that get us some perks in this sad excuse for a mountain retreat? You know, like maybe a hairdryer?!" Her body mirrored Beatrice as both stood with pouty faces and tightly crossed arms. I had to admit, the loud girl was kind of cute.

Sera passed Bea and yanked my sleeve, pulling me after her. "Why don't we let them catch up?" She motioned to the others. "I'll show you all around. I think you'll like the Hive." She spoke to the group, but her eyes were focused on me, so I followed the command.

She led us through the large atrium, well past the entryway where Beatrice and Sayor stood. Hallways like branches from a tree reach out into every direction from this central room. My brow arched with understanding. "The Hive?"

"Yeah, that's what we call the rebel hideaway Sayor built. It was pretty run-down when I was here last." Sera's face fell at the reminder of her last moments here. I'm sure they weren't pretty. I knew what it was like to be hated by your own kind; I could only imagine being attacked by people you were trying to save.

Tasha and the others followed, and soon we were walking down a narrow corridor. Others passed by dressed in everything from casual Earth clothes, jeans, t-shirts, and lightweight sweaters to Ferroean combat clothes—cargo pants and a black t-shirt. No one gave any mind to our presence.

Sammie nudged me as we strolled. "You really forgave Sayor easily, huh, Ash? If that was me, I'd have held out a little longer. Waited for a real apology, maybe even a present."

"Shut up, Sammie," I hissed. "You don't know what you are talking about."

"Enlighten me. He lied to you. Made you think he was dead. Let you sit in a cell, , and what? It's all hugs and 'go Team Rebellion' again?" She moved away from me, sidling up to the human I'd torn off of Bea when we arrived. Good. She was the last company I needed right now. Let Sammie dig her teeth into that one. That would keep him busy.

"I was never off Team Rebellion. In fact, it's the team you should have been on from the start. Did you know Gabe Sayor was an elder?"

Mark interjected, "There were rumors but, no, it was never confirmed publicly. He still went up against the Council, Ashton." Mark's voice wasn't rude, but it wasn't convivial, either. It was obvious Cash's team had doubts about my intentions, about Sayor, maybe even me as a whole. Without my brother here, Sera would have to convince them. I already betrayed too many of their trusts to be their leader. I'd be lucky if any one of them eventually learned to consider me a friend again.

"We all took an oath to the Council. But do we believe in what they do or what they have planned? Have they been forthcoming with us?" Sera said, raising my unspoken doubts and drawing attention to what I had always seen as obvious. After all, the Council sucked. "I know my mother doesn't trust them, and when I see her, she'll be able to fill in more of the gaps. She has a network of spies."

Paul let out a half-choke, half-cough. I felt the rest of the group tense as I remembered no one had told Sera yet that her mother, Gertrude, had been killed while attempting to murder Beatrice. I prayed to the Council it wouldn't be me—I wasn't even there, after all.

Sera continued, oblivious to the rest of us. "She found out that Zane was only saving Earth so he could rule it. Make all the humans his pets and playthings."

"Yeah. I'm going to go ahead and speak for my people when I say that's a hard no." Darla was practically at Tasha's heels. "We are not pets!"

"And I couldn't agree with you more, but something is coming—something to do with Earth's survival past the asteroids. Sayor knows it. My mother knows it. And I believe it to be true." Sera's conviction was contagious. "I wouldn't have given up everything I loved, possibly my very life, if I didn't." I understood the implied mention of Cash, and I pointedly avoided looking at Sera.

Mark had more questions. "So if Sayor is actually an elder, why didn't the rest of the Council members listen to him? Why didn't they have an elder ceremony for him?"

Sometimes I wanted to punch Mark. It's not that his question wasn't warranted, but he saw everything as a binary; black and white, good and evil, one way or the other. "Why would Zane admit someone on the High Council much younger than him was chosen by the Orb as an elder? Can you imagine what that did to his ego?" I paused. I was there the day Father found out. He actually backhanded Sayor across the face like it was his fault. It was only the three of us, but I was young, and it scared me. "The Orb told him to repeat a specific vow to his followers so that they too could understand they were part of a bigger purpose and larger plan. The Orb kept him away from Faye to create the Rebellion on Ferro, but on his darkest day, the day many of us were captured, he told me that his future might have been chosen by the Orb but his love for Faye was his own." I sighed. My hands dug deeper into my pockets. "I don't always agree with his decisions, but I assume he doesn't always agree with the Orb. That's what faith is, believing in something when you may not understand it or see it. I forgot that until just now." I turned my eyes toward Sammie, singeing her with my glare. "So yes, I forgave him just as I hope he forgives me for my doubt."

Sammie nodded and I could tell even under her sassy shield she wore that she understood. They all did at some level. "What is the vow?" she asked.

I repeated the phrase for her, hoping my tone carried the importance of the words the way Sayor's did: "You'll never understand what I know, and why I have done the things I have done, and perhaps you never will. Two worlds as one, this oath I take: to Ferro, to Earth, to the Rebellion."

After a contemplative beat, the human, Chris, spoke. "Look, I literally do not know what is really going on or what this is all about, but that guy—Sayor—abandoned Beatrice. He's known about her all this time and only now does she even know he's alive. So while he may be some big-shot hero to you and your rebels, he looks like any other deadbeat dad to me."

I whirled on the human, who clearly had too much affection for my brother's girl. Instead of listing all the ways he was wrong, I simply said, "You are stupid."

The girls laughed, but Chris's eyes hardened as they met mine. I almost wished he'd said something, anything, but Sera drew everyone's attention away.

"Let's discuss ground rules and why we are here. We each have a purpose." I always admired how easily Sera could take on a mantle of authority. She didn't have to force it; people wanted to follow her lead. "Tasha, you will be instrumental training our newly recruited human guards over the next four months. They need to be briefed on anything and everything Ferroean—basically, they need a truncated but advanced version of what we all learn before and during our schooling. You'll be in charge of Darla and Chris as well." Tasha tilted her head curiously at the last remark but didn't interrupt. Sera motioned to Mark. "You, Sammie, and Paul will be in charge of the rebel Ferroeans that are in the Hive. Each day you will get one of three blocks of people. Block A are the highly trained Ferroeans; many were Guards under Cash. Block B are those that would have been in the Guards Program had they not fled to Earth with Sayor. And Block C, well, let's just say they have good intentions and I wish you luck. The humans will join Block C from time to time to learn basic combat skills. I pray to the Council none commit self-harm." Mark chuckled at the last bit. He had a soft spot for underdogs.

"What about you and me?" I realized we had no part in her outlined plan.

Sera frowned. "Cash, you, and I were supposed to train Beatrice. I guess it's just up to us now."

I placed my hand on Sera's shoulder and squeezed. In a lower voice, I whispered, "Crede Mihi." She nodded. It was uncertain if my brother was still alive, but I had hope. He was the strongest person I knew, faster than a needle car, built like a Ferroean building, indestructible, and smarter than a victrics. If anyone could survive the DOAA, he could.

"Where do we sleep in this place?" Paul poorly hid a yawn with the back of his hand. He could have at least feigned interest.

"The honeycombs," Sera stated matter-of-factly.

"Honey what?" Darla burst out. "I am not sleeping in honey or with any bugs. Because a place known as the Hive with sleeping quarters called the honeycombs sounds like a really great place to get stung and I am allergic to bee stings. I swell up like a balloon. Which brings me to another question. Is there an accredited hospital here, because the doctors that took Chris and my blood on the day we arrived did not seem qualified?"

"What doctors?" Sammie asked, raising her brow and catching Sera's attention. Something unspoken passed between them and I had an idea of what they communicating to each other. If Sayor was taking human blood samples, he was trying to find Ferroean lineage.

"The ones with the lab coats in the blood rooms. Well, that's what I called them. Every cabinet in this four-by-four room was filled with blood vials. Super gross. Really poor taste in aesthetics here. Like if this is going to be headquarters from now on for your rebel people, I think they need a makeover. Something with a fierce logo. I could design it!"

"You talk a lot," I mumbled. Is this how Cash felt being around me?

"I do. Is that a problem?" Her hands shot to her hips, her chin tilting up to prove I in no way intimidated her.

This girl was something. Rather than saying anything complimentary, though, I answered, "I could find something else for that mouth to do if you need an alternative." I waggled my brow.

"Do you have a death wish?" she snarled. "I hope there isn't a hospital because when I kick the sugar snap out of you, you'll have nowhere to go."

I laughed. "What does sugar snap mean?"

Chris was inching closer and closer to Sammie, but responded in a stage whisper, "She doesn't curse. Thinks it's bad karma." He rolled his eyes.

"I like that. Sugar snap." I inched closer to Darla and whispered, "You are more than welcome to try. I'd love to wrestle you." She pushed me, and I laughed even harder.

We came to a stop and had to go left or right. Sera turned, explaining to Darla, "Honeycombs have nothing to do with honey. They are beds stacked on top of each other in a honeycomb fashion. It's where you probably slept last night. Trust me. It's the only way we would all fit in this place." Sera continued. "Mark, Sammie, and Paul, you'll be with the Ferroeans, down that way in the Blue Wing." Sera pointed to a hallway brightly lit with blue toward the right. Appropriate. "Beatrice, Ashton, Tasha, and I will be with Darla and Chris and all the other humans in the Red Wing." The opposing hallway to the left was lit in red lights. Mark, Sammie, and Paul didn't need to be told twice. They hurried down their passage as we went toward ours.

Loud as ever, Darla huffed behind me, and I turned. "Do tell me I get to sleep next to you. I can hear you all night long and when I desperately need to shut you up, I can tell you all the ways I plan to do it." I winked.

She rolled her eyes dramatically, her long lashes grazing her eyelids. "Listen here, Hollywood. You seem like trouble. And although I am very interested in hot, older, troubled alien men, you are not the trouble I'm looking for. How about you take your smooth-talking temperament back home to your planet so my best friend doesn't feel like you're confusing her all the time, and I don't start to be confused as well. I'm very aware of Influence, and if you try it on me, I will kick you in the crotch like you stole my purse. And I love my purses." She clutched the grey bag in her hands to her chest.

I fought a smile that was screaming to break free from my lips. "First of all, you and my crotch in one sentence is something I can get behind. We can talk about that later." I held my finger up signaling for her to let me finish. "But what do you mean confusing Beatrice?" My brow raised incredibly high. That was a random and strange comment from this Earthling. She hadn't even seen her "best friend" in weeks. How did she know about me?

"Well, not confusing her but..." Darla stumbled over her words. "Well, you..." She stopped in the middle of the hallway, causing Chris to bump into her. "She called me. The day you were at the hotel. She said you seemed familiar. Got a whiff of you and thought it smelled like something she used to know. That part is weird because I can't smell anything, but I do have allergies so it could just be my nose. Anyway, since she has a thing for your brother and the whole part-alien-part-human thing still has her a little messed up—it's just a lot going on inside her head and it's confusing. Ya know?"

My head turned sharply. "Say that again?"

Darla huffed, blowing her bangs up into the air. "I said it's just a lot going on inside her head and it's just very..."

I growled. "No, not that. The part about smell. She said I smelled? Like what, exactly?"

Sera and Tasha flanked me in seconds. It was as if the world had stopped. My source slowed.

"What did she say he smelled like?" Tasha asked, her voice sweeter than mine but no less worried. Her chest was pounding, and I could see it rise and fall like the flapping of butterfly wings.

Darla crinkled her nose, darting her stare from Tasha to me. "She said he smelled liked cedar and sage." Darla shrugged her shoulders. "Weird, right? Like, it's a perfectly nice smell, but I don't get any of it off of you."

Sera and Tasha grabbed my arms. Each girl pressed their fingers into my skin, but it was Sera who spoke. "She smelled the Orb."

Chapter Twenty-Two

Cash

I left the royal gardens with more questions than answers. Why did Zane all of a sudden need specially trained soldiers? Why were sources being stolen, and what could be done with them aside from transplants into a Blood-Light? Would he really kill Bea if I tried to escape? Probably. And By the Council, what did I do to piss off my mother so much? As to the last point, the only thing that came to mind was my role in Ashton's punishment. But if she forgave Zane, why would she be so cold to me?

It's not like we ever had a warm and fuzzy relationship. She thought I was reckless, and I thought she was naïve and set in her ways. Finding out Ashton was my half-brother gave me a peek into a part of my mother that I never knew existed.

I shook my head. Feeling annoyed. Being confused just pricked at my temper.

I exited the same way I'd come in. To my disappointment, Samptim had been replaced with another new recruit, and I exchanged curt nods of greeting with the pair as I stepped through the doorway. I'd wanted to ask Samptim more questions about those rumors, and I hoped the boy hadn't been reprimanded too harshly for speaking out of turn. Traveling to Earth for the first time was a rite of passage for a lot of Ferroeans. I remember how excited Tasha and I had been before our first trip. My sister spent weeks researching humans to find the right alteration to her Ferroean name Maratash, looking into all sorts of derivatives. She'd finally settled on Tasha, because it supposedly meant birthday or resurrection or something like that. A trip to Earth was a pretty important event, so it made as much sense as any other name I'd seen people take. Personally, I just liked the sound of "Cash" over my longer, traditional birthname. Casheous was a stuffy prince. Cash could be some human comic book hero. Also, settling on my Earth name didn't require the extensive work my sister had put into the project. The only real difference between what we did and Samptim's enthusiasm was that we kept our brainstorming a secret—we didn't start blabbing about names to our commanding officers.

I made my way back into the depths of the building toward my room. I needed some time to think. I needed to figure out what to do next. As soon as I opened my door and took stock, however, I understood the miscalculation I had made. My room was practically bare, and I had arrived with basically nothing. I didn't even know if my access scans worked in all the systems. The bed had already been made as well, as if I'd never even been there.

"Latmon," I called out into the air. "Personal assistance is required."

There was barely a beat before the door chimed and the studious Ferroean slipped into the room. I had never seen him out of uniform—a perfectly pressed slate-grey jacket and slacks and a band of iron around his left wrist. Like his father and grandfather before him, Latmon was the descendant of a long line of personal valets to the King specifically, and to the great families more generally. His family line, along with a few others, prided themselves on generations of impeccable service to the Council. He went to years of school to learn how to do this job. I can't even imagine that level of dedication to a position like this.

"What may I assist with you, Captain Kingston?" Latmon inclined his head to one side, a question in his eyes.

"I haven't seen my cell phone. Or my wallet. Or even the clothes I was wearing when I was captured. Can you get them for me?" I started looking around the room, peeking into the perfectly camouflaged cabinets, closets, and drawers that closed flush against the white walls of the room. I hadn't realized how much I liked Earth's diversity. Rooms were cluttered but colorful. They were glimpses into the personalities of those who dwelled there. Each Ferroean room was not. Well, except for Ashton's. Thank the Council no one was permitted into that room. Even Latmon would have been appalled. It looked more like Earth than any other place in Ferro.

"I apologize, sir. I cannot." Nothing about his face seemed apologetic.

"What?" Since when did Latmon say no? My head tilted as my brows furrowed.

The valet continued, "The clothing was disposed of, as per your mother's request. I had offered to clean them, but she insisted there was no way to—how did she put it?—Remove the Earth from them, I believe it was."

I reminded myself it wasn't Latmon's fault if he'd been given an order, but my anger flared. I ran my hand through my hair, replying through gritted teeth, "The wallet and cell phone?"

"I am afraid they did not arrive with you, sir."

"What?" I knew I was repeating myself like those chatty parrots humans liked to keep. "Did the King take them? Or were they never here to begin with?"

"That would be a question for His Majesty, sir. I was not here when you arrived." I would normally be fuming at this point, but I found my anger deflating in the face of Latmon's gentle responses. It appeared he truly regretted not being able to fulfill my requests, and his tone was the same as when he'd informed me my hybrid puppy hadn't survived assimilation to Ferro's oxygen level.

"There is every chance the DOAA confiscated them and never bothered to return them when they handed me over." Thankfully, there wasn't anything on the phone Director Dodd didn't already know. I took a breath and started to pace, talking mostly to myself in an effort to calm down. Regardless of who took them, the DOAA or Zane, either way they were gone. "Latmon, I'll need a comms device to use if I'm going to be on Ferro for a while. One tuned specifically to my source only, understood?"

Latmon pulled the small, pad-like piece of glass-metal composite called a Vitrics from his pocket, offering it to me. "I assumed as much, sir. This one has been prepared to your usual specifications, and I have made sure all of your clearances are up to date, both here and in the relevant utility buildings." He paused, then twitched. It was such a small movement that I had almost thought I'd imagined it. "As well as the observatory."

And that's when I realized Latmon was trying to tell me something without telling me anything. Instead of questioning him, knowing that this was more than he should be saying, I nodded and took the comms device from Latmon, a little dumbfounded. "Thank you, Latmon. That was very...proactive of you." I shouldn't have been surprised, but his attention to detail was appreciated.

The smallest smile played at the corner of Latmon's mouth. "Of course, sir. It's my pleasure and my duty. Anything else?"

I tapped the pad, and a personalized screen appeared in the air in front of me. The residence—like most buildings on Ferro—was equipped with universal viewers anyone could access, but a personal comms device was preferred for tapping into any data you want to transport from place to place or keep secure and private.

"You wouldn't have any sour cream and onion potato chips in your other pocket, would you?"

Latmon's head cocked to one side in utter confusion. "I'm sorry, sir. No, I—"

I cut him off. While highly efficient, our family valet was terribly obtuse when it came to humor. "Never mind, Latmon, I didn't think so. That should be all."

Latmon nodded politely, his hands clasped behind his back. "Very good, sir. Please do not hesitate to summon me should you need anything else." He turned to exit, silent as a mouse, when I thought of one last thing.

"Oh—I'm going to assume the answer is yes, but did Mother arrange one of her parties for this week?" Every time I came home, the Subaltern took it upon herself to throw some kind of stuffy, formal event for the Capital's elite.

"Why, yes sir. She is having your suit tailored as we speak. The fitting appointment is scheduled for tomorrow—it is on your personal calendar."

I nodded, resigned. "Thank you, Latmon." With another nod, the valet was gone.

I dropped into the desk chair by my bed. It was as utilitarian as everything else on Ferro—hard, cold, and uncomfortably white. Weirdly great back support, though. I held the comms device in front of my eye, letting beams of green light scan my source through my retina. There was a chime, and I waved my hand over the same sensor. As the display appeared in the air in front of me, I set the device down on the desk and sat back. Despite my well-known station on Earth and a very explicit automatic away response, there were far too many unread personal messages. The bulk were just impersonal condolences, sent once Sera's death had been confirmed. I deleted those first without bothering to read them. After that were invites to various political functions—in the Capital and on Earth, it seems—all out of date and obviously sent by secretaries that didn't realize they'd never reach me on Earth. Or maybe they did know that, and it was a courtesy invitation to the son of the King. Either way, deleted. That left only a few messages I'd even consider looking at. They were from the closest thing I had to friends on Ferro—fellow trainees from my youth and a few former Guards that went into civil service after serving their time rather than make it a career.

I wondered about my father's plan for an army. Some of those retired Guards had excellent records. Would Zane make me re-enlist them? At least two of them were married with kids already. I would not be happy if our positions were switched, but it would be just like Zane to force them back into service—and make me be the one to do the dirty work. I swiped those messages into a reserve folder to view later. I couldn't stomach seeing their faces while my mind was grappling with the thought of throwing a wrench into their lives.

One last message blinked unread. It said it was from my mother, but I recognized the sender as Drayen Rose, the Subaltern's messenger and personal assistant. My mother rarely bothered to send her own messages, preferring to meet in person. After seeing that there was nothing interesting in current news—especially not anything about stolen sources or rewritten prophecies—I took a breath, swiped to open the video, and braced myself for the message to come.

As I suspected, an image of Messenger Rose appeared in the air before me, her eyes a gentle calm grey and her face plastered with a polite simulacrum of a smile. "Captain Casheous, welcome back to Ferro." I winced at my full name. "Your presence has been requested for a welcoming social hour to be held in the Royal Audience Hall. By now, Latmon should have uploaded the relevant times and guest biographies to your formal calendar for your review. Her Majesty has also done you the courtesy of drafting a list of acceptable topics for polite discussion, as well as a number of topics that are off limits. Particularly, she wanted to remind you that Earth slang is unacceptable, and she expects you will not deign to bring shame on her with any colorful language in the presence of so many important guests."

I rolled my eyes, stifling a groan. I suspected I would never be forgiven for that year I taught all the Council members' children some human slang words.

The video continued, "If you have any further questions, Latmon should be able to assist you. It's a pleasure to have you back with us, Captain. Messenger Rose out." The video vanished, replaced with the command screen.

In an effort to keep from destroying the little furniture I had in my room, I stood up mechanically and dropped my comms device in my pocket. When I'd been going through the closets earlier, I spotted the one piece of human clothing my mother must have deemed acceptable—a vintage black leather bomber jacket with white detailing on the cuffs and stitching. I slipped into my own little piece of Earth and headed out the door.

I needed to hit something. Thoughts of Beatrice raced through my mind. Was she safe? Did they make it to the cave? If so, how did the introduction to Sayor go? Were Sera and Bea getting along? Was Sera ok? Was Ashton really the one to connect to Bea? Could they have been meant for each other all this time? All of these thoughts swirled in my mind. There was no way I could get to her without putting her in danger. Zane would kill her. I had no doubts.

Chapter Twenty-Three

Beatrice

The others had left to settle into their rooms while I just stood there staring at a stranger who was my biological father. I had so many questions, each circling at high speeds like a race car on a track. How long had he known about me? Why didn't he fight harder for my mom? For me? Did he really love her? Was I a mistake or a plan? Was one better than the other? What did he expect from me? Why had he hidden himself from me? Why hadn't he ever reached out? My thoughts were so overwhelming I couldn't grab onto only one, so I just stared.

After a minute or so, a wistful look washed over his unfamiliar face. "You are the spitting image of your mother," he said, voice full of sadness. "I miss her very much." His shoved his hands into his pockets and I was thankful he didn't reach out to me for a hug or a handshake. I didn't know how I'd react to a physical greeting, especially one as familiar as he had with Ashton.

"I do, too," I said on reflex. I had no idea why I answered him. I tucked a fallen lock of hair behind my ear as I looked down at the floor. His gaze was intense and uncomfortable.

"I'm sure you do. I can't imagine how painful her death was for you—how difficult all of this is for you. I can tell you that she gave her life for this rebellion, for you and your future. I'd like to tell you about it, as much as I'm able to, at least. Maybe that's where we can start?" He ran his hands through his hair. "I'm sure you are conflicted, full of questions and yet unbearably uncomfortable in my presence. And if it helps to know, I share those feelings."

I looked back up. "Ok." It was all I could say.

He waved his hands to the atrium, turning the subject away from us and toward our surroundings. "Before there was a Department of Alien Affairs here on Earth, this cave was initially designed for Ferroeans to live in when they came from Ferro." He started to walk, and I followed, glad for the distraction. "We came here originally to dwell."

"Ferroeans wanted to live on Earth?" I asked. No one had ever said anything about that before.

"We did originally, yes. Ferroeans aren't a fearful people. We were taken aback by the volatile response when humans found out about us. It wasn't very welcoming, to say the least. They came at us with every weapon they could." We walked down a hall lit with a yellow light. Trails of cracks crossed the cement and stone walls like spiderwebs, and the damage told the violent story of this place. It had seen more than its share of attack in its time. "This passageway leads to the cafeteria and training area. I wanted to show these to you first."

I nodded, looking at everything but back at him.

"So as I was saying, it would be an understatement to say the people we met on Earth weren't very happy about our presence, and especially about our powers. At first, they were scared because they didn't understand us. Then when they learned more, their fear grew. They felt, given our power, we would drive humankind to extinction and take over the Earth for ourselves."

"That wasn't the plan....right?" I asked, almost hesitantly. I remembered how frightened Gertrude had been. She'd claimed the Council—and especially King Zane—wanted to overthrow Earth. I may have hated her for killing Grouper, but I did believe her. My heart squeezed at the thought of Grouper; he was Sayor's estranged brother. I would have to tell him what happened. Eventually.

"It wasn't." He didn't expand on that, but rather, diverted the conversation. "Did you know thermo daggers were created by Earth?"

"No." I tried not to appear jarred by the shift in conversation. I had never thought about the origin of thermo daggers and assumed they were a Ferroean invention.

"It's true. We all use them now, but before encountering Earth the people of Ferro didn't kill one another as humans so often do. In more recent history, things have unfortunately changed. Ferroeans could still die, of course, but only when their source diminished with old age. Not even criminals were executed. Instead, their source was removed and stored away as punishment, forcing their body into a comatose state. Once the length of their sentence was over, an Awakening would be performed to bring them back to consciousness. Nowadays, the Council finds it easier to just drain someone's source with a thermo dagger and be done with it."

He opened a set of double doors, revealing what I presumed to be the cafeteria. Black tables and benches stood in two neat rows in odd contrast to the worn linoleum tile beneath. Track lighting along the ceiling sprung to life as we crossed the entryway, and I could see a line of vending machines along the back wall. As far as I could tell, there was no door or pass-through to a kitchen. Sayor walked us in a circle around the room, and I saw that three of the five vending machines were stacked with clear packages of multicolor pills, some larger than my fingernail. The fourth was full of some kind of bottled water, but the fifth was most familiar—candy bars, chips, and cookies in all sorts of oddball flavors filled the slots behind the glass. Sayor gestured to the input pad, but I shook my head. I wasn't hungry.

He continued toward one of the tables near the double doors. "Before thermo daggers, there simply wasn't any way for one Ferroean to kill the other. At least none that they knew about. People could fight and injure one another, sure. But the effects were never permanent. We were never killers because there was no way to do it. Humans are very industrious, however, and eventually someone our people had thought was an ally found a way to create a weapon that could slice through source points in the wrists and ankles using a combination of ferrous metals native to our home world. This unassuming human from Earth made the only weapon that would allow us to kill one another outside of the Council's jurisdiction."

"Until me." I crossed my arms over my chest. Sayor took a seat at the table nearest us, but I didn't join him. I remained standing as the knowledge of my intended purpose tiptoed up my spine. "I'm their next weapon, aren't I?"

He sighed. "You are."

"And you knew this—knew your birth daughter was to be made an instrument of destruction—and still allowed me to be turned into this? To be able to do what I can do?" Anger flared in my insides like molten lava.

"I did. And I would do it again. Because Earth needs you, Beatrice."

My attention was pulled away from him before I could ask why as a familiar shape entered the room. "Dad!"

My father—my real father, Robert—was dressed in jeans and a lightweight cashmere sweater I bought him for Father's Day two years ago. Ignoring the stranger to my left, I ran and threw myself into the arms of the only father I had known. I knew he never would have allowed me to be used as Sayor and my mother had.

"You ok?" He pulled away, his hands holding me by the shoulders as he looked me over with a concerned eye.

"Yes. Honestly, I'm fine." He continued to scan me. "Dad, I'm fine, I promise. I'm a little tired, but other than that I'm ok." He pulled me back in and wrapped his arms around me. Even knowing he and my mother had lied to me, I didn't care. Sayor's one gift to me was being left to Robert to raise me.

"Maybe she should get some rest," Sayor said as he stood. "Robert, would you like to take her to her room?"

My dad—my real dad—nodded.

"Beatrice, our conversation is not over, but I know you need rest and time to think. You train first thing in the morning." He pointed to the back door of the cafeteria. "That is the entrance to the training room. Meet Ashton and Sera there at seven a.m. sharp." He turned toward the exit. "Robert, if you could stop by my room after you drop her off, I would appreciate it."

Dad and I walked through the halls quietly, and I could tell it was as awkward for him as it was for me. We didn't have much time back in Cartwright to discuss everything that happened when my memory came back. I had so many things to say to him, but Cash had rushed us off. Knowing what my memories had revealed, time was of the essence and I didn't fight him, but I was in need of a father-daughter moment and thankful to finally have it.

"So, Mom and an alien?" I blurted out with a small laugh.

Dad joined me and smiled. "I know it's a lot of information and I'm sure you are angry. I wish your mom was here to tell you more since I don't have a lot of answers, but you will always be my daughter and no DNA will ever change that."

"I'm not mad, Dad. Honestly, I'm really grateful that Sayor wasn't in my life and that you are my father. I'm starting to think Mom was a little out there with this whole rebellion thing, but I do trust her." I hesitated on that last statement. "Do you?"

Dad stopped in front of a slate-grey door with a stainless-steel lever. He lifted it and waved me into the room.

Holy cannoli this was...well, not what I expected.

"Is this a bedroom or a prison cell?" I mumbled. The walls were all grey, the bed made of steel with a thin mattress on top and white sheets and a comforter folded at the end of it. A metal desk accompanied by a white chair was off in the corner, adjacent to a large portable armoire made of glass. All my clothes were stacked inside and visible from the outside, and when I say mine, I meant, clothes picked out for me. Several pair of cargo pants, maybe a dozen or more black t-shirts, several white linen pants and matching button-downs, and black boots sitting next to white fluffy slippers. Okay, the slipper thing was just weird. There was an electric toothbrush on one of the shelves and two metal hairbrushes.

"Accommodations here aren't five-star. Have you seen Darla yet? She can tell you all about them," he said, rolling his eyes. "I've been listening to her complain for the last twenty-four hours and I have considered a muzzle. If it wasn't for Chris, some of the others might have taken measures into their own hands."

I chuckled. "Actually, Chris and she were the first people I saw."

A small smile grazed my father's lips. "I'm glad they are here and aren't in any immediate danger. It'll be good for you to have them close." He took a seat at the chair in front of the desk. I plopped onto the bed, immediately regretting it. My butt hit the hard frame, causing a burst of pain to my backside.

"To answer your question, yes, I believe in the Rebellion, and yes, I believe your mother had the best intentions for not only Earth but you. I am a human, so I have a vested interest in Earth's well-being, but because I believe Ferroeans should be treated as equals, I believe the Rebellion is just. It pains me to see how some of the DOAA refer to them and how others out of fear mock them. I've met many good Ferroeans, like Cash and Tasha."

My heart plummeted in my chest. "Dad, Cash was captured by the DOAA." My voice dipped into my throat. The words physically hurt to say out loud.

Dad sighed. "Beatrice, honey, do not worry about him. There's not a living alien or human that could break him. I know he probably hides how powerful he is in front of you but unless he's drained of his source, he could take on an army by himself."

"That's the thing, Dad. He's been healing me."

Like a Jack-In-The-Box, Dad popped up from his seat. "What! Why in the world would he have to heal you?"

My hands fidgeted in my lap. The fact I had been shot, especially by Cash's brother, was not something I wanted to share with my father—or really anyone. It felt like a lifetime ago and Ashton had his reasons.

"I'm fine. I wasn't feeling great because of the overwhelming amount of source building inside of me and Cash thought it would help me." I had no idea if that was believable but since my dad wasn't Ferroean maybe he'd buy that. "You know Cash. He's super careful when it comes to my well-being."

My father's brow rose as if he was unsure of my honesty. "Are you feeling better now? Is it the headaches?"

Well that would be a good cover story. I felt my lips stretch to my ears. "Yes. And feeding helped me."

Dad walked over to where I was sitting. He kissed my forehead. "Why don't you get some rest. We can catch up tomorrow after your training. If you need anything, I'm in one of the larger honeycomb sleepers in the Red Wing. Come find me. I'm always here for you."

He was halfway out the door when I asked, "Do you like Sayor? Well, I'm sure you do not like him, but do you trust him?"

My dad's lips thinned. "Not as far as I can throw him." He smiled mildly. "And I don't have powers." And with that my dad had slipped out of the room, leaving me with an uneasy feeling. He didn't trust Sayor, but he believed in his mission. I'd take the same approach when it came to him then. I'd fight for the Rebellion, but I'd never trust my biological dad, not at least until he'd earned it.

The training room was unlike anything I could have ever imagined. It was rectangular, with walls of sheer black onyx and blue padded floors. It was open and empty, except for a variety of martial weapons hanging from stakes on a wheeled wooden partition. It was currently parked against the wall, but I could tell it could be moved easily. I hadn't wielded any weapons during my training sessions with Cash, but I had wanted to.

Sera and Ashton were having a shushed conversation in the middle of the room. They were dressed in the same outfit that was laid out for me this morning: black t-shirt, olive cargo pants, black boots. Sera's hair was braided like my mother used to wear hers, in a side fishtail, and even without makeup, she looked flawlessly beautiful.

"Hi," I called from the entrance. My stomach was full of butterflies.

Sera turned toward me, her expression blank. She focused on something below my eyeline. My hand followed her gaze and rested on the mildly sharp point of the dagger pendant that hung from my neck. She was completely focused on it.

"Good Morning, Beatrice. I hope you are well rested." She barreled forward, leaving no room for me to speak in return. "Nothing we are about to do will be easy, and I hope you know that already. Before we get started, I will say this: Do not look to me as your friend or as your enemy. My loyalty belongs to both of our worlds, and I will not tolerate anything less than your full commitment. The weight of billions of lives is in your grasp, and if you falter or attempt to abandon this training, I will not hesitate to force your hand in continuing." She was resolved, her eyes perfect steel. "Do we understand each other?"

I shifted uncomfortably from side to side. "Not sure I have a choice..." I mumbled.

She wasn't interested in my response. "We will start with basic combat training. Keep in mind, however—the goal isn't the fight itself."

I shook my head. "Not following you. I thought we were training?"

"We need you to balance the power of your source and turn that necklace purple so you and I can be time-slowing, asteroid-blasting heroes. Beating each other up is just a bonus!" Ashton smiled as he offered an answer.

My lids lowered. Intimate moments with Cash were the only catalysts for the shift in color. I didn't see how anything else would work.

"You and I will square off first." Sera ignored the wooden sparring blades and grabbed one of the thermo daggers from the wall. After testing the weight, she grabbed a second, flipped it in the air so that she was holding it by the point, and offered me the hilt. I took it hesitantly and stepped back.

Ashton rubbed his hands together. "Oh, I get to watch. How wonderful!"

"I've never used a dagger before," I admitted as I felt the hilt's energy zap my palm. It was smooth and heavy. I walked to the middle of the mat and positioned myself in a fighting stance as Cash had shown me.

"You better learn and learn fast because we don't have long. Dr. X calculated approximately six months. And I'd hate that Cash was captured—possibly even killed—for nothing." At the sound of his name and the mention he might be dead, I flinched. Looking back at her, she smiled. That's exactly what she had wanted from me. This wasn't going to be a physical fight. Her blows would be verbal, and I understood what she meant by not being my friend. She was the Rebellion's ally, not mine.

Without waiting for a cue, I shot forward from my stance, dipping under her arm with no warning. Cash would be proud.

"What the—?" Sera exclaimed as she spun to narrowly avoid my lunge. I guess she wasn't expecting me to be any good at this. Cash always said surprise your opponent.

I ended up behind her, fisting her shirt in one hand, and thrusting the dagger's tip toward her waist, just as Cash had taught me to do with my fists. But she was quicker than me, lurching to the side and avoiding my blow altogether.

"Never used a dagger before!" Her eyes narrowed with a cunning smile. "Could have fooled me." She licked her lips. "You have spirit. I like that." She prowled toward me like a jungle cat. "I wonder—did you have that spirit when you were kissing my boyfriend?"

I cringed but shook my head. "I know what you are trying to do. I won't fall for it. There's nothing you can say about Cash that's going to turn my necklace purple," I spat.

"I imagined you would say that. I guess I'll have to try harder." She circled me. "Do you know how many times Cash and I have kissed?" My heart dropped a beat, but she kept going. "Do you know how many times he's touched me, messed my hair, flushed my cheeks, left my lips swollen and damp?"

Anger flared hot inside me. "No, because he never talked about you at all." My teeth gritted. Part of that was true. Cash never talked about her for a lot of reasons, but mostly because he didn't want me to know he was my opposing source at first. Although apparently that isn't true anyway.

"Maybe it was too painful for him. I wonder—how many times has he kissed you? Or was it just feeding? There's a huge difference; you know that, right?"

My heart lurched and she took that opportunity to send her leg into a roundhouse kick. I dodged but not fast enough. She caught the edge of my chin. I yelped in pain, the sound reminding me of a small dog as I lost my balance.

"I wonder if he thought of me as he fed from you." The pain radiated through my heart and my body, causing the tiny hairs on my skin to prickle. Kicking my instincts into overdrive, I gripped my dagger tight and shoved it into her. I wanted to wound her physically the way she was hurting me. If this was what practicing was going to be like for the next six months, I was over it!

My strike was too wild, and I missed. Sera swung around, and I didn't see her fist until my jaw exploded with agony, throwing me off center. I tasted something metallic. Blood.

"Sera," Ashton warned from somewhere behind me.

"I've been his best friend and love of his life since we were children. He hasn't chosen you. He will never choose you. You were born as a weapon for Earth, not for him. Do not confuse what you had for anything more than the result of my source in your frame." She was practically growling, her eyes flowing in rivers of color. She might have been trying to provoke me, but she also meant every word she said.

Instinct crowded out the bite of her words, and it was like I was back in the training room at the safe house when the gang told me they might leave Earth without me. I had torn a hole right through the punching bag. A sense of focus and calm washed over me as I lunged at Sera. Folding the knife into my forearm, the metal pressing into my skin,

I exposed the hilt. I used all my forward momentum to bash her with the blunt pommel.

"He chose me," I spat as she tumbled. Blood and plasma dripped down her face. I stood over her, watching her wipe the goo off. "And if you think this is how my necklace will turn purple, you're nuts."

She didn't miss a beat and bucked herself back onto her feet, causing me to take a couple of steps backward.

Out of the corner of my eye, I saw Ashton step to the mat. He grabbed Sera's arm and swung her around. Her chest pressed against his. "We need to find another way. Not like this. It's not right." His voice was serious and full of concern.

Sera turned suddenly, ripping herself out of his grasp. She ducked and swiped his legs out from underneath him. Ashton went down and landed hard on his back.

"Do not ever grab me again, Ash," she cautioned. He rolled to the side as her fist drove toward him. She missed and he was back on his feet.

She stopped right then and threw the dagger onto the mat. Her face tensed as she spoke, her eyes boring into the both of us. "I'm not doing this because it's fun for me. We need Beatrice to figure out how to get the job done without Cash. If he's captured, that's one thing—we can have Sayor send a team to get him back from the DOAA. But if he's dead..." She paused. It wasn't long but it was long enough to make me realize she was hurting too. "If he's dead, it's my responsibility to save these two planets and I need the damn necklace to turn to purple." She pivoted toward me. "If I have to feed from you, berate you, brawl with you, kiss you myself, I'll do it because if we don't get Ashton and you to connect, we will all die. Every single one of us."

I charged at her. "I get that. You think I'm naïve and have no clue how important this is. I was made INTO a weapon. A horrible, lethal weapon. Can you imagine what that feels like?"

Her face softened slightly but I didn't stop. "You do not have the monopoly on pain and confusion right now. Do you know what I've been through in the last several months?" The list rolled off my tongue. "My mother kidnapped me, put an alien life source in my chest, died and erased my memories, then left the most excruciatingly obnoxious alien in charge of my well-being and—then the cherry on the top—I fall in love with him and he has a girlfriend of like forever that we had to bring back to life and before we can figure out anything at all he's captured and might be dead because of me." I threw my dagger down into the mat as well and started toward the door. The idea popped into my brain like popcorn in the microwave midstride. "Cash got the necklace to turn purple not out of anger or cruelty! You ever think he might have triggered something else?" I crossed my arms over my chest.

"Well, then, what was it?" She grinded her teeth as she asked.

"Love! He ignited love."

Chapter Twenty-Four

Cash

The walk to the Guard barracks and training center wasn't far from the royal residence. I waved off Latmon's offer to call me a needle and left on foot. The fresh air and bright sunlight mingled to help clear my head. I'd originally thought to head to the barracks knowing there would be speed bags I could lay into there, but that wasn't the only draw of the old fortress of a building. If I was once again the head of the Guard Program, as Zane said, then I would have my old office back. And if I had my old office, I'd have security clearance from there to look into any events the Council would be trying to keep out of the public eye. I'd long ago figured out how to get into more classified files than a Guard was usually permitted, and if my father knew he didn't care. The thought of doing some clandestine spying on the Council made me almost as happy as the thought of showing off in front of some young recruits.

The architecture of the city around me was practically sparkling, light refracting off the stout white- and cream-colored buildings and tall, spindly towers of silvered glass. I patted the inner pocket of my jacket and was happy to find my dark sunglasses still there. I slipped them on, more for the look than anything else. The aviators were distinctly not Ferroean design and made me stand out among the residents of the Capital. Almost everyone I saw was dressed like they were out of a human spy thriller or executive office: Crisp, well-tailored suits and ties; form-fitting pencil skirts and chic pressed blouses; dresses and tunics of rich, stiff fabric. It was a sea of white on cream and silver on grey, with only touches of black, bronze, or gold in between. Jewelry was one of the few areas my home world seemed to promote as a means of self-expression, but even then, the choices were limited to precious metals and meticulous designs. I knew I stood out and reveled in it.

I turned a corner, and the roadway opened up into a large cul-de-sac. The building that housed the Guard barracks and training center stood at the far end, just as I'd left it a few years ago. It was a blocky structure, all sharp angles and carefully engineered geometry. The bottom five floors rose out of the cement sidewalk, with two thin towers rising above. The majority of the building existed underground, though—ten floors of training rooms and dormitories all the way down. The Guard barracks were built to protect us from harm, so that we could protect our people.

I strode through the large, automatic front doors and through an archway that scanned me with a series of green beams of light. Latmon was true to his word. Like my comms device, there was a small chime as the system recognized my source, followed by a computerized voice, "Welcome, Captain Cash Kingston." My shoulders deliberately relaxed at the sound of my preferred name. Here was a place I knew I could receive respect. I shared a nod with each of the flanking security guards and swiftly approached the lift bays on the far side of the room. A command screen hovered in the air a few feet in front of each bay, awaiting my input. The training centers were down below, but my office was in one of the towers. Before I could decide my direction, I heard the sound of loud, heavy boots behind me. I spun on reflex.

My eyes met those of a tall man in full Guard uniform. The surprised look in his honey-brown eyes told me my instincts may have been a bit on edge, and I relaxed from my tense stance. The man looked familiar, but I couldn't place him.

"Acting Captain Haddock, sir. We attended a few academy classes together," he spoke, answering my unvoiced question. "They call me Dock for short."

His sharp nose and short, cropped hair struck a chord. "Of course. Comparative War Theory, and what was the other? Source Ethics?" I remembered him now, and I know why he hadn't stuck in mind. I also knew why he might have been elevated to my position. Like Zane, Dock was a real Ferro patriot and, like my mother, he hated anything related to Earth. He'd made it very clear in our classes that he found even the theory that humans and Ferroeans could co-exist, let alone be socially equal, appalling. I tried to keep my face neutral as I kept eye contact.

"Correct, sir. Welcome back to the barracks, Captain." The man's eyes were hard, and I understood there was no real welcoming feelings coming from him.

"Thank you—you said 'acting captain'? Of what?" I was pretty sure I knew the answer, but it seemed more entertaining to pretend otherwise.

"Why, sir, of the Guard Program and ULT. I was reassigned when you took up your post on Earth." Current command positions were probably one of those things I should have bothered to look into, but honestly, I didn't care. He shifted his weight from foot to foot a moment, waiting for some kind of response. When I didn't give him one, he continued, "As per my orders, I have vacated my—your—office on the tenth floor. I have moved into the Second's office a floor down. I hope this wasn't presumptuous of me. I wasn't notified that anyone other than yourself would be returning."

He was referring to my team, and I immediately missed having Tasha as my Second. Nevertheless, it was clear the man was worried about his job. What a trivial concern with the worlds at stake. "No, of course. I'd be happy to have you continue as my Second." I wasn't sure if this was true, but for now it was easier.

Dock didn't seem happy with my reply, but at least he didn't look angrier. "I will endeavor to prove myself to you, sir. I was just about to review drills with the recruits—would you like to join us?"

It was a courtesy I knew he was hoping I'd say no to. "That would be excellent, actually. I have a few things to take care of in my office first. Then, why don't you have the recruits ready for inspection in, say, half an hour?"

I could swear the man's lip twitched ever so slightly, like he was holding back a sneer. "I will see you then, sir. On the Open Training Floor." He stood, waiting.

I finally realized he was waiting for me to formally say the words. "Dismissed, Captain," I said quickly. He turned on his heels and marched away. "Good job, Cash," I said to myself. "Already making friends on your first day back."

I looked back at the floating screen and selected the option for a personal bullet to the tenth floor. One of the smaller, single-person pods popped up from an automatic doorway in the floor of the closest bay and hovered there, waiting. I climbed in and took hold of the safety rails on either side. Once I was settled, the bullet shot upward of its own accord, so quickly my brain didn't even have time to register the change before I'd arrived at my floor. I climbed out and headed to the direction of the Captain's office. Dock did not seem happy about having to leave it, and I couldn't blame him. I just hoped he hadn't messed up the place in my absence.

Another retinal scan, and I was through the automatic doors and into a room I'd always considered a sanctuary before I left for Earth. It was a corner office, and two of the walls were floor-to-ceiling windows of crystal-clear glass, chemically treated to adjust for the sunlight and darken as needed. The floors, ceiling, and other two walls were traditional white tile, but the antique Earth desk was dark, well-polished mahogany. There were a few other touches of dark wood in the room, all souvenirs collected by various Captains. Some brought back pieces for the aesthetic, others as a show of conquering Earth, and a few out of respect for human craftsmanship. More than any place in the royal residence, this place was mine.

Struck by the thought, I dashed across the room and opened the double doors of a tall wooden hutch that matched the desk. To my disappointment, the human snacks that had always filled the shelves were replaced with bottles of nutrient-infused water and Ferroean meal bars. At least they were the near flavorless kind, and not the terrible attempts on Ferro to simulate berry, citrus, or, worst of all—mint chocolate.

I took a bottle of nutrient water and closed the cabinet doors a little harder than necessary. Luckily, I knew from experience that the antique furniture in the room could take a much worse beating. With a few precise waves of my hand, I opened three files in the air above my desk. One folder was the current trainee roster. I gave it a quick glance and saw a few familiar faces amongst the advanced students. At least two had been on my short list to bring to Earth with me, and several had just entered training a few months before I left my post here. The rest were new to me.

The second was a dossier on Dock, filled with commendations and accreditations for some articles he had written. I couldn't even read the titles they sounded so boring. There was no evidence he had ever left the Capital, let alone visited Earth. He may have gained rank, but his combat experience was nonexistent.

The third folder contained all the information officially known about the prophecy and the Orb, threats from the Rebellion, and relevant training directives. It was no surprise that nothing on the prophecy was new or useful, but just more of the same rhetoric we were taught since childhood. Information on the Rebellion had been updated with some current terrorist attacks and acts of sedition, but I'd have to dig deeper for more specifics. I thought I read something that might be related to source stealing, but the details were vague. It was clear I'd have to dig deeper for more useful information. I glanced at the trainee roster again, and then headed back to the bullet bays. I had some fresh meat to intimidate. At least that would distract me from thoughts of Bea. If anything happened to her, I would never forgive myself, but most of all I'd never forgive my brother.

The Open Training Floor was five levels below the surface, but the ride on the bullet took no more than a few seconds. I still had half a bottle of nutrient water in my hand as I exited the pod and came face-to-face with the training room floor. No walls or doors separated the bank of lifts from the rest of the room—instead, there was an empty track of solid cement and then a floor of blue mats all the way to the other side of the cavernous floor. The walls were matte black ceramic aluminum, bifurcated with a line of track lighting that circled all the way around. More floodlights shone down from the high ceiling. For the sake of versatility, the training room took up the entire footprint of the main building above, with only the occasional pillar blocking line of sight. There were areas for open sparring, specific weapons training, cardio, and anything else a soldier might need, but with a few swipes, the whole floor could be converted into an obstacle course or the set for a training scenario. I even added some black lights the last time I returned from Earth after visiting something called "laser tag."

"Captain on the floor!" Acting Captain Dock's voice rung out from several yards away and I stifled a groan. Respect was important, but I never found invoking rank to have a positive effect on building a cohesive, capable team.

I took one of those centering breaths Tasha had taught me years back and strode over to Dock and the squad of trainees. Twenty faces in four rows of five stood in front of me at various levels of attention. I spotted Samptim in the second row. He was actively avoiding eye contact as he stared dutifully ahead. I wondered if it was because of our conversation in the corridor yesterday. He had most likely been reprimanded for gossiping. "At ease," I barked but couldn't help but notice how stiff Dock remained. I bet he made them stand at attention anytime they weren't sparring.

I started pacing around the group, taking in what we had to work with. I honestly had no concerns—if Paul could make it through training, all of them could. It was really a matter of where best they'd ultimately be assigned. Regardless, it was good to keep them on their toes.

After a complete circuit, I stopped in front of the group, my hands comfortably clasped behind my back in a stance my instructor had always taken. "As you most certainly know, I am Captain Kingston. You can call me Captain or Sir officially, but I hope to quickly get to know most of you well enough that Cash will be fine as well. What I don't know is what you have heard about me, my work on Earth, or my capabilities. And honestly, I don't care. All of you are here because you—or someone you've trained under—believe you have the mental and physical fortitude to hold the most prestigious honor of becoming an elite Guard of Ferro. With my training we will see if that is true."

I pulled my Ferro dagger from my boot sheath, idling balancing it in my hands as I continued to talk. "I see we have a good mix of seasoned and new students. Who can tell me why that is?"

Two hands darted up, and Samptim's eyes went wide as he inched his hand up to join. "Recruit Samptim," I said, singling him out. "It's a pleasure to see you again."

He kept his soldier cool about him. "Unit Level Training—otherwise known as ULT—is four-pronged," Samptim answered, meeting my eyes now with a bit of excited nervousness. "It consists of group lessons, advanced lessons, individual lessons, and open sparring."

"Very good. What is the point of group lessons?" I looked out across the trainees and picked out a girl with a side-shaved haircut in her otherwise tousled locks. "You, Re-cruit...."

"Recruit Cardel, Captain—Sir." Her youthful voice almost broke mid-sentence, but she kept attention.

"One or the other is fine, Recruit Cardel. Go on, please," I answered, feeling the words of my teachers on my lips in a way I hadn't in years.

"Group lessons allow for all trainees to work as a unit as they focus on a particular skill or weapon style. Those with more experience are expected to help those with less in the associated drills," she recited from the training manual. How boring!

"Very good," I looked out amongst them, unimpressed, but having to keep my Captain cool. "I haven't had a chance to read through your dossiers yet, so you all have a chance to impress me." I flipped the dagger in my hand, effortlessly catching it by the hilt. "Grab a practice dagger from the wall rack and divide up into pairs. Let's see what you can do."

"Samptim," I said, still focused on my own thermo dagger. "Come with me. Let's talk."

"Captain Cash?" Dock asked, causing some of the recruits to gasp. Questioning me was forbidden. I ignored him and kept my pace in the other direction. Samptim caught up. His eyes wide, his face pale as he stepped in line with me and walked.

"Am I in trouble, Captain?" His hands trembled at his side. How old was this boy they had standing guide at my quarters? I'd look into his file when I get back to my office, but my guess was around fifteen.

"Not at all," I answered and meant it. "Actually, I'm happy that you'll be in my training. I wanted to learn more about what you said the other day."

Stumbling over his words and his feet, Samptim rolled out excuse and after excuse for his overshare, none I believed and or wanted to hear. I waved my hand as I came to an abrupt stop. "Do not fill the air with words you think I want to hear. Tell me about the rumors even if you feel they are nonsense." I put my hand on his shoulder and gave a gentle squeeze. "Let me judge their value."

Samptim gulped the sound a frog made. "Well, Captain, it's just scuttlebutt but..." He paused, looking all around, even at the ceiling. His voice lowered. "The Rebellion is rumored to have spies here on Ferro. Which I know is crazy in and of itself because King Zane would know." Samptim straightened his spine and drew his shoulders back. "He's the most aware and fierce king we have ever had." I rolled my eyes inside their sockets, thanking the Council for my Aviator shades.

I removed my sunglasses and held them out. Smudges grazed the lenses. I grabbed the hem of my t-shirt and started to massage the smears out. "And what do the rumors of the Rebellion have to do with stealing sources?"

I held them back up to make sure the smudges were gone, and I caught Samptim's reflection in the frames.

Samptim's eyes tensed and drew upward but what caused me to stop breathing was his uncontrollable irises flashing pink, red, and orange, a strong reaction to my inquiry. "The Rebellion is building an army of Blood-Lights."

Chapter Twenty-Five

Ashton

It had been a month of training with Beatrice and not once did her necklace draw in enough opposing source energy to turn purple. We knew the necklace was working; it swirled a violent magenta when we made her angry, and blue-green when she needed her source drained now that Cash was no longer feeding from her. But no matter what we tried, it never turned solid purple.

Eventually, Sera decided to open Bea's trainings to everyone in the Hive. The rebels, both human and Ferroean, were hard on her. Crowds from all Blocks stacked themselves into the training room, sitting on benches, chairs, and the floor, all desperate to get a peek at Beatrice's acclaimed and growing fighting skills. We were all impressed with how quickly she'd been advancing since that first day on the mat with Sera. At one point, the space grew so overcrowded that Bea accidentally struck a human who had stumbled into the training area. The poor earthling was fine after we healed him, but the decision was made to stagger audience attendance from that point on.

Block A was allowed to participate Monday and Wednesday. These were harder days for Bea because the residents of that block had previous training. Afterward, Tasha would spend entire evenings healing Bea from the battering she took. Training against the residents of Block B on Tuesdays and Thursdays was better suited to her skills. They had solid training but no experience in real combat. That naivety helped her deal with the unexpected. Block A all moved and fought as a united force, but Block B made things up as they went, demonstrating an opponent's originality. Friday was a nightmare. Block C was made up of human rebels and completely inexperienced Ferroeans. Many times, I asked Sayor if we could release them into the wild. It was Mark, always Mark, that stood up for them, like they had some hidden reservoir of potential underneath all that mess. They resembled untrained puppies chasing their tails and wetting the floor. After a number of disappointing sessions, Bea admitted she felt too guilty working with them. She wasn't even worried about hurting them; she was more concerned they'd hurt themselves. Most of Block A spent Friday nights healing Block C from their unending injuries. But the most curious I had been was when someone from Block C gained enough strength to leveled up to Block B. Yes, it made sense the humans would progress and get better—if they didn't, we weren't doing our jobs—but there was a nagging feeling that something else was going on and I couldn't put my finger on it.

Sera resigned from training with Bea and took a more active role with Sayor, working closely on a plan as if Bea had her powers under control. We still didn't know when the asteroids would hit and where we needed to be positioned. All Dr. X could tell us was that there would be three days of an eclipse, a harrowing three nights of darkness—the universe's way of letting us know the time had come.

Sera felt badly about her first day of training with Beatrice and I agreed she may have proceeded poorly. I'm not sure if Bea forgave her or not, but she seemed to have understood her motives, nevertheless. They kept their distance from one another for the most part, and I suspected the absence of any real intel on Cash was exacerbating the void both were suffering from in their own ways. Bea busied herself with sparring day and night and Sera with researching the asteroids, burying her nose in every book she could find.

Sayor was growing increasingly impatient. His daily check-ins had been less friendly with each passing day and his fear more evident. He looked drained with worry, and if the dark circles under his eyes weren't enough, he was starting to lose track of days by working through the night without any rest. If Bea didn't learn how to ignite her power, she and I wouldn't be able to connect and there would be no saving the planets. We were getting desperate.

One afternoon during a Block C training—excited to be removed from that debacle—Sayor called Sera and me into his office.

"I've received word on Cash," he said, reclining back into his leather chair.

Sera leaned forward, her palms flat on his desk, her braid swinging around her shoulder. "Is he alive?"

"Yes. He's been back in Ferro in the Capital since the day he was captured. Apparently, Zane bargained with the DOAA for his life."

"So, let's go get him," Sara barked. "Now! What are we waiting for?"

Sayor shook his head. "It's not that easy. At all wormhole entry points, Zane has guards scanning people's sources. He's not unwise. He is looking for us to come and retrieve Cash."

Sera started for the door as if Sayor hadn't been speaking.

"Seraphina Laylan! Stop!" Sayor stood. Her hand was raised, about to waive the door open as she froze. "You'll never understand what I know, and why I have done the things I have done, and perhaps you never will."

Sera turned slowly. Her skin pinched around her eyes. "Two worlds as one, this oath I take: to Ferro, to Earth..." She started to the finish the pledge. I cut her off.

"Screw that. We are going to get Cash." I held my hand up to Sayor, readying myself to telekinetically throw him backward. It wouldn't hurt him physically, but from the look on his face the threat was as much a betrayal as wielding a thermo dagger against him.

"And I expected no less." He took his seat, deflated. "Be sure to tell Beatrice before the two of you leave. I'm sure she will want to accompany you and I do not want to deal with the aftermath if you leave her behind."

As if an avalanche of realization hit me, I thudded into the chair in front of his desk, my bravado evaporated. "By the Council, you knew we would react this way! You *want* us to run off and tell Beatrice. You are so desperate that you would let the three of us go to Ferro to free Cash because you don't think we can get Bea's source to ignite without him." I pounded my fist into his desk. "How long have you known Cash was on Ferro? How long have you known he was alive?!" I roared into his face. Cash wasn't the only one with a ferocious temper.

Across the desk, Sayor was calm. He showed no sign of being roused by my question or accusatory tone. "I've known since the day you arrived back at the Hive."

Before I could tell him how insane he was or threaten to kill him, Sera was already vaulting over the desk, toppling the chair, and taking him to the ground. Papers and other office supplies fell around them. Sera straddled Sayor, fist raised to crash into his face. Red and yellow fluid dotted her knuckles.

I darted around the desk, wrapping my arms around Sera's waist and pulling her off Sayor's supine form. She struggled against me, her legs flailing in the air. "How could you? Haven't we suffered enough?" Her voice was hoarse, anger and despair fighting for control.

I held her tight, both to comfort her and to keep her from hurting Sayor any further. I spoke softly, trying to relay my understanding of how messed up this all was. "I'm going to put you down. Please do not go after him again. It will not change anything." She growled but relaxed, and I took that as a confirmation she'd behave. I released my hold on her, and she crossed her arms over her chest, her eyes as deadly as any thermo dagger as they focused on Sayor. I shook my head, matching her stare at the man I'd considered my mentor on the floor. "You have some balls, Sayor. We should kill you. I don't care if we are falling into your trap or whatever else you have planned, but we will tell Beatrice and take her with us to free Cash. And thanks for the heads up about the scanners. I guess telling us the truth from the beginning and trusting your team was too hard for you. What else should I have expected from someone that would let those that care for him think he was dead."

Sayor stood, wiping the yellow plasma from his face and pulling his clothing taut. "If my job was easy, don't you think there would be Ferroeans lining up for it? The pledge is the pledge for a reason. If you two had any idea what was coming and what we are really up against out there, you wouldn't question me." He turned to Sera and it was the first time I saw Sayor let his cool, collected mask slip. "And if you think you are the only one who has sacrificed, you are extremely mistaken. The woman I love, I could never have. The child I dreamed of, I could never raise. And the planet I love would never accept either of them. So don't you for one minute think you are above the mission or that your pain is more important than anyone else's. It's not a competition of trials." He picked up some of the fallen papers from his desk. "But if it was," he glared at her, "I'd win."

We immediately left Sayor's office to find Beatrice and found her and Darla in her bedroom. Beatrice was the only one other than Sayor to have her own room. Not that it was anything to gloat about. It was more like a prison cell. Sayor felt that it was important that she stay away from the Ferroean rebels. They had mixed feelings about her—not only was she a relative newcomer to the cause, she also had the unique ability to kill them with nothing but her source—even if she didn't quite know how yet, but I had my suspicions. Being around the human rebels was no better, except that they each wanted to be her. They bombarded her with a hundred questions daily the short time she was with them, so Sayor had a small room fashioned for her. It had a bed, a desk, and a small closet just like Sayor's.

I leaned my hip up against the doorframe as Sera walked in and took the desk chair, her body still tensed and buzzing with angry energy.

"Hey Hollywood, bored of Block C day?" Darla snickered. It was no secret I couldn't stand Block C, especially since she was one of its members and had more skills with her mouth than her hands. She may not have been the worst of the group, but she was not leveling up to Block B any time soon either.

"Not when you're the one on the mat, my little Sugar Snap," I teased despite myself. As long as she kept calling me Hollywood, I'd keep calling her the makeshift curse word she'd said our first day here.

"I literally hate when you call me that. Do you need to be here right now? Bea and I were just talking about how annoying you are."

"It's nice to know you talk about me, Sugar," I snickered.

Darla crossed her arms over her chest. "I do not talk about you. I can't stand you. You make my skin crawl. I get a fever in your presence. You are too tall. You are bossy. You are..."

"Handsome, sexy, cute, the man of your dreams?" I waggled my brow as Darla's dipped downward.

Beatrice rolled her eyes. "She *does* talk about you constantly, but I haven't figured out if it's because she really likes you or really hates you."

"What can I say? It's a mystery," Darla murmured, throwing her head back against the wall.

"Anyway," Sera said, drawing the attention back to the task in front of us. "Beatrice, we need to tell you something." Beatrice sat up straighter. "It's about Cash. He's..." Sera paused and glanced my way. She thought into my head. *Don't tell her Sayor knew. Unlike us, she has the power to kill him. And she might not even know she's doing it until it's too late. We don't know what she's really capable of yet.*

I hadn't thought about Bea as a weapon until Sera said something. She was right. Bea might not want to be what she was to our people, but just like the Ferroean rebels were scared of her, so should we be. I nodded in agreement.

"He's what? Oh my god, is he dead? Please tell me he's not dead." Moisture welled in Bea's eyes. She grabbed the covers on the bed, balling them into her palm.

I traveled farther into the room. "He's not dead. He's alive." I moved Darla's legs and placed them on top of mine, sitting on the edge of the bed. I was only half surprised she let me hold on to them. "The day we left him at the DOAA, he was taken back to Ferro. Zane made a deal for his life."

Bea's eyebrow rose as did her voice. "What deal?"

I shook my head. "I have no idea and truly I doubt, even if Sayor knew, he'd tell us." I rubbed Darla's leg with my thumb. I hadn't meant to it just happened. She tensed for a moment but then relaxed. "You want to go save my brother or what?"

"Did you even have to ask?" Bea's smile extended her whole face.

"I'm going too," Darla said.

"You can't, Sugar," I responded, and I meant it. All the humor I typically had during my endearing conversations with Darla was vacant. "Don't even argue with me. You're a human, you don't fight well, and you'd be a distraction." Darla's legs moved so fast I didn't have time to catch them. She kicked my hip, throwing me off the bed, and stood.

"First of all, don't call me that. Secondly, I am NOT leaving Beatrice. And thirdly, I'm not a distraction unless you make me one. If I get caught, what will they do to me?"

"Kill you!" I pushed myself off the ground, rising to my feet and rubbing my rear as I stood. "My people would kill you or make you their pet. And I'm reserving that right for myself, Sugar." I let the humor slip back into my voice, but it only softened my tone so much. She could not go to Ferro.

"You are so infuriating. And I'm not yours!"

"Darla, I don't think it's safe if you come with us. I'm sorry," Bea said, removing the covers and standing. She was in white drawstring pants and a white button-down top, the night apparel of Ferro. I don't know why I thought it was so odd Sayor had these clothes for her, but I did. Except for the occasional guard uniform during practice sessions, I hadn't seen any of the others wearing Ferro-sanctioned clothing in the Hive.

"So, what now?" Bea asked as she moved to get clothes from her closet.

"There's a wormhole here in the cave, so we can leave immediately. Wear your combat gear and bring your thermo daggers. It'll be a fight at the entrance when they figure out our sources don't match our shells. Apparently, Zane has scanners at all entry points, waiting for us to try," Sera said, explaining the position we would be in upon arrival.

I rubbed my hands together like I was starting a fire. "Oh fun, we haven't almost expired lately. I was beginning to weary at the lack of death-defying moments." I rolled my eyes.

"Are we going to tell the others?" Beatrice asked, looking at a pouting Darla. Darla's hands were shoved so deep in her pockets, the outline of her fingertips was visible at the seams. Her hair was covering some of her face, but still allowed me to see her watering eyes. I understood the sadness and worry she wore in the creases that framed her face.

Sera chimed in. "Darla can tell them after we leave. If they know before we go, they will either try and stop us or come with us, and we can't chance their lives with what we will have to do." Sera gazed at the door before letting her eyes reach mine. "I fear we will have to stay on Ferro and complete the connection there. It's where we will save both planets or where we will die. I certainly hope we can stop both asteroids from that location." She paused. "Given the time difference the likelihood..." She couldn't finish her sentence.

"We will stop the asteroids. We can't do it without Cash, and this is the only way how. We have to get him back," I said confidently.

I stepped outside so Bea could get dressed. "Hey, Sugar Snap, wanna keep me company?"

Bea motioned for Darla to go and she did. I half expected her to tell me all the reasons she wanted nothing to do with me, but she didn't even put up a fight. She leaned up against the wall and sighed.

"Don't be sad, Sugar. I promise I'll come back for you if for no other reason than to remind you of all the ways I can quiet you."

Darla shivered, and I didn't think it had anything to do with being cold. "You really are utterly annoying, extremely rude, giraffe-like, and it really pisses me off your hair, unlike mine, doesn't need a blow dryer to look all perfect and fluffy." Her arms crossed her chest. "But with all that being said, I'd appreciate it if you came back alive." My mouth opened and she covered it with her hand, her whole hand. "Do not ruin what I said with something ridiculous and moronic. I don't have the energy to kick you in the crotch like I want to right now."

I licked her and she groaned, taking her hand off my mouth.

"You know how I feel about you and my crotch in the same sentence? Are you trying to sweet-talk me so I'll kiss you good-bye?" I closed in the distance between us.

"You wouldn't dare." Her voice was low.

"I would and you know it," I said, lowering my head closer to hers. Cocooning her in, I placed a hand on either side of her.

She pressed her back into the wall, causing her spine to straighten. "You like Beatrice." Her voice was as slow as a whisper.

I barked a laugh. "You're kidding me! I've never been interested in Beatrice. And since my brother got captured, I've acted more like a big brother to her than anything else."

"You kissed her! That's a gross brother-like thing to do then," Darla countered.

Ok, she had a point but..."If I'm being honest here, I was just testing this connection out that she and I are supposed to have. And when I did, I felt nothing for her. But I do think I figured out what is really happening between her and me."

"And what's that?" Darla's voice was low and cautious. "A love that grows over time with watering and proper sunlight?"

I barked a laugh. "There are other ways to grow a flower, Sugar."

Darla's nose twitched.

"A story for another time then." My heart felt heavy remembering the flower my mother gave me as a child and the significance behind its responsibility. I shook away the thought. Another time was right. I moved my head even closer to Darla's, bringing our lips a mere inch apart. I felt our breaths mingled as one. Darla placed her hand directly over the source in my chest cavity, keeping some distance between us. Energy buzzed through me, and it felt like my half-human veins were on fire.

"Tell me what is happening between you and my best friend? Or would you like a kick in the pants?" Her lips pulled and I could tell she was trying to fight a smile.

"Whatever you want, Sugar." I backed up an inch. Her bottom lip jutted out. Whether it was conscious or subconscious, she was missing our close proximity. "I think it's that our sources are directly from the Orb because only sources harbored in the Orb smell like cedar and sage and only descendants of the Orb can smell them. Which would mean someone has been playing source thief on Ferro." I placed my hand over hers on my chest. "This puppy. It's definitely not mine."

Chapter Twenty-Six

Cash

Standing in front of the great double doors reserved for esteemed guests, I took a deep, resolved breath. The palace guard eyed me curiously, but I needed a moment before proceeding. I'd never encountered a battlefield more treacherous than one of my Mother's insipid homecoming parties. No occurrence was too small or unimportant for Subaltern Tali Kingston to remember it with one of her signature social hours complete with obnoxious levels of Ferroean pomp and circumstance.

"Is it everything I'd hope for in there?" I asked, meeting the Guard's vacant stare. He and the other Guards were wearing whites today, the traditional formal attire for all Royal events. Everything from their shoes to their gloves and caps were stark white, except for the chrome buttons that outlined their embroidered collars.

"Why yes, Captain Cash," the Guard answered, eager to be of assistance. "I think you'll find your mother's welcome home party more than adequate for your liking."

My mouth tipped up in a half smile. "I take it they are serving sour cream and onion potato chips, then?"

The Guard's brows jerked together in confusion. "I'm not sure, Captain. But I can have a Guard find out. Would you like me to—"

I waved my hand dismissively, cutting him off. More than ever I missed human sarcasm. Ferro's mind-numbing personalities had the potential to kill me if these asteroids didn't. I motioned for him to open the doors.

In truth, I had to begrudgingly admit that the Royal Audience Chamber was the grandest of all the rooms at the Residence, possibly on the planet. Not that I'd ever say so out loud. According to our history books, Earthen architectural styles had a profound influence on the governmental constructions of Ferro. Sera had dragged me to the Metropolitan Museum of Art on our first trip to New York City, and pointed out all the similarities and differences between our buildings and those of ancient Earth. Built with both indigenous Ferroean and precious Earthen materials, the Audience Chamber was meant to receive and entertain large numbers of guests. It had the high, vaulted ceilings of a Gothic cathedral, but lacked any of the intricate details, carvings, or finial accents ancient humans were so very fond of. Arched alcoves lined the walls, allowing places for small groups to sit and converse, broken up by large windows that looked out into the Crystal Gardens on either side. Today, the electromagnetic screens had been dimmed, and a gentle breeze carried the faint sound of chimes and the rich, green scent of fresh-cut leaves into the impressive space. A great dais occupied the very center of the room. Long ago, a royal throne may have occupied a space like that, but now acted as a stage for speeches and entertainment. A small string quartet that was a favorite of my mother's was playing from there now, the classical music filling the room with ambience.

"Casheous." My mother's voice sounded behind me. I pivoted. "You look very handsome, my son," she said, eyeing the outfit she had picked out for me: grey dress slacks and a white button-down. I left the grey tie in my room. The smile behind her teeth—if one even existed—was hidden, possibly because of the missing tie. "You remember the parents of Marketus, Samdomion, and Paphater, don't you?" I didn't miss the insinuating tone meant to remind me to behave.

Mother, who was dressed in a tight-fitting, long-sleeved, rose-tinted dress, was standing with Mark, Sammie, and Paul's mother and father, both dressed in understated but wholly refined attire. Now *their* smiles were nowhere to be found. Flickers of colors broke at the edges of their irises, but they controlled it from flowing freely. The Flannerys couldn't even feign happiness for my return home without their children. Not that I blamed them.

Mr. Flannery's mouth twitched as if he wanted to say something. His knuckles were white enough that I wondered how long the crystal goblet he was holding could take the pressure without breaking. With pinched lips, Mrs. Flannery addressed me instead. "Welcome back, Captain Cash. Will your team be returning anytime soon?" She cupped her hands in front of her waist and, like her husband, her hands gave her tension away.

I bowed my head in respect. "It's lovely to see you both again. It is my greatest hope my team joins me in the near future. I, however, am not privy to the King's plan." They could be angry at me all they want, but I didn't have to shoulder the blame alone. My mother's frown fell so fast and far, I feared her lips would hit the floor. Unfazed and unsurprised, I casually scooped a goblet of pale-blue frost wine from a passing server's tray. I continued in my most professional-sounding voice, "I had not wanted to leave them in the first place. As I'm sure you would never question the King, neither would I. I do hope for their speedy return as well." That should satisfy dear old Mommy. Showing support of my father was not unfamiliar to me but lying about still having any faith in him was.

Mr. Flannery stepped forward, ready to say whatever he'd been holding onto, but he paused when a hand reached for his arm from behind. It pulled him backward, and as Mr. Flannery turned, the woman came into view. I was struck by her beauty before I recognized her. Satiny dark-brown hair spilled over her shoulders, covering the thin straps of her rather scandalous white and silver dress. The bodice hugged her waist so tightly it pushed her chest up so high I had to question how she breathed. But it was the bright glint of humor in her green eyes that plucked at memories from my childhood. They were the same mischievous eyes that peeked through the slits of doorways to eavesdrop on Mark, Paul, and me as we plotted our boyhood schemes. The same doe-eyes that begged and pleaded Sammie and Sera to play with her, too.

"Father, I'm sure Cash is tired from his travels. Must you really make him feel worse about leaving my siblings behind?" She sashayed in front of me toward my mother, completely ignoring my existence in a pointed reversal of those childhood memories. "Tali, you look stunning as ever. And this party!" She waved her free hand gracefully in the air, indicating the entirety of the room while the delicate, well-manicured fingers of her other hand curled around a goblet of her own. "How do you manage to make everything look so beautiful? If I ever marry, please tell me you will help me plan my wedding? I would be honored to have something half as splendid as this."

Despite myself, I erupted with laughter, making the girl and my mother glare in my direction. "Jellybean, is that you?" I asked, having lost any interest in maintaining that professional facade.

She rolled her eyes. "I like to be called Jill now. Thank you."

I kept laughing. "You may like that, Jellybean, but until you travel to Earth you are stuck with your Ferroean name. It's a—"

"Rite of passage to be called by an Earth name. I know, I know!" she cut me off, saying exactly what I had intended to say. She threw her hands in the air, her own well-mannered mask lifted. I was glad her glass appeared to be empty. "I'm the only Ferroean to have been born and given a human candy as a name all because my parents left my naming in the care of a child!"

Mrs. Flannery's hate-filled glare toward me softened as she spoke to her daughter. "Do not blame me. Samantha named you while I was on ferrophene. I had no idea until I saw the legal papers, and it was in fact your father who signed them. We did not advise her on that name, and I believe she misspelled it accidentally due to the circumstances."

Jellybean's hand flew to her hip as she reached out and placed her empty goblet on a passing tray. "Who travels to Earth nine months pregnant and has a craving for jelly beans, then two seconds through the wormhole goes into labor, writes their child's name on a candy wrapper, and hands it to a four-year-old? Of course, Samantha misspelled it. She never turned it over and saw what you wrote. She only saw the candy name on the front of the packaging and handed it to the nurses!"

"Well at least you don't look like a jelly bean. Sammie's gonna wish she named you Marshmallow when she sees you. And Mark and Paul are gonna whip some—"

"Casheous, enough," my mother hissed. Her cheeks reddened at my attempted use of Earth slang.

"Come on, Casheous, why don't we go for a walk," Jellybean said, my mockery quickly forgiven as she looped her arm through mine. "I've had enough of memory lane for one night."

We casually walked away from our parents, arm in arm. "Wow," I said, giving her a once-over. I threw back the frost wine I was still holding and set the empty glass on a nearby pedestal. "Your brothers are gonna lose it when they see how well you can fill out a dress. And Sammie might just try to extinguish your source so there's no competition," I teased. Jellybean was one of my favorite kids growing up. Unlike her siblings, I appreciated her inquisitiveness, but as Captain and surrogate older brother, I was just as much to blame for her being left out of most of our excursions. She was just too young at the time.

"She doesn't have to worry about that," Jellybean said as she hugged me in closer to her side. As the warmth of her body pressed up against mine, I instantly missed Beatrice, and I began wondering where she was and what she was doing, and that it better not be arm in arm with my brother. "We don't play for the same team's attention." She winked at me.

"That'll break a lot of men's hearts, but you just brightened up every woman's day," I said as I squeezed her back.

Jellybean might not be part of my crew, but she was a piece of them, and for the first time since I had been back in Ferro, I was having a decent time.

"Just don't mention it in front of my mom. She ignores it's real, so I just ignore her. I figure it will work itself out eventually."

It was a party like any other my mother would throw. Servants in dull grey aprons carried trays of carved crystal cups filled with the fermented drinks our people loved so much—some a light and clear icy blue, and others a deep, effervescent amber. While serving human-inspired food had long ago become fashionable among the elite, Mother felt eating while talking was crass. Instead, a few of the servants held trays of small, jewel-like capsules that melted on the tongue and filled the mouth with various fruit, spice, and floral flavors. They honestly weren't bad—kind of like human gummies or hard candies—but they were certainly not food, either. The thought made my stomach rumble in protest. It had been two days since I'd had real food, and no number of nutrient pills and powders would replace that.

All around me, Ferroeans drank and lounged, laughing and pretending amusement at each other's anecdotes. There was no hint, not even a glimmer, of anticipation for what might occur when the asteroid hit, or what it even meant that I was back without my opposing source alongside me. The average Ferroean had little reason to fear death normally, so perhaps it was harder for them to muster it now, or maybe they believed it was all just a political ploy by the High Council and the elders. Whatever it was, the nonchalant appearance of calm was nothing but alarming to me.

We walked past the front foyer, where my father was talking to two Councilmen. Each was in a dark-grey suit tailored perfectly to their bodies, white ties, and black, newly-polished shoes that reflected the lights from the ceiling like mirrors. They nodded as they saw me. I nodded back out of respect.

Jellybean dragged me to the corner bar, where she asked the server for two glasses of mulled amber wine. "We need to talk, but not here," she whispered. She took the two offered goblets, handing one to me and taking a sip of her own. The warm wine was fragrant with the spicy scent of a type of ginger you could only find in the wilds south of the Capital.

"I'd be equally thankful to get out of this place as I would for Earth food right about now, but my mother would notice my absence." I stared in the Subaltern's direction, watching her movements intently. She floated across the room, stopping at each gathered group. Her conversations lasted less than a minute before she'd move on to her next prey.

"Would she though?" Jellybean asked, her brow raised. "Your mother is up to something. Notice when she stops at the groups of three people or less. Watch what happens." She pulled on my arm conspiratorially, directing my attention in the right direction. My eyes followed as my mother made her way to three women. They were in a strange formation, almost as if they were waiting for my mother to fill in the fourth spot. They'd lean in and a flash of light sparked, so small you'd miss it unless you were looking for it.

"They're sharing information from their sources, in a memory exchange. Why?"

When Ferroeans died, they could hide their last moments on this planet for their loved ones. It could be anything from a simple *I love you* to something more drastic like their murders. The downfall was it could only be seen and heard once. It was what Faye left me in Sera's chest cavity when she asked me to protect Beatrice. But to do it when you were alive was risky; essentially, it was like being struck by lightning. It wouldn't kill you, but it could do some damage to your source, causing it to dim faster than expected. Basically, it took years off your life and there was no way around that.

"It's archaic, but it's effective, and your mother does it at every event she throws. And recently, there've been a lot of events. If they are exchanging secrets that your father or any of the other High Council cannot know about, this would be the only way to do it. It must be pretty important to risk so much."

"You're not kidding. But what secrets could she be telling? I mean, the only scandal on Ferro is the..."

Jellybean finished my sentence. "Rebellion." She took a sip of her wine. As a protective older sibling, I wanted to smack it away, but she placed it back down as if the taste disturbed her. "Your mother couldn't be further from the Rebellion than I am from men." She rolled her eyes. Subaltern was known for a kind word to your face and a silent insult to your back. She was political and loyal to the High Council—stubborn and stuffy, not defiant and radical.

"Let's get out of here," I said. I needed air and I needed answers. The latter were harder to get from my mother, so I'd settle for air.

"There's more than just your mom being secretive," Jellybean continued, and I couldn't help but notice she reminded me of a mix of Mark and Sammie—collected, but in control. "Since you've been gone, the Capital's security has tripled. Did you see the vitrics message the other day? All citizens in possession of thermo daggers had to bring them to the observatory. And all wormholes are being guarded with scanners to make sure Ferroeans match their sources. Which would only mean—"

I cut her off remembering my conversation with Samptim. "Someone's been stealing sources. And if it's the Rebellion—"

Jellybean stole my thunder, finishing my thought. "They are building an army."

Jellybean threaded her fingers between mine. "Come on. I have something else to show you." She dragged me forward out of the hall, through the front doors, passing the razor-sharp glass fashioned to look like grass in a perverse attempt to replicate Earth's flora. Although beautiful during the day when the sunbeams cast rainbow colors over the walkways, at night it was a deathtrap. Many Ferroeans were known to have fallen after a particularly long day to find themselves covered in plasma from hundreds of their piercing tips. Luckily, the injuries were easy to heal, but ego and clothing, not so much.

"So tell me! Tell me everything that's happened during your mission! I'm dying to hear." Now, this was the excitable Jellybean I remembered.

As we headed along the raised walkway that connected the royal compound to the protected courtyard surrounding the Observatory, I told her everything that had happened since our crew had begun our mission to Earth: How the five of us enrolled in Cartwright High School and observed human teenagers. How Sera gave up her opposing source, forcing her into a coma until I managed a successful Awakening. How Faye hid Sera's source in Beatrice Walker, a Blood-Light I managed to fall in love with harder than I'd ever fallen in love with Sera. How I was captured and brought back here to Ferro, leaving them both without any idea what I was thinking, and leaving me wondering where they were and if they were safe.

Jellybean nodded thoughtfully as the words spilled out of me. I realized how badly I'd needed to talk to someone about all of this, and she was the only person I could be truly honest with here. When I finally finished, we'd almost reached the end of the promenade. There were no stars in the dark sky like on Earth, but the moon shone with golden light and the city around us was bright and dazzling with tiny specks of globe light.

My surrogate little sister gave my arm a squeeze after a moment of silence. "I'm really hoping I'm there for that reunion. What are you going to tell Sera? She's going to lose it when you tell her you chose a Blood-Light over her."

I sighed. "I'll always love Sera but what I have with Bea, well, it's different."

"And different is better?" she asked.

"Not better, just more real. No one told us we were supposed to be together. In fact, it was the opposite. Falling for her wasn't easy knowing what she possessed inside of her was stolen, but it wasn't her fault. I fell for who she actually is."

Jellybean nodded. "Sounds kinda romantic if you ask me."

"Well no one did." I punched her lightly in the shoulder with a sly smile, shoving her away and breaking the too-tender moment. Enough of the sincere love stuff.

The Observatory loomed before us, and for the first time, I realized it looked like that large silver golf ball thing in that human amusement park. The one with the mouse. The building was shaped into a geodesic sphere that served as the symbolic structure of the naturally spherical Orb inside. The angles and edges were made of special blue-green glass. You could see from the inside out, but not from the outside in.

"You want to go to the Orb?" I asked incredulously. This was not the type of place anyone went to for fun or excitement. It was the closest thing to a church that we had on Ferro.

She nodded feverishly. "Yes! And whatever I do, please trust me."

I looked out over the courtyard surrounding the Observatory. It was nearly empty at this hour of night, but having run the Guard's Program, I knew better. Two Guards flanked the outside doors, and two Guards were stationed on each of the ten floors inside. Twenty Guards wouldn't be a problem. What would be was when the alarm went off and we were surrounded in seconds by every Guard in the Capital. I'd never find my way back to Earth if I ended up being sentenced to ferrocades without my source.

"You know I want to, but I can't. I can't risk it." I started to turn back, dreading my mother's party once more.

"Wait. You don't understand." I pivoted to object to Jellybean's request, but she kept speaking. "Cash, they chose me."

My brow raised ever so slightly. Did she mean what I thought she meant?

"The Orb. It speaks to me. I'm an elder."

Chapter Twenty-Seven

Beatrice

My hands shook with anticipation while I tied the laces of my black combat boots. Sera spoke in a controlled voice about what we would encounter upon re-entering Ferro through the wormhole. Apparently, King Zane had set up security at every entrance point in preparation for our likely return. My mind was spinning with thoughts of Cash and the anguish he must be in. Was he being tortured? Was he in a prison cell, weak and injured without my source to live on? Was he confused about his feelings, about mine? I was hoping for the best, but I knew I had to prepare myself for the worst. We should have never let him sacrifice himself for us. We had to rectify that mistake. Now.

"You ready?" Sera asked as I stood, stretching my ankles on reflex from all those years of track practice. I braided my hair quickly, tying it off at the ends with a black elastic and throwing it over my shoulder.

I grabbed my pair of thermo daggers from the shelf in the tiny closet and flipped them in my palms once, checking the weight even though I knew it was perfect. I slipped them easily into each of my ankle sheaths. "Let's go get Cash."

We stepped through the doorway and found Ashton and Darla closer than I would have imagined, her back against the hallway wall and her cheeks dusted a light pink. I suddenly felt awkward seeing the two of them like that. "Are you ready? Or do you need more...?" I trailed off, fidgeting with my words.

Ashton pushed off the wall quickly. "No. We are good. Let's go." His eyes were calm and his voice void of its usual flippant humor. That in itself might have scared me more than what we were about to do. If Ashton was worried, then I was petrified.

The four of us walked in silence down the hallway, preparing ourselves for the unpreparable. The warm, orange lighting switched to a dreary purple as we made a right down the corridor towards the Hive's control room. I'd never had any reason to go in this direction until now, and the way Sayor described it to me was as if no one ever did. It felt eerily quiet and unused.

"Where are we headed?" I asked in a hushed tone as I followed Sera around a sharp bend. Her thermo dagger was bouncing off her cargo pants as it hung from the weapon belt at her hip.

"The entrance to the wormhole is in the control room. No one has access to the transport but Sayor and me." Her eyes were steeled forward, focused on what was ahead of her.

We turned another corner and found ourselves in front of a rather unassuming door, no different from others throughout the complex. In a swift motion, Sera held her hand out toward the door handle, blowing it off the frame with the power of her source. It bounced violently off the wall and whipped past my head, finally clattering on the ground.

I crossed my arms, having almost been impaled by the metal hardware. "That's your idea of access?"

She shrugged her shoulders at me. "I meant access to the wormhole. Sayor's the only one with the key to the actual door." She turned toward Ashton and Darla behind us. At some point their hands had linked together, and I realized I couldn't remember the last time Darla got that close with anyone. She went on plenty of dates, but usually taunted those couples that would prance down the hallways hand in hand. I wanted to address this immediately, but it felt like the wrong time to ask my best friend if she had lost her mind. "Say your good-byes," Sera said, her voice void of emotion. "We don't have much time."

As if on cue, the corridor filled with the sound of a wailing klaxon, and red lights whirled from a beacon above the doorway. We each glared at Sera as we realized alarms had been set off.

Sera frowned at the flashing lights, then hissed. "I didn't think Sayor would add an alarm. He really trusts no one. We gotta go!" She grabbed Ashton's arm and pulled him away from Darla and through the door into the control room. My eyes met my best friend's just as Sera slammed the door. Neither of us had the chance to properly say good-bye, but a look of uncertainty was written all over Darla's taut face. Knowing I might be breaking her trust, but needing to connect with her somehow, I used my newly found telepathy to tap into her thoughts. *You better come back, Bea. You all better, even stupid Ashton. Devil's Doritos, I like him. Is perfect hair an alien trick, maybe? None of this feels right. The Hive already feels more dangerous without them.*

214 ~ DANA CLAIRE

Before I could process Darla's reservations toward the Hive, Sera's stern tone grabbed my attention. "Ferro is very different from Earth. You must control any look of surprise. Do you understand?" She busied herself pressing device buttons.

The utilitarian room was just a little bigger than a walk-in closet and mostly empty. The wall to the left must have been for security. It was covered in video monitors, a third focused on rooms in the Hive but most on the outdoor areas near the entrance and along the road we'd come in on. Control panels covered the opposite wall, a haphazard mix of human and Ferroean material and design that was rather common throughout the complex. A central control panel had a sheet of glass standing upright on top, like a translucent screen that was currently clear. As Sera moved to that device, the screen came to life with glowing words and numbers. I strained to see past it, to the wall beyond. It seemed out of focus, and as I stepped past the screen, I realized it wasn't just an effect of the glass. The wall ahead of us was pulsating, coming in and out of focus like one of those pictures you could strain to see an image in. Only I couldn't find an image.

"Bea, move!" Sera struck a final command and threw herself toward me, pushing me toward the unnatural wall. All of a sudden, what had been weird stone erupted into a swirling mass of color and light, shaking the room and causing cracks in the floor below me. I looked down, careful to adjust my feet around the fissures as the three of us stood before something that should have been impossible. Sera threaded her hands into mine and spoke into my mind. *Close your eyes and don't hold your breath. Try and stay calm.* My lids shut as she pulled me forward. There was a feeling of pressure against my whole body, and then one of release. The darkness roared around us, a wind pulling me this way and that, the ground falling away beneath me, the world gone around me. My legs paddled against the viscous air like a child struggling to stay afloat, and panic crawled up my spine as my braided hair whipped across my face. I couldn't feel Sera's hand in mine anymore, but I focused on her command, squeezing my eyes tighter until I managed to push most of the panic back down. I breathed slowly, deliberately, as if there was pressure against my lungs. Within seconds, the wind calmed. My feet found solid ground.

When I opened my eyes, I was on a floating platform surrounded by a starless purple-black sky lit only by a single moon. Without clouds or even birds, the empty sky felt like it had been painted above me. Where it had been day on Earth, it was clearly nighttime on Ferro and I was under an alien sky for the very first time.

Nothing I'd seen so far could prepare me for the strangeness of this place. Behind me, the air shimmered slightly like oil on water, and I knew that was where we had just come from, now inactive and stable. The floor beneath us was an almost ceramic white, the moon bouncing off and providing as much light as the globes that lined the edge of the platform's perimeter. Looking ahead, I could see distant skylines of what I presumed to be the Capital. We were nowhere near Cash.

Sera and Ashton flanked me on either side. There were two Ferroeans immediately in front of us, each holding some kind of device in their hands. At least six guards huddled together past them—shoulders relaxed and casual laughter echoing between them. No one seemed alarmed by our appearance, at least not yet. The only sign they would even care about our existence came from their neatly pressed Royal Guard uniforms; white slacks with matching white jackets buttoned on their left side all the way up to their necks. Thermo daggers with ornamental chrome hilts hung at their sides.

I saw long capsules of some kind on the far end of the platform, possibly some kind of vehicle or way to get to the ground? It reminded me of a tram car without a track. I suspected it was our only way off this floating island. Between the drop to the ground and the distance to the Capital, jumping certainly seemed more like a death sentence than a viable option.

I realized Sera was still holding my hand and I silently thanked her with a gentle squeeze. I wanted her warmth and the assurance that it offered. I hadn't realized how badly I didn't want to die before seeing Cash again—how much I wanted to live alongside him, whether it be here or on Earth. I knew that we shared that feeling, and it brought an odd sense of comfort. We may not have seen eye to eye, but we both shared a purpose. We had to evade these guards and make it to the Capital, together. I believed to my core that Cash was the answer to unlocking my full power.

Most likely sensing my fear, Sera squeezed my hand back twice. *We've got this. Whatever you do, when they scan over yours or my source, run toward the end of this platform and board the needle. It's the thin transportation vehicles lined up at the end. Do you see them?* I nodded, recognizing she meant the odd capsules waiting there. *Wave your hand across the side of it. Our source opens the invisible magnetic door. Ashton and I will take out the guards.* She paused. *We can do this. Failure is not an option.* I dipped my head slightly in a silent response as we slowly advanced, and the two Ferroean Guards moved toward us, their demeanor casual.

As the two stepped forward, a strange sensation bubbled up through my veins, traveling throughout my body, and I stilled. My source stirred and my bones—*oh, my goodness.* My bones shifted under my skin. I could feel them crack and reshape. But into what? My knees wobbled, finding it hard to move forward.

Bea, you're hurting my hand. What are you doing? Sera spoke into my mind. She subtly released our grip, transferring her hold to my elbow, steadying me. *You've got to keep it together and keep moving.*

Ashton stepped behind me. His breath was at my ear as he whispered, "It's ok. Stay calm. You're acclimating to the iron-rich core of Ferro. Your veins are filling with source and ridding your body of blood, and your alloy is replacing your bones. If you think you were strong on Earth, you're a gladiator on Ferro. Deep breaths."

I sucked in air, steadying not only my breathing but my body as I willed my right leg to advance and then begged my left leg to follow.

"If it makes you feel any better, it's happening to me too," he whispered.

"Then why aren't you walking like a newborn deer?" I grumbled.

Ashton chuckled. "Because I'm a buck." I turned to glare at him, and he shrugged. "You set yourself up for that one. I can't even be blamed. It's like you don't know me anymore if you think I'd let that opportunity slide."

I rolled my eyes. Sera ignored Ashton and tightened her fingers around my skin, warning me to stop talking.

"Alright, who's next?" The older guard with seafoam-green eyes looked over at Sera amicably enough and held the scanner out to her at chest level. Floating words hung in front of his face lit in blue. Instead of screaming *traitor, source thief, rebel,* as I feared, he called another Guard over. "When was our last com check?" He shook the electronic device like Darla would do to the whipped cream bottle before adding it to our ice cream sundaes—violently. "I think this scanner is broken."

Sera looked back at Ashton with a raised brow and then back at the Guard. I didn't dare turn. "Is there a problem, Officer?"

"Seraphina Laylan, correct?" the officer questioned in his deep bass voice. His brow rose to his barely-there hairline.

Sera's eyes were as large as serving dishes at the mention of her correct name, but she didn't miss a beat with her words. "That's correct. Is something wrong?"

The guard shook his head again. "I am contrite. I believe our image calculator is malfunctioning." He flipped the hanging picture in the air to show Gertrude's face to Sera. At the sight of my kidnapper, I stifled my gasp.

Sera's name and photo were under her mother's and next to a Gerraldyne Laylan's name. His masculine face was topped with the same black hair Sera had and same pointy chin. Red highlighted words, *source removal three ferro-cades,* were written under him, next to the unhighlighted words *immediate family members* under that.

"Your source's transcript is computing as Gertrude Laylan. She is your mother, correct?"

Sera's shoulders tensed while my heart sank. My breath caught in my throat. I wished I had the intelligence to know what a scanner could tell you, or the guts to have admitted to Sera back when we first got to the Hive that her mother had died before her Awakening. But I'd been living moment to moment for weeks. My life had become so consumed with training, the Rebellion, and thoughts of Cash that until these few seconds ago, I had not remembered we killed her mother—information that might have been important to relay to her before coming back to her home world.

I kept my face set in a mask of stone. Sera dropped her hand to her belt, and it stayed there on the hilt of her thermo dagger. Panic writhed in my chest, but I pushed it away, and steeled myself, lifting my chin.

For a moment—one long moment—we all stood there. Sera released her weapon, and her shoulders dropped. She cracked her head side to side.

"Yes, she's my mother and when she finds out your scanners are broken, the High Council will have your sources. If I were you, I'd head down to logistics and get it fixed now. Next thing you'll tell me is your vitrics is defective." She sighed, playing the part of frustrated High Council daughter, but I knew better.

She spoke into my head. *Tell me my mother isn't dead. Tell me you didn't know the source inside my chest was hers.*

My heart beat faster than it ever had during the last four weeks, and I made myself look as calm as I could be. *Please let us explain in private. Please.*

The four remaining guards had joined the conversation and the tension in my gut increased. Ashton's voice came into my head and my ears simultaneously. "If it's broken, I suggest letting us proceed. We have business with King Zane." He pointedly added, looking at Sera. "And her mother." His voice dragged me away from the memory of

Gertrude's death and what we had done to Sera, but I couldn't stop the sick feeling of bile rising in my throat at the thought of how we had been lying to her.

The Guards nodded and let us proceed.

We walked to the end of the platform, each step heavier than the last. Once we met the needle, Ashton waved his hand at the invisible door, and it lifted. We got inside and the door sealed shut, leaving us alone in the small space together. Sera whirled on us, her eyes swirling with dangerous rage. "Who killed my mother?"

There was no point in lying to her, so I answered. "Cash."

Chapter Twenty-Eight

Cash

Lost in thought, I stared beyond Jellybean, my eyes fixed on the Observatory. It was the oldest and most revered place in Ferroean recorded history, and yet it was a near mystery to everyone. Well, except to the elders, but even they didn't seem to have a full story, only the bits and pieces the Orb revealed to them. It didn't matter how many times I'd visited this sanctuary, each time I learned something new. I suspected tonight would be no different. If Jellybean was speaking the truth, then she was the youngest elder to have ever been chosen by the Orb.

My gaze dropped to meet her stare, and her wide green eyes swirled with excitement and joy. Over the last many ferrocades, those chosen—Sayor included—considered the distinction of elder to be a damned fate. It was clear, however, that Jellybean saw her revelation as a gift, something to rejoice over rather than feel burdened by.

I opened my mouth to speak—ask her how this happened, when this happened—but faint words sounded in my mind, causing me to shiver. *Brother, oh dear brother,* Ashton's voice sang out, *you may want to hurry to the land-*

ing docks at the Capital if you can hear me. Remember when father found out I was part of the Rebellion? Well this...it's worse.

Ashton and I had always shown incredible aptitude when it came to sharing our thoughts over extreme distances. We weren't given the option of failure in this area. Zane oversaw our extensive telepathic lessons with the addition of unique punishments and extreme scrutiny no other guard would have ever received. We were the heirs to the King, an honor I had valued until recently, even if Ashton had never revered it. Zane's creative cruelty varied from extra hours in logistics, the seemingly harmless tinkering, mind-numbing until punctuated with the far-too-frequent electrocutions from faulty devices, to more physical punishment, like hours strength training our telekinesis or defense training with real thermo daggers while blindfolded. We spent most of our adolescence healing each other from the resulting injuries. Many times, Ashton would take the blame for our shortcomings, and while I'd argue with Zane over the truth of it, Ashton would receive the brunt of the punishment. I understood now why. He was really punishing Ashton for who he was, not what he had done. But telepathy from one planet to another? Even I doubted we were that talented. I swung around, taking in a one-eighty view of the carefully curated gardens around us. Either he was about to pop up from behind an emeraldine hedgerow, or I had indeed lost my mind.

Jellybean tilted her head, watching my distracted movements. "You hear something, don't you?"

In about five minutes we will be at the Capital's landing docks. I do hope Father hasn't kept you in a hole rotting away, because if you can get your butt to the docks, we may still have a chance of going undetected. If you don't, well... There was a brief pause. *Make that three minutes.*

I grabbed Jellybean's hand in mine. "Remember that reunion you wanted to be there for?" Before she could venture a reply, I'd already pulled her with me in a sprint. She stumbled slightly, barely able to keep her pace with mine. We'd just reached the edge of the public gardens on our way to the Observatory. We would have to backtrack to the Capital's front gate if we wanted to make it to the docks. Ornamental trees and blankets of pink and purple flowers blurred past us as we ran.

I heard tearing noise as we bounded over a short dividing wall. Her dress had ripped from a risqué but fashionable slit at the knee to a full tear to her upper thigh. She waved it off but took the momentarily pause to slip out of her high heeled silver shoes before taking off once again with me along the graveled walkway. The footwear dangled from her fingers, reflecting light across the crystal leaves around us. "Are they here?" she asked. Her feet moved faster under her small frame now that the dress and shoes weren't restricting her gait. If the terrain bothered her bare feet, she didn't let it show. "Are they really on Ferro? How did they get through a wormhole? Aren't they all hidden on Earth? By the Council, aren't the wormholes all guarded here on Ferro?!"

"I have no idea," I replied between breaths. "But if Ashton isn't at the landing docks, you better get my head examined because I'm hearing voices." Even as I admitted my own doubts, I mentally shouted out to my brother. *On my way. What's happening? Why are you here? Who's with you?*

Nothing. He never responded. He didn't have to. I stopped dead in my tracks, Jellybean knocking into me. The front gate of the capital was open and under the intricately spun gold and chrome archway stood my brother, my ex-girlfriend, and my girlfriend.

The three were shoulder to shoulder, pinched expressions hugging their faces. If this was a rescue mission, I'd hate to see a kidnapping.

Loathing and accusation glistened in their glares. As if their eyes were adjoined, six irises focusing on my hand entwined with Jellybean's. I dropped her hand, realizing how it might look with her dress torn and sweat glistening on our brows, but it was too late. Bea had already stepped backward, the sight physically throwing her off guard.

Dressed in her full armored tactical gear, Sera crossed her arms, tucking the hilt of her thermo dagger under her bicep. Her cheeks painted red as she spread her feet slightly farther apart on the cut gravel pathway.

"You look pretty cozy for a guy whose been suffering imprisonment and torture. Is that a new suit?" Sera's smug tone wasn't missed. "Having a nice time this evening together under the moonlight?" she cooed, nodding to Jellybean.

Our childhood friend immediately stepped forward, her green eyes narrowing. I grabbed her arm and pulled her back. Something about Sera wasn't right, and I knew how trained and powerful she was. I wasn't going to let Jellybean into the line of fire. "I don't know what's going on or where you got the information that I was locked up and being beaten but I'm fine." I waved my hands down the front of my body. "And the suit is curtesy of Subaltern Tali, thank you. You know how my mother loves a good party."

"She always did excel at the niceties of Ferro," Sera growled. The moonlight shone from behind, setting Sera's outline aglow, yet she was anything but angelic. Her lips—the ones I've kissed a thousand times—were set in a thin line.

Behind her, Bea was a deer in headlights. She shook her head silently in disapproval as her hazel eyes narrowed in on Jellybean. I wanted to scream how stupid this was, how dumb these girls were acting when we'd literally just run to their aid. But as much as I wanted to say nothing had happened and as angry as I was that this was our first moment together since I was captured, relief was flooding my source. Everyone was okay. Even if for some unknown reasons they were all inherently pissed at me.

"Maybe introductions are best?" Jellybean offered. She extended her hand, but no one moved forward. Realizing her failed attempt in melting the invisible icicles that hung in the air, she mumbled, "This is so not the storybook reunion I'd imagined."

"You killed my mother, Cash." Sera released her arms and they fell at her sides, the right still holding the thermo dagger. It glinted off the overhanging lights, sending rainbow reflections across the garden.

I whipped my head toward Ashton. At least he had the decency to wince. He hadn't told me what the hell I was walking into as he spoke into my mind. *A heads up would have been helpful.* I ran my hand through my hair, pulling on it before I released it.

I haven't spoken that far in a long time. Did the best I could. He shrugged his shoulders.

"You don't have anything to say? You. Killed. My. Mother." She dragged each word out longer than the last, increasing her volume so much that the last was practically a shout.

My stomach turned over—not just because Sera learned I killed her witch of a mother, but because I had already made my choice. And what if that choice caused her more pain? Even if she doesn't want to be with me, which I wouldn't blame her, how could I tell her I love Bea now?

"I did kill Gertrude. I am sorry." I took a bold step forward. Having this conversation with Sera was inevitable but extremely untimely. With all the imminent danger, my mind wasn't focused on who I've killed to keep my team alive. But be that as it may, it was my responsibility to tell her and I failed her. My hope was we could rescue the planets and then I could carefully explain what happened after the billions of humans and Ferroeans were safe. This, perhaps, had been a foolish hope.

Sera matched my step. "That's the best you got? You killed my mother knowing all that I had been through, all I have lost. I already have no father because of you and your family?"

Ashton moved closer, but I warned him to stay back. *Don't intervene. No matter what. Let her do what she needs to. She's my responsibility.* He nodded, retreating protectively toward Bea instead.

"Nothing I say can bring your mother back. And as for your father, I had nothing to do with that." I motioned for Jellybean to go to Ashton's side and, without argument, she complied, holding her dress together as she hurried across the sidewalk. "Gertrude was angry with Zane, with some of the High Council, for your death. She knew it was a setup and wanted your source back at any cost."

"Do you blame her?" Sera said while flipping her thermo dagger in her hand threateningly. "Your father sentenced my father to three ferrocades without a source all because my father suggested we should hear the Rebels out. He wanted them to have a fair chance in a High Council hearing." Her knuckles whitened against the hilt of the dagger while she shifted her weight forward. "So yeah, I'm sure my mother was mad at your dad and the High Council for many things."

"You are blurring the lines of truth." I ran my hand through my hair and pulled for the second time in the last five minutes. Her anger overshadowed her logic. "Gertrude's actions have nothing to do with your father's. She would have done anything to get your source back. She wanted to kill Beatrice. She almost killed Tasha. And she *did* kill Grouper." I matched her step forward with two of my own. If Sera yearned for a physical fight, I'd appease her, but she also needed to hear the truth. Not because I hoped she'd see my reasons, but because I owed her at least that much.

"She killed Sayor's brother? She killed Grouper?" She paused; her grip loosened around the weapon. Her shoulders trembled, despair shattering her resolve. "She was my mother, Cash, my mother!" Sera's voice broke and tears appeared suddenly, streaming down her cheeks. Whatever dam her anger had built against her grief, it was broken.

I didn't know Sera was alive when I killed her mother but it wouldn't have changed anything. Gertrude wouldn't have stopped until she killed Beatrice and took back the opposing energy source. She was a threat to our civilization and a traitor to our kind but as I watched Sera crumble before my eyes, I questioned, could I have done it differently? Was there another solution?

"I am so sorry." I reached out my hand, silently asking for her weapon.

228 ~ DANA CLAIRE

She dropped to the ground, her thermo dagger strewn to the side. "I don't have anyone left," Sera said in between sobs. I lowered to my knees beside her and wrapped my arms around her shoulders. I pressed my head into hers and pushed away the satin black hair caught in her tears. "You have me. You'll always have me. I love you, Sera. I always will." And that was the truth. I had loved her from the day we were told who we were, that our destinies were intertwined. And I always would love her, even if I was *in love* with someone else. "Crede Mihi," I breathed, stroking her cheeks with my thumbs and wiping the moisture from her skin.

"Well, this is interesting," a voice of amused annoyance rang loud behind me. My spine stiffened.

Sera and I lifted our heads to see Ashton, Beatrice, and Jellybean's wrists already in illuminated cuffs. Their mouths had been bound by amperes, electrode rings creating fields that blocked our powers. A one-time-use restraint that was annoying and painful as hell. I could see the electric current of the device crackling in the air around them and I cringed.

"King," I growled.

Chapter Twenty-Nine

Ashton

A tall, sniveling man with a Captain's insignia on his uniform stood shoulder-to-shoulder with Zane, two of his personal guards positioned on either side like bookends. By the nervous look on the Captain's face, I could tell he was somewhat surprised the entire concourse wasn't swarming with reinforcements. Protocol for any kind of illegal or undocumented entry into the Capital usually triggered the mobilization of a whole battalion, but Zane hadn't followed that rule in response to our ruse with the wormhole sensors. *Protocols are the backbone of our civilization*—Zane's words at every Guard graduation. I was amazed they weren't tattooed on his chest.

"You certainly know how to make an entrance, don't you?" Good Ole Dad's pointed words matched his pointed glare in my direction. Even after all this time, it cut into me, and I had to shake off the memory of being a small boy reprimanded by my father for the smallest infractions. He was dressed in full formal attire, diamond-inlaid chrome buttons trailing from collar to waist in a perfect line, mirroring the style of the formal whites of the Royal Guard uniforms on either side. His suit was tailored-made, the sharkskin-grey carrying a bit of shine, the hemlines crisp and folded at his wrists. His boots looked brand new, they were so perfectly polished, and a thermo dagger I'm sure he'd never had a reason to use was strapped ornamentally against one. Its hilt was also chrome, and it glinted in the light like his buttons.

I stupidly shook my head, causing the ampere to prick my skin and sting into my gums. Amperes were like a dental visit in a nightmare, specially designed to cause so much fluctuating pain you could barely think, let alone use telepathy or any other ability your source could grant you. My jaw throbbed, the muscles spasming uncontrollably from the relatively minor jolt of electricity my movement activated. I jerked my iron-bound hands in reaction to the pain, and my hatred for the man who pretended to be my father doubled. I glanced at Bea and Jellybean, silently begging them not to make the same mistake I did. Bea blinked her eyes acknowledging my plea, but Jellybean rolled hers, as if to say she wasn't the idiot I was. They stayed still like statues, and I was grateful.

Cash stood, his hand guiding Sera by the elbow up alongside him. Sera wiped her cheeks and flipped back her raven hair over her shoulders, instantly pulling it together. I almost shouted "that's my girl," but caught myself before activating another painful jolt.

"Always a disappointment." Zane shook his head. "Your constant need for the spotlight and attention, boy, is exhausting. Such a pivotal time for our planet, and you've decided to once again make this about you—"

Cash cut Zane off, crossing his arms over his chest. "King, with all due respect, Ashton and the others were given word I was under duress and came to—"

It was Zane's turn to interrupt. "What, rescue you? They had...concern for your well-being?" His brow lifted, emphasizing his point. "On your own planet, in your own home, under the protection of the King—your father, of all people?" Zane's lip curled slightly into a sneer. His relentless taunting was a worn-out welcome mat. If I wasn't controlled by the wretched device he'd ensnared me with, I might have done something worth regretting later.

Zane turned his shoulders toward the Captain at his side. The man still hadn't wiped the wide-eyed expression from his face. "Captain Haddock, am I known for cruelty toward my sons, my people?" he asked, his voice a parody of concern and beneficence.

Cash rolled his eyes, causing my source to leap in my chest. By the Council, I never thought I'd live to see the day Captain Cash Kingston publicly disrespected our good old dad. If my hands weren't restrained, I might had given him a round of applause.

Zane missed the gesture, but that toady Haddock didn't. His lips thinned while his forehead furrowed. "No, my liege, you are not." He swallowed, and then added, "But if I may be so bold, perhaps you should have." He glared at Cash with hate-filled eyes, his implications clear.

Cash lunged at the cowardly threat, but Sera grabbed his arm as a small animal noise slipped from Beatrice, only to be cut short by a jolt of what must have been near-paralyzing pain.

"Stop, just stop!" Sera's voice was low but forceful. Cash pulled back at her command, but his shoulders remained tense and his veins popped along his forearms. His eyes stayed frozen on our father. Part of me believed he needed to pretend Bea wasn't bounded by an ampere, so he avoided her gaze, but the other part of me knew he was challenging Zane with his unwavering stare.

"Captain Dock, while I appreciate your support, Cash is still a Ferroean captain." His voice lowered. "And *my* son."

"My apologizes, Your Highness," Tic Tock Idiot Dock bowed at Dear Old Dad.

"King Zane, if I may address you?" Sera asked, her formal request ringing out in opposition to the otherwise awkward intensity of our situation.

Zane nodded and waved his hand. His wedding band caught the moonlight, producing gold dancing specs on the ground, and a sliver of despondency inched up my spine. Mother. What would her current disposition be when I saw her? Possibly the same, but a shard of hope pecked at my source for her to have changed her outdated ways. The last words I spoke to her echoed in my mind before my capture: *If you keep your oblivious blindfold over your eyes, you will have no one else to condemn for my death but your own negligence. I'd hate for you to have to buy Tasha a puppy when I'm gone because you'd have no one else to bring her happiness. Ignoring what is really happening here will surely cause your source to dim sooner than your callous heart.*

Sera broke my thoughts of Subaltern Tali with the practiced speech of a trained Guard and loyal Ferroean. "We were under the assumption that Captain Kingston was detained unlawfully here in the Capital. Not by you, sir, but by the rebels living amongst us. It is the oath we have taken as Guards to protect and serve. As it may seem unsettling to find us the way you did, our intentions were for Ferro and for our leaders' safety." She acknowledged Zane and Cash together, as if they were a unit and not currently at violent odds with one another.

Zane narrowed his eyes for a moment, and it almost seemed like he was appraising Sera's words. Too quickly he dismissed them and turned to the three men around him. "Each of you: As your King, I order you to swear to the Council what you have heard and will see here tonight will be taken with you to the expiration of your source."

All three men performed a formal salute, placing the palm of their hand over their sources in a quick, practiced motion. They dropped their heads in a nod, and then returned their eyes back to their King in subservience. "Guard Piteon, take Seraphina Laylan to her family estate and secure the perimeter and take first watch over the property. Someone will relieve you in the morning." My father's voice was flat. He rotated his whole body toward Sera. "While I'm still assessing the situation, I appreciate your input and will consider your words moving forward. You are dismissed."

Guard Piteon strode forward, signaling Sera to lead the way, but a growling Cash stood protectively in his path. Sera placed her hand on Cash's bicep and whispered something in his ear even my excellent hearing couldn't pick up. Void of any emotion, Cash relented and moved out of the Guard's route.

Her lips thinned as she addressed Zane. "My King, I have a request."

Zane's brow lifted so high I wondered if it would touch his silver-streaked hair. "You press your luck, but go ahead."

"I'd like to see my father." She swallowed and tucked a strand of hair behind her ears. By the Council she knew how to play the part. I'd known Sera my whole life and this timid, nervous, usure version of the girl did not exist. "I'd like him to be Awakened so that I—or a designated representative—may tell him that my mother has expired. He was High Council once and he deserves…"

Zane's eyes widened, by my guess more at the insolence of the request than at the revelation of Gertrude's death. "He deserves the sentence he got." His words were sharp, daggers to Sera's joints.

She sucked in air but before she could protest, Zane waved his hands. "I will see what I can do." His lips curled. "I'd tread lightly, Seraphina Laylan. If you ask a favor of the King, you are indebted to him."

"Yes, Your Highness." She bowed, placing her hand over her source—her mother's source—and pivoted on her heels to follow Guard Piteon toward the arched gateway. She eyed her thermo dagger on the ground and, to my disbelief, left it there.

Cash watched her walk away. His fists circled into balls, forcing the energy of his source into rapid pulsations under his skin.

Zane turned to the other personal Guard. "Take Jellybean back to the Flannery home. Explain nothing about the events of this evening but assure them her safety is Tali's number one concern. As a guest of the royal family, we felt it in her best interested to be escorted home by a Guard, especially due to the late hour." Zane snapped his fingers and the restraints on Jellybean's wrists dissolved. She rubbed them, soothing her aching joints.

"Miss Flannery, I'd like it if you stayed away from my family while they are visiting. Clearly, we have some personal issues to resolve that will not be public knowledge. Do I make myself clear?"

Jellybean didn't move. The ampere around her face would burn her if she did.

Zane arched his neck, anticipating her response. "It's not polite to keep your King waiting." By the Council, he wanted her to be harmed.

A tear escaped her eye as she nodded, and the ampere around her face surged. Her face contorted with pain, and she clenched her eyes shut against the new tears pouring from them.

"Was that necessary?" Cash grunted. "You could have removed the ampere."

"You are dismissed," Zane said, shooing away the Guard and Jellybean and flouting Cash's comment. "The ampere will dissolve once she is outside the radius of my Influence," he added as reassurance. If the Flannery parents found out Zane had restrained their youngest daughter, the High Council would be alerted and an investigation started. I wondered how Jellybean would play this out. The streaks of mascara and the pain on her face would be hard to write off without explanation.

Zane walked over to Bea, tapping his pointer finger against his lips. "So. You are the Blood-Light who is going to save Ferro and Earth." He walked around her, a circling lion assessing his prey. Bea's eyes widened. "You don't seem likely to be a weapon." Of course, he would say something so ridiculous. It's not like thermo daggers looked like Godzilla, but they killed us too.

"Release them," Cash barked. "There's no reason to keep them bound like criminals."

Zane flicked his wrist at Cash. "Don't be dramatic. I needed amperes so that these two don't communicate with you telepathically." He motioned to Captain Dock to grab the weapon on the floor that Sera left behind. "It's the same reason I chose not to release my hold on Jellybean until she was out of her meager range." His lip curled. "But more importantly, my hold on them is the only leverage I have to keep you on your best behavior." His smile extended, reaching his ears. "You may be the most physically powerful Ferroean, Casheous—"

I cringed when I heard my father use Cash's birth name. The insult was not missed by Cash as well. He growled like a grizzly bear but kept his lips tightly closed.

"But I am mentally more formidable and will always be two steps ahead of you."

Cash didn't miss a beat. "Didn't know this was a competition. Would you like to have a measuring contest later too?"

Zane snapped his fingers, and my ampere tightened its hold on my face and hands. I screamed—well, it would have been a scream if my vocal cords were able to work—as I fell to the ground, hitting my knees first and crashing onto my side, agony emitted from my heels to my head. Bile crawled up my throat but was pushed back down when my insides realized there was no way to release.

"Ok," Cash said, holding his hands up. "You made your point."

"Lovely," Zane replied, smugness coating his word. He snapped his fingers and broke my ampere. It snapped and zapped my mouth while dissolving into thin air. I rolled over on the ground, rubbing my face where it had paralyzed the muscles and had done the most damage. I pushed into the cold concrete up to my knees, and my insides cringed. The sulfuric acid re-emerged and expelled in front of me until there was nothing left. My throat burned and I took my time to stand, wiping my mouth with my forearm. I held my father's eyes, refusing to acknowledge the pain around my wrists and face. "What up, papa bear?" I coughed the remnants of my purge onto my tongue and spit them to the side. "Thanks for the exceptional welcome home treatment. Mother would be proud." My smile bared all my teeth. "Miss me?"

"Like a hemorrhoid," Zane muttered. He motioned to the last Guard standing, that sycophant Dock. "Have both of my sons and Miss Walker accompanied back to the royal home. Show Miss Walker to Tasha's room. As for Ashton, alert Latmon to his presence but no one else. He will not be permitted to leave his room until after eight p.m."

I rubbed my hands together, grateful for the heat it caused and dramatic effect. "Oh, a curfew, it's like Guard training all over again. Please please please tell me there will be recess."

Zane ignored me and continued. "Then at eight o'clock every night, escort him to the private training room, where he will meet Miss Walker and Cash."

"Why the training room?" Cash asked.

"I imagine the three of you need to prepare. Figure out how to save these two planets and all that. If that's not too much trouble?" His smug smile had given way to boredom, as his taunting always did.

I gazed over to where Bea had been as quiet as a mouse. "Not to be the obvious one out here, but what about Beatrice's ampere? Anyone want to remove them?"

Zane was already straightening his suit jacket, preparing to leave. "No."

Cash growled.

"They will be removed when she is back in Tasha's room." He held up a finger. "And if any of you misbehave,

I will put them right back on her, like a dog." He snarled, showing his teeth. "Do not test me, boys. There are worse places she can go than to your sister's room."

Chapter Thirty

Beatrice

The second Captain Dock threw me into Tasha's room, and as I staggered, the restraints evaporated. I stretched out my jaw and took a deep breath that felt like the first in hours. The bright, white room was overwhelming after the darkness of the night outside, and I had to squint to make out my surroundings as I rotated around. For what was essentially a cage, the room was at least as large as my bedroom at home, but entirely too spartan. Despite floating like the one in Ashton's apartment-slash-prison cell, the bed looked normal enough at least, and was covered with plush ivory and white bedding. Two perfectly arranged bookshelves flanked either side of the plush, ivory-dressed bed, the spines sorted by color from white to grey to blue to black. There was a desk, and a chair, and a door to a little attached washroom, everything neat and proper and monochrome. However coordinated Tasha's tastes might have been, four white walls and recessed strips of white light caged me in. Like Ashton on Earth, I was a prisoner.

The closet was opened and filled with well-tailored clothing in the same colors as everything else. White, silver, grey—a navy shift dress was about as exciting as it got for Tasha, apparently. It was also filled with the same black training gear I was used to wearing at this point. White cotton pants with a thick, cream-colored drawstring and matching long-sleeved shirt were laid out on the bed. I recognized them as the same style I'd worn in the Hive. I tried to find some comfort in the familiarity, but the monotony felt too much like forced assimilation. I never knew you could crave a color, any color other than dark blue, like I did in that moment.

A soft knock at the door shook me from my musings. A muffled but clipped voice followed. "Miss Beatrice, my name is Latmon; I am the royal servant to the Kingston children. May I come in?"

I backed up as far away from the door as possible, searching for a way to defend myself if this was a trap. "Yes," I said, contemplating how hard I could hit a Ferroean with a book.

The door slid open, and the man strode in dressed in a white Guard's uniform. He was holding a brightly lit tray surrounded by an inlaid ringlet of blue light. His red hair was short and neatly combed with product. "It's a pleasure to make your acquaintance, Miss Beatrice." He looked around the room. "It feels like ages since I have had the pleasure of serving Miss Tasha. I'm sure she would be quite content to share her room with you in her absence. Is there anything I can get you?" Latmon extended the tray he held. There was a piece of tented paper, a candle, and a set of regular matches—the kind you would get in a motel.

"Why am I here? What are they planning on doing with me?" I placed my hands at my side, ready to grab my thermo daggers, but they were gone. "If it's to bore me to death by trapping me in a monotonous cage, they might be succeeding."

Latmon's face was stoic. "Ah, yes. Earth is full of color, so harsh to the eyes." He shook his head. I wondered what Latmon thought of rainbows and parrots, but I dared leave that question for another time. "As for the intention of the royal family, I believe that is an inquiry for the King. I am only here to serve." He eyed the paper on the tray, inclining his head meaningfully toward it. "If that'll be all then?" I reached out and snatched the paper teepee, and he set the matchbook and candle on a silver tabletop that, like the bed, was floating inexplicably. "For your sleeping pleasure," he said, answering my puzzled look. Latmon bowed and slipped out through the automated exit. I followed him, desperate to reopen the door, but it had sealed shut. I was locked inside, again.

My shaking body sunk into the plushness of the ivory white mattress and I opened the folded note:

I hate that the first time I saw your face it was...well, it was a messy situation. We have a lot to discuss. I've learned things here that, unfortunately, have created more questions than answers, but something bigger than the asteroid is coming and it's one of the reasons I didn't try and get back to Earth or send word to you and the others. Tomorrow, when we are to practice, Ashton, you, and I will make a plan. For now, rest. You will need it.

P.S. The matches are not for the candle. They are for this note. Burn it.

Credi Mihi

Cash

"More questions," I mumbled into the vacant room, wondering if there would ever be a time we could retrieve answers only. I bit my bottom lip with anticipation to see Cash tomorrow. I knew that shouldn't be my focus but I couldn't help the list of inquiries I had built up in my mind over the last month without him and then to see him for the first time with *her*. I heard Zane mention her last name and wondered, could that be Sammie, Paul, and Mark's younger sister? Even if that were the case, why did they seem so close? And Sera...my heart nearly stopped when he told her he loved her. Did that mean he chose her? And like that? I hand-clutched the note to my heart. My eyes closed. What had he been doing all this time in Ferro? Why couldn't he have sent word? A collision of questions impaled themselves, rear-ending each other in my mind.

I took out the match and lit the paper on fire. Flames danced as the particles crumbled into the wax. The scent was cedar and sage. I was starting to get used to that aroma.

I stood and trailed my hand along the small desk, when a sudden flash of light startled me. A hologram popped up of a woman with red curly hair and a sleek suit jacket with matching pencil skirt. What I assumed was her name appeared below her: Messenger Drayton Rose. Her face plastered a polite but tight-lipped smile. "Miss Walker, welcome to Ferro. I am the personal assistant to Subaltern Tali Kingston." I frowned, having no idea who or what a subaltern was. "Cash and Ashton's mother, to answer your question." She shook her head at me, like a disappointed principal. "Your presence has been requested for a welcome breakfast in the Royal Dining Hall tomorrow. I shall have Latmon bring you suitable clothing." She squinted her eyes and seemed to scrutinize my physical form through a judgmental glare. Although not physically present in the room, her gaze caused goosebumps to prickle on my skin. "You'll never fit in Miss Tasha's wardrobe, regrettably." Her voice lacked any remorse as she shook her head in a disapproving manner. "No matter. We will find an alternative and send it along. Please rest and be ready at oh-seven-hundred sharp. Should you require immediate assistance, you may call aloud for Latmon by name." She gazed down at something below her and then back up to the screen. "Her Majesty has also requested you refrain from bringing up the following subjects during her meal: no Earth slang or pejoratives; no talk of the impending asteroid; no questions about your stay; and no questions or comments regarding the Subaltern's family history, including but not limited to her Earth visits. Additionally, it would be in everyone's best interests if you simply avoid speaking to King Zane as much as possible. Any questions?" Without waiting for me to respond, she said. "No? Superb. Please rest." The video evaporated before my eyes.

In an effort to not pace the length of the room, I changed into the set of pajamas laid out for me and slipped into Tasha's bed. I couldn't imagine how I could sleep after the day I had. I was wrong.

I woke to a sharp knocking at the door, the volume steadily increasing as the knocks repeated. "Miss Beatrice? Are you ready?"

I scrambled out of bed, having no idea what time it could be. I'd shut my eyes for a second—a minute at most. "I'm getting dressed. Be right there!" I yelled, seeing a set of clothing that hadn't been there last night hanging over the desk chair. Someone had been in the room when I was asleep. I didn't know whether to be creeped out or thankful. I threw off my sleepwear and eyed the outfit that had been picked out for me. It was a one-piece white jumpsuit, with seams down the trousers and a modest halter top that tied at the neck and around the waist. I was glad to see it had a built-in bra, because there was no way my sports bra would work with this thing. I slipped into it like a glove and threw my hair into a quick bun before running into the bathroom. I prayed for mouthwash but was happy to find a brand-new toothbrush, tube of toothpaste, and—bonus—deodorant. I washed up as fast as I could and hoped the no-makeup look was in style for Ferroean prisoners.

"We must leave, Miss Beatrice. The King and Subaltern do not accept tardiness." There was the click of the lock and then Latmon was in the open doorway as I walked out of the bathroom. "The Royal sons, Cash and Ashton, will be joining us in the corridor if you are ready."

I held my chin up high and walked out of the room. Cash and Ashton were dressed in what I now assumed to be standard attire for Ferroean special events. Their suits were like Latmon's and Captain Dock's, only stark white with a line of chrome buttons instead of gold.

Latmon led the way as Cash and Ashton flanked me. Cash slid his hand in mine and spoke into my thoughts.

Be very careful with telepathy at breakfast. My mother and father are extremely trained and while tapping into each other's heads is frowned upon here on Ferro, it happens all the time. Do not think for one moment those two will not be trying to pick apart your brain. Keep your shields up no matter what, even if that means having to keep Ashton and I out of your head. Ok?

I squeezed his hand and he squeezed back. My shoulders released a half of an inch as we continued down the hall. *You look good in Ferro clothes.* He raked over me with his intense gaze, sending goosebumps to my arms. *You look really good.*

I blushed, letting my eyes meet the ground in front of me. Out of all the times Cash could be charming, this was his moment? I chuckled to myself as the situation's weight tugged at my shoulders.

The corridor came to a t-intersection, a tall, chrome-inlaid doorway straight ahead. Two Guards waited there, showing not even the barest hint of emotion. They were all business, their thermo daggers dangling at their sides.

"Captain Cash, Captain Ashton," the Guards said in unison. They stared at me, unsure how to address me. Cash spoke, "This is the opposing source to my own, Beatrice Walker. My girlfriend."

Girlfriend? I questioned through our minds.

Cash ignored me, leaned in, and whispered, "She's also the infamous Blood-Light prophesied to save our planet and she has the ability to kill us in one blast." He stepped back in line with me and said, "Have a lovely morning."

The soldier's pale and fear-struck expression said it all. I was not welcome here. We turned right and I pressed my shoulder into his. "Was that necessary?"

Cash smiled. "Nope. Not at all." He lifted my hand to his mouth and kissed it.

Don't you think you should at least have asked me? I pushed into his mind. We had so much to discuss and now was his moment to be comfortable with titles.

I didn't think you'd care.

I twisted my head and stopped walking. Ashton practically barreled into me. "You didn't think I would care?" I released his hand and crossed them over my chest. "How romantic! The guy I like tells two alien guards I'm his girl-friend before he tells me?" I shook my head. "Really, Cash?"

Ashton released a low whistle. "Totally saw this coming." He turned to Latmon. "Got any popcorn, Alfred? This is always entertaining to have front row seats at."

"Popcorn, Sir?" Latmon questioned. He pulled out a device and pressed several buttons.

"I'm sorry I didn't get down on one knee with a dozen roses and chocolates for you just to ask you a question I already know the answer to." Cash's tone dripped with sarcasm.

"Oh, you think you already know the answer, do you?" I shook my head so hard my neck cracked. "Maybe I changed my mind."

Cash laughed. He actually had the balls to laugh. "You must be kidding me? How stupid of me to think with the impending asteroids and potential end of the world scenario you might be ok with a simple, 'Hey this is my girl-friend' instead of a parade down main street."

"We don't have a main street," Ashton offered.

"Technically, Capital Street is our main street," Latmon responded.

"Shut up," Cash and I said at the same time.

Latmon straightened his spine. "My apologizes, Captain and Miss Beatrice, but we really mustn't be late." He placed the device he had been holding in his back pocket and started forward.

The four of us continued down the hall in silence until we reached two large white double doors with massive handles bigger than my head. Latmon waved his hands and they opened. Inside was a large rectangular dining room perfectly sized to fit a huge white and light-grey marble table capable of seating at least twenty people comfortably. At the head to our left, King Zane sat in a huge antique straight-back chair that was distinctly not Ferroean, ornately carved so that it would have fit in just as well in one of those British period films. Blue letters like the ones that popped up in Tasha's room hung in front of him. He swiped at them as he read, ignoring our presence. A regal woman that I presumed to be Subaltern Tali Kingston, wearing a beige satin gown, sat to his left. She was sipping from what appeared to be a wine glass, but there were no place settings or food on the table.

Tali glazed right over me as she stared, no seared, Ashton with her blue eyes. Ashton ignored her and casually walked around the table like he had done it a hundred times, and this wasn't his first encounter with his mother since his capture.

"Sit," Zane said, not looking up from whatever he was reading. Ashton took the seat next to Zane while Cash sat next to his mother, making me the fifth wheel. Either sit next to Ashton or Cash or all the way down at the other end by no one. I chose Ashton, and Tali noticed.

Tali's perfectly styled brow lifted. "Changed your mind, have you, dear?"

I blushed under her scrutiny but remained silent.

"Mother," Cash growled, gazing up at the sky and shaking his head.

Zane cleared his throat. "Cash didn't ask her formally to be his girlfriend, but just introduced her to our personal guards as such, and she's now angry with him. It'll work out by the end of the meal. She's already thinking she made a poor decision sitting by Ashton in front of us, and Cash is brooding over there because he believed he had done what she wanted and now she's being ungrateful." Zane paused. "Scratch that. Not ungrateful, he says, being dramatic."

My mouth hung open. Zane had been reading our thoughts since our exchange in the long hallway. His powers far exceeded my expectations.

Tali smiled and it seemed genuine. "Casheous has always had trouble communicating." She placed her hand on his forearm. It pulsed under her palm. "As a mother, I read his mind more than any of my other children. I still do."

Cash grunted. "That's because you cheat." He yanked his arm away from his mother and stared at me. "If Tali touches you, she can break your shields." He glared at his father. The signature curved, sinister smile intensified. "It's a secret no one but our family knows."

"Ah, that was true until about thirty seconds ago. Are you baiting me, son?" Zane swiped the words he was reading away and lounged back in his chair. He removed his reading glasses from the arch of his nose and extended his hand out. Without an exchange of words, Latmon placed a white linen cloth in it.

"How?" I asked from my seat, making that the first word I had spoken to Cash's parents. Part of me wanted to smack my head for making a poor first impression on my body-guard-boyfriend's parents and then the other part of me was angry I even cared, seeing they were our enemies. My palms were sweating with nowhere to wipe them. I wondered if I held my hand out would Latmon oblige me.

"She's family now, Zanith." Tali took a sip of her drink as she spoke to her husband. "If Casheous has deemed her so, it is so." Her voice hardened with finality. "And he has." Taking a lighter tone, she continued speaking directly to me. "We have no idea how I am able to read minds by touch and how no one's shields block me, but my mother could do it, and so could my grandmother. In fact, it's why I was betrothed to Zanith. He needed a powerful woman by his side."

"You mean a weapon," Ashton mumbled.

"A weapon or a damn curse?" Cash countered, raising his brow to meet his hairline.

"A curse I wouldn't mind inheriting," Ashton spoke louder.

"You'll have to fight Tasha for it on her eighteenth birthday, the mature Ferroean year." Cash rolled his eyes.

"Enough!" Zane commanded.

Tali ignored her son's comments and waved at Latmon, who was in the shadows. "We will take our breakfast pills. Refill my wine glass and bring more for the others." She returned her gaze to me. "Did you know Zanith and I had an arranged marriage?" She focused on Ashton but didn't say anything. It was clearer than a cloudless day they need to hash their crap out, but I agreed with their unspoken truce. Today was not the day.

"Forced as it may have been, it worked out for us in the end, didn't it, dear?" Zane said, not even bothered by the fact Tali admitted their marriage was not one out of love for each other.

"True. But isn't it nice that Casheous and Beatrice are bound to one another and they are actually in love, Zanith?"

Zane massaged the cloth over his lenses, holding them up against the light to examine them for smudges. "You drink entirely too much," he grumbled, never meeting his wife's eyes.

Tali held up her glass, sticking out her perfectly manicured pinky. "That, indeed, I do." Another sip.

"I'd drink too much if I lived here," Ashton mumbled. Cash chuckled under his breath.

"Well, thank the Council this is no longer your home," Zane snapped, quieting the room. Latmon served Zane first, allowing him to smell and taste the wine before pouring the rest of us wine glasses. "Now that we have that needless conversation behind us, Beatrice, why don't you tell us about you? I am curious to know more about the only Blood-Light created that can kill our kind. Earth has a thing for weaponry," Zane said. He breathed on the other lens, then wiped it clean.

"Zanith, really? Must you bring this up at breakfast? I specifically requested in my Messenger Drayton Rose's memo to avoid talk about such things."

"Well then, how convenient for me that I don't take orders from you."

Tali responded by finishing the contents of her wine glass and ushering Latmon to refill it.

I stared down at the pill that had been placed in front of me. Ashton elbowed me in the side. "See? This is why Earth has a lot more perks." He dramatically eyed the pill in front of me. "That's your breakfast." He nodded his head toward his mother. "And that's why she consumes so much alcohol."

"That and she hides behind being drunk," Cash quipped, grabbing his oval-shaped meal and throwing it back with a mouthful of wine.

Tali glared at Cash but addressed Ashton. "Hush, Ash. Earth's perks, as you call it, are their downfalls. You get used to eating for fuel rather than fun," Tali said as she delicately picked up her pill and placed it on her tongue, swallowing it back with a long draught from her refilled glass. "How do you think I stay in such great shape?"

I turned my head toward Ashton and whispered, but of course everyone could hear in such a small space. "Why does she call you by your Earth name?"

Ashton's smile extended across his face as he threw his arm around the arch of my chair and leaned back. The two front legs lifted from his shifted body weight. "Ash is my birthname. Ashton is my Earth name."

Cash shook his head. "The naming of a child on Ferro is very important because it's given to you by your parents, their choice. But your Earth name is equally as official and significant because it's your choice." Cash crossed his arms over his chest. "In a place where we don't see many choices, this is a true gift."

Zane coughed, bringing the attention back to him. "Are the three of you done blathering? Because if you are not, by Royal authority, I will have amperes brought in here and placed on every single one of you."

Cash growled. Ashton stared casually into space but Tali did something completely unusual—she smiled. It wasn't a grin of support but more like a dare. I was starting to see a lot more similarities in Ashton and Tali than their looks; she just hid them better.

"As I was saying, Beatrice, tell us about yourself." Zane's voice returned to cool and carefree.

I sat up straighter, taking a cue from a fearless Tali. "There's not much to tell. I was a normal high school kid until my mother drugged me, imbedded a Ferroean opposing source in me, and sent Cash to protect me from the DOAA and..." I paused for only a moment, then lifted my chin and stared directly into Zane's eyes. "...You." I grabbed my pill, placed in it my mouth, and swallowed, glad I was used to taking aspirin without any water to wash it down. It was tasteless yet sticky as it passed through my tongue and onto the back of my throat, dissolving into cotton candy-like crystals.

"Ah, and what do you think of me now? Friend or foe?" Zane placed his glasses on his face, adjusting the sides around his ears.

I didn't dare look at Ashton, Cash, or Tali. I kept my concentrated gaze on Zane. "I think you are not to be trusted. I believe there may be good in you, but I don't see it living in you now. And I believe at the end of the day, there will be a large war because of it."

Zane crossed his arms over his chest, tilting his head ever so slightly. "In another time, or even world, I may have liked you." The room was so quiet the only sounds were shallow breaths. "It will be a shame when you die."

"I do not believe I would feel the same." My hands balled into fists under the table. "And I do not intend on being the one to perish."

Ashton let out a low whistle, but it was Cash I was cautious of. His expression had twisted into something I had only seen once, the anger and hatred plastered on his face when he killed Gertrude.

Zane laughed. He threw back his head and actually laughed. "You think you are strong and that you are a worthy opponent? Do you know what you are even fighting for?"

"Do you?" I pushed my body away from the table.

Cash stood. Power rippled down his arms in successive waves, causing his veins to pop.

"Sit," Zane demanded to his son.

"No, I will not. I don't know what game you are playing, King, but this ends now. Let Beatrice and Ashton go back to Earth." I willed Cash to stop talking. I would not leave without him. Never again. "And I will stay here and do whatever task you'd like of me. Run the Guard Program and stay on Ferro under your rule. No arguments."

Ashton and I stood at the same time, blurting out similar objections.

Zane waved his hand. "As tempting as your offer sounds, I can demand that of you now. You hold no leverage over me." His voice deepened. "You will work with Beatrice and Ashton, train with them, and make sure we all survive the asteroid." He looked around the room, appraising the three of us standing. A fissure of power surged the room and the lights flickered. He stood and slammed his hands down on the table. The wine glasses rattled. Tali grabbed hers before it fell. "If the three of you do not do as I please, I will have Robert Walker"—he glared in my direction as the oxygen left my lungs at the mention of my father's name—"and every other human at the Hive killed."

Chapter Thirty-One

Cash

We were retrieved at exactly eight in the evening for training. I'd been alone in my room since we'd been escorted back from our awkward breakfast. By the disgruntled looks on Ashton's and Bea's faces, I could tell they were still just as affected by Zane's threat as I was. As if we needed a guide in our family home, Latmon led us through the twisting hallways to the set of large gunmetal-grey double doors in the western wing of the royal home. They swung open as we approached, the lights inside flickering on to reveal the auxiliary training room Ashton, Tasha, and I had used to supplement our Guard Program training. I hadn't seen the room in ages, and I doubt anyone else had been in there in quite some time. Well, scratch that—someone had been there to remove all the weapons from the cases that lined the walls. Smart King.

"Well, breakfast was fun," Ashton teased as he idly played with a few hand weights that had been left in the corner. I hadn't seen him in Guard fatigues in a long time, and now he looked somewhat out of place wearing them instead of his usual clothing.

"A delight," I groaned, unable to make light of the morning conversation. I finally had a chance to examine Beatrice without guards or parents over my shoulder, and I studied her from head to toe in search of any sign she'd been mistreated. She seemed fine physically, but it was obvious the mention of Zane's name rattled her.

As if she was reading my thoughts, she answered, "I'm fine. Your dad's a giant jerk, and he knows my weaknesses, but I'm fine."

I nodded. Bea didn't need consolation or a hug; she needed answers and solutions. We all did. That's what I was hoping we would find this evening. "Good. I'm glad to hear it because we need to do something that could possibly get us all locked up in holding cells and amperes." Ashton put down the weights, raising one eyebrow in curiosity. I gave them both a sly half smile. "Interested in learning more about this upcoming war?"

It was no surprise to me that both Ashton and Bea were on board for a little field trip. Zane may have removed the weapons from the training room, but either he never knew about or forgot that there was an emergency exit out the back. Ashton still remembered how to disarm the security alarms, so getting outside from there was a breeze. We just had to be back before Latmon came to escort us back to our rooms. We had a couple of hours to get what we needed from the Orb and get back.

As we approached from afar, the Observatory looked like a single, monumental building, but really it was its own complex full of various departments and activities. The ten-story geometric sphere stood at the center of the Capital like a treasured gem. Its size was exaggerated by an expanse of flat, open space that surrounded it for several blocks. The Observatory Grounds, as they were called, were punctuated only by the occasional memorial fountain or carefully curated shrub or tree. The Grounds belonged to the people of Ferro—a great public concourse for the community to gather, host tasteful art displays, or even hold the occasional wedding ceremony. It was always a peaceful place, inspiring reflection and an almost religious meditative mindset in both design and purpose.

Jellybean was exactly where I had asked her to meet us. She waved hesitantly as we approached. "Hi, Bea. I really wanted our first meeting to go better than the other night. Thanks to my big sis Sammie, my name is Jellybean, but hopefully in the not-too-distance future you can call me Jill." She extended her hand to Bea.

Bea bit her lip, flashing me a look.

I'll tell you later, I sighed telepathically.

Not missing a beat, Bea took Jellybean's hand "I'm Beatrice Walker, as you already know." She gazed at me briefly. "And apparently his girlfriend."

Jellybean pulled her into a surprising hug. "By the Council, when did he ask?" She released her.

"He didn't," Bea said, rolling her eyes. "He just assumed."

I wanted to throw my hands in the air and yell mercy but at this point I'd take the abuse if we could just move on from it.

"Cash, really? That's so lame," Jellybean said wrapping her arm through Bea's and guiding her toward the entrance.

I followed next to a smiling Ashton. "Say one word, brother, and I'll..." Ashton held his hands up, cutting off my threat.

We walked into the front door with ease thanks to Jelly-bean's parents. I requested her to steal their High Council card to get us through without detection.

The Observatory community obligation extended to the first floors of the Observatory itself. Security guards were always posted at frequent intervals but decreased in numbers during the evenings, but all Ferroeans were welcome to enter during daytime hours. The first five floors of the building not only housed a great repository of geological artifacts as part of its Museum of Natural History, but also a rotating art gallery, several exhibition and lecture spaces, and a floor devoted specifically to the story of the Orb and the Capital itself. Several basement floors even housed a great public library, as well as a prized archive of historic documents preserved behind glass and in specially designed cabinets.

From this point to the highest floor, the center of the spherical building contained the Orb itself. This great, glowing ball of rotating light and shadow contained the sources of all those who have passed.

"Whoa," Bea said as she gazed up. "How is it so bright? What does it run on?"

"Sources," Ashton answered, following her line of sight.

"These sources are interred by an elder during a ceremony on one of these floors, depending on the status of the family," Jellybean answered as we rounded the bend. "We are all from High Council families, so we are able to be on the seventh level. When our source diminishes, this is where it goes. Sources as a whole create the light, but by themselves, they are dim. Kinda like our society. We are stronger together, united."

"How many levels are there?" Bea asked, still gazing in awe at what she saw.

"Ten. And we are going up to the top!" I added, threading my hand into hers and leading the way.

Visitors were allowed to commune with the Orb and show their respects on the sixth floor, where they were divided from it by glass and other transparent alloys, and Council members and their families were able to host private events and meetings on the seventh floor. The remaining highest three floors were open only to those chosen by the Orb as elders and a scant number of specially trained members of the Guard. Here were places for meditation, stations where elders could record and review revelations, and sitting areas were elders could meet with one another as needed. These floors were a sanctuary, and no one dared trespass there—until today.

"You have the amperes," I asked Jellybean.

She dug into her back pocket and pulled out two of the application devices. "Each has enough charges for three amperes. It's all I could manage."

I released Bea's hand and slipped the devices into my pocket, being careful not to trigger either. Then we took the stairs up to the tenth floor. I motioned with my hands for the girls to stay put and for Ashton to follow me. Handing him one of the application devices, I sent words into his head. *Mouths. Go for their mouths first, then wrists, then ankles. There are only two Guards on the tenth floor. We have exactly seven minutes from the time we tie them up to when they will have to check back in.*

I opened the door and sent a surge of power to the first guard's throat, causing him to stumble backward and hold his neck. Having his hands out of the way, I slapped an ampere around his mouth, grabbed his arms and crossed them behind his back, and cuffed another ampere around his wrists. Then I swiped his legs, bringing him to the floor, and tied up his ankles. Finally, I went back to the door and let the girls in only to watch Ashton struggling with his Guard's limbs.

"Need a little help?" Bea asked, smiling.

Ashton's lips dipped down. "I've got it. He was like a fish out of water wiggling around all over the place."

We pulled the Guards back into the shadows and forged on toward the side of the Orb. Our faces glowed in its reflection and if there was time I would have basked in its radiance for hours. This was one of my favorite places to explore as a child and I'd never been to this level before.

"I need you to ask the Orb about the pending war." I turned to Jellybean. "How did it happen last time when you spoke with it?"

"Wait. The Orb spoke to her?" Ashton pointed to Jellybean, his mouth creating an "O" shape.

I dropped my chin, acknowledging his question.

"I honestly just snuck up to the eight floor and kinda hung out. Then it started speaking to me in riddles. The first one was the one we have all heard before: *Two worlds will be in danger, and if you choose to save one, they will both perish.* Then they said, *A Blood-Light born without a source will empower an opposing source and save Earth.*"

For the first time, I really paid attention to the second prophecy and noticed something peculiar. "It didn't say anything about Ferro?" Wanting to smack myself in the head, I asked a question I should had asked previously. "Did it ever mention our planet?"

Jellybean squinted. "No, it didn't."

260 ~ DANA CLAIRE

"Sayor said that too. Those are his exact words and he also never mentioned Ferro." Ashton stepped closer to me. His voice lowered. "What are you thinking?"

I tapped my bottom lip but before the words spilled out of my mouth, Bea spoke. "The threat isn't the asteroid. It's the war!"

She was not only beautiful but, By the Council, smart. Exactly what I was thinking. "Every few thousand years, opposing energy sources are born from an original's bloodlines: Sayor, Kingston, Malloy, Laylan, and the Flannery families. Only one of these bloodlines can carry opposing sources. Both Seraphina Laylan's and my source set the prophecy in motion—both born with sources of a unique color constituting an imminent threat of destruction. The prophecy says that two worlds will be in danger, and if you choose to save one, they will both perish." I took a deep breath. "What if the danger wasn't the asteroid but the impending war?"

I whipped my head around to Ashton. "What did Sayor say the Orb said about two Blood-Lights?

Ashton's brow rose, practically kissing his hairline. "He didn't. He assumed."

I shook my head. "Maybe we all assumed. Do you remember what Gertrude said—'There is no prophecy. It's a fabricated story the Council created to keep the opposing energy sources on Earth, guaranteeing Earth's safety.' Maybe she meant the asteroids were not the prophecy. Maybe she knew the Council used that as the threat so no one would discover the real threat was the war?" An avalanche of maybes fell out of my mouth, yet they were making a lot of sense.

"Yes, but if that was true then why did the prophecy need us to connect flesh-to-flesh?" Bea asked.

I peered up to the ceiling as the pieces formed in my mind. "To release your memories. It's how you regained the memory of your mother, The Hive, Sera's Awakening. What if the asteroid wasn't why the opposing sources were created but rather just another hiccup in the road on the way to the real threat? What if the actual danger is the loss of two civilizations? Gertrude said Zane and the High Council wanted to rule Earth. What if it is exactly that? Then Earth—its peoples and freedoms—would need saving."

Jellybean put her finger to her lips in a request for silence. She closed her eyes a moment, and I could only imagine she was listening to the Orb in her mind. Her nose scrunched. "I don't understand," she said out loud. Before I could ask, Jellybean gasped and clutched her chest, as if the words she was hearing caused her physical pain. "Ferro is going to crumble no matter what we do. Our orbit around the solar system's black hole is degrading. In less than a year we'll be feeling the negative effects—there is no way to stop it!"

In unison, Bea, Ashton, and I screamed "What?"-

Jellybean's eyes welled up with tears. "It's only a matter of time before Ferro won't be able to support Ferroean life."

An ancient and haunting voice I had heard when Beatrice and I were connected flesh-to-flesh spoke as if it were always speaking to me and I was just now realizing what it was. The Orb.

Two worlds are in danger of extinction. Save them both and join the people of Earth with the beings of Ferro. Become one on planet Earth. Crede Mihi.

Chapter Thirty-Two

Beatrice

Three dark nights passed.

A lonely star. That's how the asteroid appeared. On Ferro there were no constellations, birds, clouds. The night always appeared as a purple-black canvas. As I stared into the abyss lit up with a bright white light, I knew this was it. Ferro's astronomers had been monitoring the skies with their instruments and satellites, and they knew it was coming. No matter what they did, though, they couldn't get exact coordinates. Cash said it had something to do with the asteroid's composition. It really shouldn't have been a surprise to any of us that the harbinger of two worlds' destruction wouldn't be just another hunk of space rock. It was something else. Something unknown to either of our people. And everything that had happened to this point, my life and the lives of those around, came down to the next couple of minutes.

It seemed so clear now. In the last three dark days, Ashton, Cash, and I had practiced in the training room and attended pill dinners with only Tali until today. We rushed outside from our training session as the rumor a star was visible in the normally black sky. Of course, we were always supposed to be on Ferro for this. On Earth, it would have been too late. There were never going to be two asteroids. There was one. One apocalyptic mass of stone and mineral and interdimensional energy that would destroy Ferro, and then send a shockwave of power and devastation through the strange, otherworldly wormholes that tied not only our planets, but our fates together as one.

I inhaled fresh, unpolluted air of Ferro. The cool breeze tickled my nose and grazed the back of my throat, too clean and sanitized to be familiar to anything I knew on Earth. Little time stood between my breaths and our impending future, each one symbolizing an audible clock. Tick tock. Tick Tock. Inhale exhale. Inhale exhale.

"Are you ready?" Ashton asked as he held out his steady hand. His hair wafted in the night breeze, and there wasn't a hint of gravity on him except his royal garb: white pants and a white jacket, the last button on top unopened. His blue eyes roamed over me and landed at my necklace.

I followed his gaze and picked up the usually black stone. Colors swirled and whirled. Reds, yellows, and oranges slithered around each other, the energy snapping at my fingertips as they passed. I allowed my eyes to traveled up to Cash. The asteroid hadn't flared with fire yet—the sure sign that it had breached the atmosphere. We had to wait until the exact right moment—that time just as it came close enough for my opposing source to reach it. Too soon, and we'd expend the energy too early. Too late, and there wouldn't be enough distance for us to slow down time and destroy it before its gravity and strange energies started wreaking havoc on Ferro's ecosystems. Already, the electricity of the city around us had already gone out, leaving the Observatory behind us and the asteroid above us as the only sources of light. In the distance, I could see the platform we'd landed on when we first came to rescue Cash, even if rescue hadn't really been needed. It was hard to miss. Ever since the light appeared in the sky, the hazy, swirling mirage around the wormhole had grown, tendrils reaching up to the sky as if to meet the asteroid.

Cash followed my gaze. We didn't know what effect the asteroid was having on the Earth's entries to the wormhole, but it couldn't be good. "You ready, Bea? You can do this," Cash said, straightening his bomber jacket and closing the distance between us.

I let my eyes drop and my head shake. "I don't have a choice, do I," I said, my words a statement rather than a question.

Cash grabbed my chin and held it in his hands; his grip was strong but tender. "You always have a choice. Always." His irises churned and pulsed. Greens, blues, and purples stroked the black center.

He was right. I chose to be here. I chose to try. I chose to save my friends and my enemies. I chose action rather than idleness. These were all my choices. I was not just a weapon but a gift, bequeathed to not only Earth but to Ferro. I would honor that intention and fight with everything I had inside of me, human and alien together.

I would not fail Ferro. I would not fail Earth. I would not fail myself.

I thought of all the sacrifices my mother made for this moment to happen. For the sacrifices of my fathers, both by blood and by bond, and all that they had endured. The sacrifices Sera made, all she lost and deserved the chance to find again.

And so, I was not afraid.

All my training crashed into me, as if every lesson from Cash; from Sera; from Ashton; from each Ferroean, Blood-Light, and human member of the Rebellion and the Guard were a net gathered up to catch me as I rose to fulfill my purpose. The strange energies from the asteroid radiated through my source like running water, rushing through my veins and pushing against my skin. Something like electricity hummed and danced at my joints, lighting my source on fire. I pressed the heel of my palm against Ashton's. His thick lashes lowered, closing his eyes and softening his facial features, taking in a similar breath to mine moments ago.

The skies filled with needles, at least fifty. Ashton saw it too as he said, "What's going on up there?" Two descended off in the distance not too far from us. Guards spilled from the needles, advancing quickly toward us, thermo daggers in their hands.

Cash unsheathed his weapons. "Whatever it is, I'll hold them off."

"Moment of truth, Beatrice Walker, the prophetic Blood-Light." Ashton winked, displaying his signature charm. In another world, Ashton was the Prince Charming in a fairytale; handsome, witty, and kind, saving the princess from the evil creature. I hoped that our revolution would give him the chance to be that man and feel real freedom, maybe even find a princess of his own.

Cash flipped his thermo daggers in his hands, posturing for an attack. He was all that stood between Ashton and me and Zane's legion, an army coming straight for us for an unknown reason.

I pressed my hand harder into Ashton's and my body spasmed. My skin responded to his compelled ethereal vitality. Gritting my teeth together, I unleashed my power; a flash of purple doused the sky, the energy emanating through and from the pendant of the necklace that hung over my source. I beamed—excited and proud. But it did not last. As quickly as it appeared, it dissipated, short of its target, just as it always did when we practiced. The warmth on my palms dulled. I wanted to scream at my source to get it together. We didn't have time for this now.

My brief display of power slowed the guards for only a beat before they continued moving toward us. Their eyes, each illuminated by their own sources, pushed forward in sync. Above us, I saw a flash of fire as the asteroid broke through the atmosphere. It was getting closer, and I was out of time. The smell of cedar and sage consumed me as the Orb's powers surged in response, sending a great glow of light from inside the Observatory so bright you could see from the outside in. But yet I couldn't hold my will long enough to activate my powers. My limbs, my veins were splayed wires, already shorted and fizzled out.

"You said the necklace turns purple out of love?" Ashton asked, angling his head with that casual style he possessed, watching in awe at the uncooperative pendant meant to channel my power.

"I was just guessing." I shrugged, my eyes hopelessly caught in the descending light of the asteroid. "The only constant is Cash." Remembering how during practice it flickered as Cash trained Ashton and me, I bit my lip. It only held purple in intense moments surrounding Cash, and I had guessed his love was the ignition. But could I be wrong? Standing here with him, feeling as much love and desperation as I've ever felt, I wasn't sure.

Ashton pushed his hand harder against mine, causing me to sway slightly. "I want to tell you a story." Ashton looked down at me, the force of his gaze pulling my eyes to stare steadily into his, the intensity mesmerizing.

My breath hitched. The world stopped as if we were the only two people. My skin tugged onto his like a child to its mother's skirt. My flesh bound itself to his for a brief moment until Cash barked in the background, breaking my concentration. "Now? You want to tell her a story now?"

Ashton ignored him and continued. "Stay with me, Beatrice. This is important." I nodded. I felt it through our bond, and I trusted Ashton. "The day I found out my mother was pregnant with twins..."

"By the Council, Ashton, now is not the time," Cash growled, his back toward us, his weapons held out for battle.

"Trust me, brother," Ashton snarled at Cash. With a smoother tone, he continued. "Like I was saying. That day was hard for me. I was angry and confused, young and adorable as well, but scared that my mother would give more attention to the two little Ferroeans in her stomach than me." A small smile tugged on Ashton's face as he recalled the memory. "I think my mother sensed something was wrong because she asked me to follow her into the crystal gardens out to the perimeter by the stone wall. She took me to the shaded area where the Hellebore flowers blossomed."

"We are running out of time," Cash begged, his back close enough that I could reach out and touch him if I wanted to.

Ashton threaded his fingers into mine and held our hands higher to the sky. My skin begged for his to join and the voice that had been rather muted for the last several months spoke for the first time. *Connect. Become one.*

"The Hellebore flower is an interesting flower. It looks delicate but is tough. They bloom in late winter to early spring, even popping up through harsh conditions like snow. The colors ranging from pure white to deepest pink to almost black. They are the only botany shared by both Earth and Ferro, even far from the sites of wormholes." I understood the importance of his claim. The flowers were like us—born of both planets, belonging exclusively to neither. "Looking at the miraculous flower, my mother asked. 'Do you know how this flower has become so tough and sustainable?' I had no idea, so I shook my head and she answered, 'Because of the shade.'"

Ashton's eyes settled on his brother as he finished the story, and I could see them filling with moisture as he spoke. "She told me that I was Cash and Tasha's shade, that the only way they would survive is if I protected them. She said they will grow to be 'tough as nails' if I am to them as shade and harsh conditions are to the Hellebore flower."

My throat choked as I held back my own tears. Ashton had lived his entire life looking after his siblings because he thought that's how they would grow and prosper. It was the responsibility his mother gave him so many years ago. It was why he joined the Rebellion, so that he could give them a better life. This bond between us opened the doors to his heart, his source, and as if I was him, I felt everything he felt. The sadness of Tali, the shame of Zane, and the un-conditional love he had for Tasha and Cash. Love cocooned Ashton all these years, drove him to this path, and it would save our worlds.

Cash slowly turned to his brother, his face almost un-readable except for his eyes. The iris slivered with colors of gold, silver, purple, and yellow.

"I have lived my life hoping to be the shade for you," Ashton continued.

Cash cut him off. "You have, brother. You have." He dropped his weapons and placed his palm against Ashton's other hand. Recognition flashed before me, before us. And that's when it happened. My necklace pulsed purple. The world completely stopped, our powers activated, and noth-ing and no one moved.

As if Ashton knew this entire time that our shared love for one another would set this world free, he motioned for Cash to join my other hand, creating a circle. There was no end. No beginning. The three of us stood, palm to palm. The silent voice spoke again loud enough to be heard by all and I realized for the first time it was the Orb communicating with me, with us.

For the Flesh craves what is contrary to the Source, and the Source what is contrary to the Flesh. Join. Become one. And you will save all.

Power coursed through my source, bubbling at my fin-gertips. My flesh joined with Ashton's, who joined with Cash's, who joined mine. We were one. Purple light burst through the necklace and into the sky, crashing into the white light of the asteroid. For a moment, time remained slow, and then resumed with an explosion of blinding light where the two sources of light met. As it burst from the inside out, molten fragments of the hulking rock disintegrated under the force of our powers. The sky clouded over, filled with ash and stone that would likely rain down on Ferro for days to come. It would not be pleasant. But the world—both worlds—would survive.

As I released my palm from Ashton, he wrapped his arm around Cash, and they embraced. My heart swelled. Tears cascaded down my cheeks, and I let them run unabated.

Cash released Ashton and turned toward me, his energy wild. He took me in his arms, and as if the rush of emotions weren't enough, he held his hands to my face so that all I could see were his own eyes filled with wonderment. My heart and source paused until he crashed his lips against me. Then the beat and rush of my insides took over, flushing out any hesitation. I wrapped my arms around his neck, and I melted for him, into him. We kissed unlike any kiss before. I opened my mouth as his tongue brushed against mine and grazed my teeth. His hands worked down my shoulders and around my waist pulling my body flush to his. These kisses were full of love and happiness, relief and exhaustion, sadness and pain. They were everything we had felt over the last year and then some. When I pulled slightly away, he kissed the corner of my mouth, the side of my chin, and trailed down my neck. Hazy black rain fell from the sky, littering his hair and shoulders. My source burned hotter than the dancing ambers now adhering to my face, onto my clothes as he continued back up to my mouth. I would have forgotten there was a world if Ashton hadn't made a grumbling noise behind us.

When I looked up coming out of the haze I had been in with Cash, I saw that we were surrounded.

Captain Dock stood next to King Zane.

"You are under arrest."

Cash, catching the soot-soaked rain, barked out, "Who?"

"All of you."

Chapter Thirty-Three

The Escape—Ashton

Pacing back in forth in my Ferroean holding cell, I rehashed our last moments. I shook my head and mumbled, "A little appreciation for saving the world before an arrest might have been more thoughtful." This may not be my first time in one of these metallic cages but at least the last time was for a reason I understood. Then, I'd actively joined a rebellion against the government. This time? It just didn't make sense. Time in my titanium prison cell was irrelevant. Exhaustion and claustrophobia clawed away at my insides. Eventually, I gave up trying to understand it, curled up on the rigid metal cot, and drifted to sleep.

I awoke to a pair of guards slapping ampere restraints to my wrists and jaw. They jerked me to an upright position, nearly taking out my teeth with the damaging device. I had no choice but to obey. They led me out of the holding tank, marched me down the strangely empty streets, and brought me directly into the one place I didn't expect to find myself ever again—the Royal Estate that stopped being home the moment I joined the Rebellion.

None of the Guards were ones I knew, but they certainly recognized me. The two Ferroean lackeys who flanked me gripped my biceps so hard that I was confident they'd leave their fingerprints imbedded into my flesh. Their eyes stayed forward and focused as we roamed the hallways until we reached my childhood bedroom. I could only believe their utter silence was at the direction of Captain Stuffy Pants Dock.

After they unceremoniously tossed me into my room, it took about three minutes before someone dissolved my electromagnetic chains. I surveyed the room, thankful nothing had been touched since I was last in here. I walked into the bathroom and ran my wrists under the cold water, dulling the heat from the device on my skin. I splashed my face several times, waking up my senses. Droplets clung to my chin as I lifted my head from the sink.

I growled an inhuman noise. A second reflection to my own stared back at me. "Mother." The word tasted bitter on my tongue. Not wanting her to touch me, I dropped my mental shields, giving her immediate access to all of my thoughts and feelings about her. The word 'traitor' floated loudly at the top.

"Ash," she said, handing me a washcloth. I ripped it from her grasp and dried my face, then tossed it back at her. I stormed out of the bathroom, letting my shoulder ram into hers on the way out. She stumbled back a bit but regained her footing, even in heels. Such talents. "Yes, well, I see you're upset." She crossed her arms over her chest, tapping her delicate fingers on her biceps. "Would another time to chat work more conveniently for you since you're so busy brooding?"

I tossed myself back onto my bed, the soft comforter a plush net to my aching body. "I'm wondering several things at the moment," I said, staring up at the white ceiling which had been repainted to cover the blue scene I'd once painted—complete with fluffy white clouds and little black birds. I guess it reminded mommykins a little too much of Earth.

"And what would they be?" She played my game. Good. I deserved at least that.

I rolled onto my side and used my arm to prop up my head so I could stare Tali down. "Do you like being used and abused by that man? Was slumming it on Earth in the bed of a human so terrible you choose prison life on Ferro?"

"Tone, Ash, tone!" she warned, pointing her perfectly lacquered nails at me.

"Let me rephrase. Do you like what you see in the mirror?" Her head tilted as her lips puckered. "Because until Cash and I saved the planet and my mother and father completely turned on their two sons, I was very excited to look in the mirror every day and see this gorgeous, chiseled face, high cheekbones, perfectly angled nose, pouty lips." I used my free hand to outline my head. "But now..." I pushed myself upright. My voice lowered. "Now, every time I look in the mirror, I see you." I paused, letting it sink in and making sure she followed my train of thought. "And I HATE myself for it." I practically spat out the last part, my voice laced with thick venom.

She uncrossed her arms, extending her spine upright. Our matching blue eyes stared each other down until I saw a small muscle in her jaw feather. "You'll never understand what I know, and why I have done the things I have done, and perhaps you never will." Her saccharine words were pronounced with ease, as if she had said them a hundred times before.

I jumped from the bed at the sudden revelation.

Tali held her finger to her mouth and stalked forward. She touched her hand to my arm. *Two worlds as one, this oath I take: to Ferro, to Earth, to the Rebellion,* she spoke into my mind. My knees wobbled as I reached for a steady surface and clung to a nearby chair. *I have a story if you'd be willing to listen?*

I think I nodded in reply, but there was every chance I just meant to. Paralyzing shock took over, and I felt heavy and numb.

My mother continued, her voice gentle. *I was twenty years old and traveling with my parents to Earth for the fourth time. I had met a man; his name was Arnie. He was tall, handsome, and kind. He was my first love, my first experience, but he was also a dream.* She sighed. *I was betrothed to another on Ferro and would never see Arnie again. My parents had made it clear this would be my last trip to Earth since I would belong to Zane moving forward and a Subaltern was not permitted to leave her duties. So, I asked Arnie to give me a gift, something no one could take from me, something that would remind me no matter what lay ahead who I am and what I once was.*

I swallowed hard as I asked, *And what were you once?*

My mother smiled, possibly the only real smile I had ever seen on her beautiful face. It took my breath away as she answered, *I was free.*

She pulled me into her arms, and we wrapped our arms around each other, my fingers clinging to her hair. *Ash, you were the gift Arnie gave me. You remind me of who I used to be and who I really am. You are hope for the future, our peo-*

ple's and Earth's. Wetness coated my shoulder as she continued. I didn't dare move for fear of losing this moment. *I am the one who put you in Sayor's path. When I found out he was an elder from your father, I went to him. I knew the Orb would want peace between our two worlds. I knew it in my source. You were half human and although on Ferro your true genetic makeup was hidden, I knew better. A Blood-Light of your strength and training would be an asset to Sayor. Plus, he always adored you. Part of me wondered if he thought maybe you'd end up on his side regardless of my interference. I made him promise to never tell you of what I had done. To leave me out of it. And he did as I asked.*

She pulled away and cupped my face in her hands. *I stole the purple opposing energy source of the last generation inside the Orb. I didn't know if a regular source would be enough and I'm still uncertain if the borrowed source even made a difference.*

I had no idea the source inside me was an opposing source, but I'd had a feeling it wasn't mine. The day Darla admitted that Beatrice said I smelled like cedar and sage my suspicions got the best of me. Only a source held inside the Orb smelled like that.

Sayor helped me, and then we implanted it in you. Her eyes softened with the memory, possibly pride as well. *The Orb told Sayor it would be a Blood-Light who saved the planet, but they said only when the source and the flesh opposed each other. The Orb can be very misleading—flesh is what they mean when they say human. We concluded there needed to be two Blood-Lights. Sayor and I didn't realize that Cash had to be the defining factor to push both Beatrice and you to your full potential, but I am sure glad you all figured it out.*

Things were falling into place, but I was still confused. *Why did Zane tell you about Sayor being an elder? Has he confided anything else about his plan against Earth?*

My mother smiled, her face brightening like an early-morning sunrise. *Darling, I can break through anyone's mental shields. There's not a Ferroean who can think something that I can't hear. When Sayor told your father and you that day about the Orb choosing to speak to him, your father unknowingly told me.* Releasing my face with her right hand, she tapped me on the nose. I twitched in response. *Sleeping next to the enemy has many perks when you are the only Ferroean who has my abilities. Shields are glass inside the minds of our people, and I am the rock.*

I bit back surprise at her confession. She's been a spy for the Rebellion all this time and I never knew.

She dragged her hands down my shoulders and held onto my arms. *You were made for greatness, my son, as you have already shown by protecting our planet with your brother and Beatrice Walker. You will go on to safeguard our people.* Our eyes locked. Tears streaked her painted cheeks, leaving residue in their wake. Usually so practiced at hiding her own emotions, her eyes darted around suddenly, dispelling any fears someone might see her.

I have so many questions. I spoke into her mind.

Her smile faltered but did not fade. *I only wish I had the time to answer them.* Noise from outside my room alerted both of us that we would have company soon.

His name is Arnold Ashcroft... And with that, she slipped out of my room and sealed the door shut.

I don't know how much time passed—a few weeks, maybe even a month—but when the door opened, I was happy to see Jellybean and Cash on the other side. I worried immediately about the stubble on Cash's face and the dark circles under his eyes. It would appear my accommodations were way better than his.

"Well, you look good," Cash said. "Have a nice two-month stay at the Ritz-Carlton?"

I shook my head. "Two months?" My eyes raked over his body. His hair was longer and disheveled and his body more toned. Prison. "Where were you held?"

"The Holding Tank," he growled.

"For the whole two months?" My voice rose in disbelief. He nodded. The Holding Tank was used as an overnight stay, a week at the most, before trials or during sentencing. Ferro didn't need prisons, just cryogenic storage facilities for those who have had their source removed as punishment for a crime.

I turned and looked at Jellybean. "I was pretty much on house arrest, but Sera and Tali easily convinced my parents I was required as an escort today. So here I am, escorting the prisoners." She winked. "In an escape."

The three of us ran out of the royal complex and up the stairs to a boarding platform. A needle floated there, idling as Cash waved his hand, opening the side door. Beatrice and Sera were inside at the helm, both rested and well, like me.

"Tali broke me out of the holding cell the following week. It's a long story," Bea offered as she saw my face twitch with questions. "And we really don't have time for it now. But when we are home, I'll tell you everything."

The needle soared through the city, its destination the same wormhole entrance we'd come through months ago, but this time there was no easy access. Although no guards were present, most of the floating strip had been destroyed. We pulled up as close as we could.

"It's not super stable. The asteroid must have damaged this area. Looks like it's been closed off for some time," Sera said, surveying the lack of road and the ash-covered remnants of what was left. We hauled out of the transport and ran carefully down the short runway to the distorted backdrop.

"I'm not going back," Sera yelled as she clutched Bea in a surprising embrace. Bea wrapped her arms around her in response. And for a moment, I was concerned I had already gone through the wormhole and ended up in a parallel universe. I couldn't help my gaping stare. Sera released Bea and looked in my direction. "Go on, Ash. Go home to Earth. Be the change Ferroeans need you to be." She stalked over to me and gave me a brief hug.

"Crede Mihi, Sera," Cash said as she passed him without regard. He grabbed her hand and gave her a gentle tug.

She turned and smiled. "Crede Mihi," she said as she released his hand. It wasn't a smile of sadness but rather one of acceptance and whatever I had missed, it felt like Sera was already healing.

"Age before beauty," Cash said, waving to me to jump through the wormhole.

"Oh no. I insist." I bowed mockingly. Cash said something to Bea I couldn't hear and they jumped through. I turned to Jellybean. "Follow me, kid."

I leaped through the swirling array of blue color and white light as the Ferroean landscape blurred around me. I closed my eyes and breathed through my nose, paying careful attention not to clench my teeth. A welcome feeling of tension caressed my whole body, and then one of liberation. I was going home. The darkness filled my surroundings, a gust of energy pulled me in several directions, the floor fell away, and the Ferroean world—the world I knew I'd never see again—was gone. My torso floated in the air as my spine reformed with bone and blood, my source no longer the base of my skeleton. My humanity ripped through my body, sending shockwaves through my fluid veins. I squeezed my eyes at the sharp pain of transformation and managed to embrace it, knowing what it meant. I breathed slowly, deliberately, as pressure filled my lungs with air. Within seconds, the wind calmed around me, calmed in time with the process of my natural assimilation, and my feet found solid ground.

My eyes opened, causing my mouth to drop. Cash and Beatrice were already through the wormhole, glaring at an armed militia dressed in training gear: navy shirts and gray cargo pants. Apparently, a new look for the Hive. I studied the room and unless it was possible to move a wormhole, this was not the same as the one we left. There were no control panels or even a door. It was an empty room that pooled into a narrow hallway now filled with guards.

"What in hell's bells is going on here?" I asked, crossing my arms over my chest.

Chapter Thirty-Four

The Escape—Beatrice

Metal walls. I was surrounded by a steel fortress. Where was I? I patted down the sides of the room, trying to locate an exit. The memory of Ashton's elevator with bolts that lined the seams sparked, and I realized I was in a prison. A long table I sure as heck hoped was not a bed was against one side and a toilet against the other. Nothing else.

I don't know how long I managed to keep calm but by the time what felt like hours, possibly a day, passed, my skin crawled with confusion and anxiety. Why arrest us? No one answered any of these questions as the three of us were hauled away, each being thrown into different needles with no idea where the others were headed.

My screams had gone unheard and my voice was hoarse. I'd just about given up hope when an invisible door opened seamlessly in the wall opposite what could vaguely be considered furniture. Two Guards walked in, followed closely by Subaltern Tali. She snapped her fingers, and ampere restraints clung to my wrists and jawline.

"If you don't fight them, you won't be injured," Tali said with a controlled tone. "Officers Samptim and Piteon will

help me escort you back to your room at the Royal Estate."
Without another word, she turned and exited, and one of
the two—a younger one I think was Samptim—tried to lead
me out by the elbow. He wasn't rough about it, but I
shrugged him off me, nonetheless. The quick movement
sent a small shock of pain through my wrists. After that, I
let him gently guide me when necessary, and he seemed to
know better than to let his hand linger longer than needed.
The four of us walked down identical metal halls filled with
metal doors. Wall after wall was made of pure stainless
steel. If this was their prison, and I assumed it was, it was
actually very disturbing.

We rounded a bend and the door opened to the outside.
I squinted at the harsh light, carefully lifting my forearm up
to my head to shield the illumination. I managed to do so
without triggering the torture device. Wherever we were, it
was an area of the Capital I had never seen before. I wasn't
sure if I felt more afraid in the cell, or out here with a hu-
man-hating Ferroean and her two henchmen.

Tali turned, a stern look of decision on her face. "Thank
you, Officers, you are dismissed. I can take it from here."

"But Subaltern Tali," Guard Piteon argued. "It's against
protocol."

Tali waved her hands dismissively. "A Subaltern escorting
a prisoner through the city streets is not against procedure."
She stared him down, evidently irritated at the show of
even the slightest doubt of her authority. "As you already
are aware, I outrank you." Her voice was cool yet threatening
enough to cause the poor soldier to immediately tense up,
most likely regretting his foolish decision to speak out.
"Might I remind you that questioning a superior *is* against
protocol?"

He bowed and pivoted on his heels, taking a stunned Samptin with him.

"Military," Tali sighed, flipping her reddish-brown locks over her shoulder. "Walk with me, Beatrice." She snapped her fingers and the amperes dissolved.

I rubbed at my wrists and massaged my face as we strolled down a quiet, spotless thoroughfare. The tall, angular buildings were nestled between streets lined with homes. It felt odd, like it should have been bustling, but instead, not a single resident could be seen.

"Since you and my boys somehow managed to halt our obliteration, the Capital has been on lockdown. No one in or out of their homes for the next two months." Clearly, she read my thoughts. "And before you think it, Ashton is home in his very own bedroom, but I have yet to find Casheous." Panic tore at my throat but before I could muster words, she continued. "I need you to listen to me and to pause your emotional side for a moment. Can you do that?"

"Yes," I answered, lifting my chin in line with hers. I had a feeling I was going to need Tali if I wanted to find Cash, so it made sense to let her speak, for now.

She stared at the cloudless sky for a minute. "I have always considered this moment. The last time I would see my sons. Meeting a future daughter-in-law." I blushed at her forward comment. I had no idea what my future with Cash held, but for her to verbalize that notion meant she felt he and I had potential together. "Ending the charade I've been playing for far too many years..." She sighed. "Nothing prepares you, you know. For a moment like this." We rounded the corner, coming to a row of sharp-roofed townhomes, staggered but attached. "Seraphina lives in the third one in, grey door. She will help you escape and return back to Earth when the time is right."

"What happened to you?" I asked, seeing for the first time the wrinkles of her worried skin, the age she hid so well under her manicured appearance. All building up a fa-cade that hid who she really was.

"A long time ago, my freedom was taken, and I've been fighting my way back ever since. I hope Ash, Casheous, and you can right my people's wrongs."

Her words felt final, as if her days ended right here and now. "Why won't you come and help us? You'd be a great ally and we could use your abilities."

"I'm better served here." She waved her hands around. "All of this is my home. The good and the bad. It'll be where I die when it falls." She placed a hand on my shoulder. "Beatrice, it is my choice to stay here till the end. It's the last bit of freedom I've been gifted."

The door opened, and Sera stood in its frame. Her long, dark hair lay over her shoulder in a loose braid. She wore a cream-colored suit buttoned up and fashioned off with a thick collar. She gazed at me briefly and then her eyes flew to Tali. She ran and embraced her. Tears rained down their faces. "I've missed you. Everything is so..."

Tali nodded but didn't say anything; instead, she pulled Sera back by her shoulders and gave her a reassuring smile, then kissed her forehead. Pivoting toward me, she said, "I've never been much at good-byes. I will alert the Guards to your escape in an hour, but no one will find you here. Sera and you should prepare. Earth is a bit of a disaster right now and..."

"We aren't a secret anymore, Beatrice. Humans are call-ing it an invasion. The shockwaves of the asteroid breaking our atmosphere caused major damage to Earth, opening up new wormholes and destabilizing old ones. The DOAA believes we did this intentionally. Some countries were completely wiped out and others left in shambles."

Tali welcomed us both into an embrace, soothing my hair with her hand. "It's up to you now, ladies. Crede Mihi."

And with that she slipped away faster than the blink of an eye.

"Come on in. I'll catch you up on everything." Sera waved me in. I followed her into the hallway and up three flights of stairs. If this had been any other circumstance, I might have complained about the long haul, but I knew my objection to the excessive steps was pale in comparison to the perilous position we were in.

The living area was lined with floor-to-ceiling windows, allowing for the perfect view of the Royal Home in the distance. I placed my hand on the glass as if I could touch it. Sera tapped me on the shoulder and handed me a bottle of water.

"What happened?" I asked. My eyes roamed over the empty city. While it appeared unharmed, like Earth, Ferro was also in ruin.

"Whatever the three of you did stopped the worst of the asteroid's destruction, but it still caused major damage before it was destroyed. Whatever energy it was giving off, coupled with the power of your combined sources, created a ripple effect between our two worlds." She paused, taking a sip from her own glass. "There are hundreds of wormholes now, some as small as the one beneath the Hive, but others as big as sinkholes. It decimated the infrastructures of many of Earth's urban centers, destroying cities, crippling governments, devastating supply chains. Thousands died.

Maybe millions. We haven't received word on the final count yet, and it's hard to say if we will ever truly know."

I shook my head. Deaths, so many deaths, when all we were trying to do was save them. "I understand why Earth blames Ferro, but can't we explain they could all be dead right now?" We saved way more than were taken. If we had done nothing, everyone would be gone."

"People fear what they cannot understand, and unlike Ferro, Earth had no idea it was in danger to begin with. It doesn't matter how successful we were—the damage is done." She took another sip, finishing the contents. "And now we have a little over seven weeks. You'll rest. We will train. And then we will go back to Earth, whether they want us or not. There is a war coming and they're going to need all the help they can get."

The next four weeks flew by as Sera and I prepared, slowly finding a good rhythm, both in our fighting and our friendship. She was no Darla by any means, but we found moments of laughter and girl talk. We even started our own Friday night routine. The first week we were together, Sera introduced me to an underground black market that specialized in real food so that we could get a break from the constant meals of pills. Even Sera, who grew up with them, thought they were horrid, and she obviously wasn't the only Ferroean who felt that way. Goods were in high demand, but Sera had a particular "in" with someone I could best describe as an old Earth cheesemonger-slash-butcher. One particular night, he'd managed to get us everything we wanted for one of my favorite childhood meals—ham and swiss sandwiches on rye bread.

As we stood in the kitchen that Friday with our smuggled goods, I finally asked a question I had been pondering since I first arrived at Sera's house. "How long have you known Tali was on the Rebellion's side?"

Sera handed me the knife and mayonnaise container as she laid the cheese in between the ham slices on top of one side of the rye bread. "Tali told me the day Ashton was taken into custody, the day she thought her betrayal had gotten him killed."

My eyes widened. "You knew all this time and never told anyone?" She understood that by anyone, I really meant Cash. We avoided directly talking about Cash and the impending war as much as possible, only broaching the bigger picture when Tali sent intel. Sera took the opportunity to break that unspoken agreement at least this once.

"Cash and I weren't always transparent with each other. We were raised to put the mission first, and Cash was aligned with Zane. I never trusted the King, but I trusted Tali." She paused, then laughed. "Oddly enough, so did my father and that's pretty much what got him imprisoned."

I handed her the knife back and slid the mayonnaise and mustard jars closer to her. "I'm sorry about your dad."

She cleaned the knife on a paper towel before dipping it into the mustard. "It's Ok. I'm proud of him for sticking to his thermo daggers and for challenging the Council." She scooped up a large lump of the yellow condiment, coating the other slice of the bread. She looked over to my workstation and gave me a mocking cringe. "You're really bad at making sandwiches. There's mayonnaise everywhere." She shook her head. "You're on cleanup duty tonight."

I chuckled. "Fair enough. I'm not the best cook, and to be fair, my dad always made the sandwiches." I smiled, and briefly hoped Robert was doing okay back on Earth despite everything going on.

"This is barely cooking. It's basically just aiming." Her lips pulled up at the ends. "Thank the Council you are better with thermo daggers than making sandwiches." She married the two sides together and cut them in half, then leaned over to my sloppy sandwich and did the same as if she didn't trust me to do so without further messing the countertop. "Cash and I had more issues than I think we were willing to admit. He would have never seen Zane for what he was if I hadn't been 'pretend killed.'" She shrugged. "It's partially why I agreed to the Awakening."

I didn't know what to say so I placed my hand on hers. "Cash loves you and I truly believe you would have convinced him either way, but he will never forget your sacrifice." I squeezed her hand. "And neither will I."

Her eyes moistened but no tears were shed. "Come on. Let's eat before you waste any more of our illicit contraband to the counter. This is precious, after all." We both chuckled as we sat down to a satisfying meal.

It took another two weeks before Tali located Cash, but relayed he was under the watch of Zane's top guards, making it impossible to contact him. So, we waited and waited until we got the call.

At the end of week eight, a picture of Messenger Drayton Rose appeared in Sera's home. I hid in the darkness of the bedroom as they spoke. "Subaltern Tali has requested your presence at the Royal..." There was a brief pause. "That's odd," I heard Messenger Rose mumble. "My apologies. Subaltern Tali has requested your services to drive the Royal Needle to the holding tank to retrieve a prisoner. She needs a seasoned Guard to accompany the escort. You are not to speak to the prisoner. The Guard is outside your residence now. Good day."

"Good day," Sera said. Moments passed before I walked out of the room. "You ready to go get Cash?" she asked.

I laughed. "Why is it we are always saving him?"

"Men need to be saved sometimes, especially that one."

We hurried to the needle that was floating outside Sera's childhood home. The invisible door opened, and Jellybean leaned up against the side. "Wanna lift?" She winked in our direction as the stairs descended to the cement ground.

When we got in, Jellybean hugged us both. The three of us stood there, arms wrapped around each other. We didn't know one another well, but we didn't have to. In times of despair and trouble, those who were strangers could often be the best of friends when they had common ground. "Can we please leave this planet? House arrest is driving me stir crazy."

"That's the plan. Now let's go get Cash and Ashton," Sera said.

When we arrived at the Holding Tank, as they called it, Cash was outside by himself. The stairs descended and he casually walked up them. Not only was he wearing uncharacteristically human clothing, but it was an outfit I would have never seen him caught dead in while on Earth. A faded cartoon mouse on a royal blue background stared out at us from the center of his chest, and his jeans looks a few sizes too big. My mouth opened but before I could formulate words, Cash spoke.

"Don't even ask." He held his hand up. "It's been a wild two months and I am ready to leave this planet for good. Let's go get Ash."

I could feel my cheeks indent as I smiled seeing him here in the flesh, alive. I rushed him, my arms wrapped around his neck, and I kissed him. A brief touch of our lips together, and definitely not enough to quench the thirst I had for him but enough to hold me over till we were safe. He grinned, wrapping a loose hair around my ear and sending words into my thoughts. *I've missed you like the sun misses the sky after it sets. Are you Ok?*

"You need a haircut," Jellybean said from behind me, cutting into our moment.

I didn't let go but spoke into his mind. *I'm fine.* Then out loud said, "Actually, he needs a freaking shower—forget a haircut."

"That's funny, Bea. Real funny." Cash smirked and flicked my nose.

Jellybean and Cash slipped into the Royal home and out with Ashton in under five minutes. Impressive. Ashton looked like a deer in headlights when he boarded the needle, so I offered him a brief version of my story. "Tali broke me out of the holding cell the following week. It's a long story. And we really don't have time for it now. But when we are home, I'll tell you everything."

The needle soared through the city to the outskirts where the wormhole we arrived through existed. As we hauled out of the transport and down the destroyed vacant runway to our exit, I could sense Sera's hesitation and slowed my own pace.

"I'm not going back," Sera said. She grabbed my arm and swung me around into her limbs. There had been so much between us from the moment of her Awakening to now. So much I wanted to tell her. She had become my friend and in the last six weeks, a good friend. She seemed to understand as she whispered into my ear for only me to hear, "I knew he chose you the day I was Awakened. And even though it hurts, I'm really happy for both of my friends." She pulled away, avoiding my gaze, and turned to Ashton. "Go on, Ash, go home to Earth. Be the change Ferroeans need you to be."

Sera started to walk away when I saw Cash grab her hand. "Crede Mihi, Sera," he said. She turned and smiled. "Crede Mihi."

"Age before beauty!" Cash waved to Ashton to jump through the wormhole.

Ashton laughed and bowed. "Oh no. I insist." Cash grabbed my hand and said, "You ready to go home?"

Before I could answer, he pulled me through with him into the swirling array of scenery. I closed my eyes in anticipation of the darkness and breathed carefully through my nose. A jarring feeling of nervousness crawled up my whole body, and then simmered. Since this was only the second time I'd transported through a wormhole; I was still getting used to it. The blackness consumed me as my body swayed back and forth, the floor fell away, and the Ferroean world, the world I had just saved, was gone. My body floated in the air. The only grounding was my hand still intertwined with Cash's. I squeezed to confirm he was real. My limbs cracked and snapped, reforming with my bone and blood. My source pulled away slightly, allowing my human connective tissue to regrow. I pinched my face at the intense ache of discomfort flowing through me. I breathed slowly, deliberately, as weight pushed into my chest. Within seconds, the wind died down, my feet found solid ground, and the pain ebbed.

My eyes opened and I gasped as Cash growled.

"You are under arrest," a guard of some sort said. He was dressed in a navy t-shirt, grey cargo pants, and two thermo daggers made an "X" across his chest.

"Who the hell are you?" I could feel Cash's power and source surging. I took in my surroundings realizing this was NOT the Hive we left but something new altogether.

"We are the Blood-Light Army. And we will use force if we have to. There is no clemency for what your people did to us, and we will never forget."

Words were having a hard time formulating on my tongue as Ashton appeared. "What in hell's bells is going on here?" Couldn't have said it better, Ash.

"You will never believe this, brother," Cash growled.

I saw his blond hair and then his familiar blue eyes as the sea of guards stepped to the side to let him through. All the glimmer of humor his facial features normally held were gone and replaced with accusation. "Thanks to whatever you did in your world, you ruined ours," he spat.

"Chris, what did they do to you?" I barely got the words out. I stepped forward to go to him, but Cash hauled me backward, sending words into my head.

Do not engage him. Something's not right.

Chris smirked. "They gave me a future, which is more than I can say about the humans, who never stood a chance." He huffed. "Things have changed in the nine months you've been gone."

I gasped. The time difference between Ferro and Earth—it completely slipped my mind.

"I'm the leader of the Blood-Light Army! And if you do not play nice, we *will* kill you." He glared in my direction. But it was the words he spoke into my head that affected me the most. *Just like you killed my mom, Peggy.*

My heart dropped into my stomach and bile crept up my throat. My only saving grace was being on a pill diet didn't allow for much substance to be released. I trembled in Cash's hold, not knowing if it was a smart idea to mention Chris had powers. *What's wrong? Why are you shaking? Talk to me!*

Weakened by the news Peggy was dead, and Chris was able to use telepathy to speak to me, I didn't respond to Cash but clung to Jellybean's interruption. Like a bowling ball, she rolled through the wormhole onto cement floor. She wasn't given much preparation for her wormhole experience. She held onto her chest as I lowered to the ground to help her sit up.

"Where are we?" she gasped.

Chapter Thirty-Five

The Escape—Cash

Zane and Captain Dock paced in front of me as I sat in a metal chair in a containment room, the ampere cutting into my jaw and wrists. The low hum of pain caused by the device prevented me from tapping into their minds, but from how their eyes shifted and skin crinkled, I knew they were speaking telepathically. Both looked disturbingly out of character, their usually pristine jackets crumpled and scuffed, the metal buttons undone and flopped open to reveal the sleek standard-issue body armor beneath.

Finally, after about an hour, given the fact I had nothing to do but try and keep time, my amperes dissolved and they stood in front of me, assessing me. "Your restraints can go back on as easily as they were removed if you make any attempt at fighting us," Captain Dock said.

I rubbed my wrists and cracked my neck. "That all depends on what you've done with my brother and girlfriend."

Zane held up his hand. "They are fine. I swear to the Council both are completely unharmed."

I nodded. That was enough to get me to behave until I learned more.

"We had a bit of an issue with the degree of power the three of you exhibited," Zane said while rubbing the sides of his temples. I tilted my head. OK, not what I thought he was going to say. "All of the wormholes have been compromised."

My mouth hung open. What did that mean? "Humans slipped through?" Zane nodded. "Can't you just send them back with a bit of Influences to wipe their memories?"

"We've been trying, yes, although the sheer number of humans is making that a difficult prospect. But it's more than just that. The asteroid itself was exhibiting a power signature that disrupted the wormholes' integrity, and that might have been bad enough. However, it seems the instability allowed your combined power to radiate out through those openings between our worlds with unexpected and heretofore unanticipated consequences. The simultaneous activation of hundreds—perhaps thousands—of wormholes of various sizes had catastrophic consequences, including but not limited to volcanic eruptions, seismic tremors, and atmospheric disruptions." Noticing my sidelong look, he clarified. "The combined energies caused devastating mudslides, country-sized earthquakes, and a hurricane front that wiped out the entire eastern seaboard and not an insignificant number of island chains." He shook his head. "In other words, Earth reacted rather poorly to being saved."

That's why there were so many needles and guards. They weren't just coming to arrest us. The guards were rounding up the stray humans who fell through the literal cracks, and possibly containing any Ferroeans that might have noticed so they could cover up the incident. Rumors that a new species was accidentally invading Ferro would not have gone over well with the general populace.

"We received alerts from every major wormhole station the second Beatrice Walker unleashed her power. We had to distribute all the guards to round up not only the humans but any Ferroean that was out. Ferro has been under lockdown protocols since we arrested you."

He waved his hand toward a metal wall that was a shade lighter than the gunmetal-grey of the other three walls to the room. It wasn't my first time here—I knew that color meant it could function as a view screen to other areas of the Holding Tank. The surface blurred until it refocused into a clear picture. I bit back a gasp.

Hundreds of humans were huddled together in what I could only describe as abject terror. With the ampere gone and my focus on them specifically, I could now pick up all their thoughts and fears at once, causing a severe overload of my telepathic talents. That's why Zane was rubbing his temples; the barrage of thoughts affected him too.

"Send them back!" I shot up to my feet. "They can't stay here. They won't survive our atmosphere for very long without assimilation."

"Sit," Dock ordered, and I growled, showing my teeth.

"We can't send them back. I said things were proving difficult. Influence simply isn't working on them." Zane ignored Captain Dock's order, continuing our conversation. "Their minds are too fragile, and they've seen far too much already. If we sent them back, who knows what would happen. There could be mental breakdowns, physical repercussions, permanent damage—not to mention the greater sociopolitical implications."

"Send them back anyway! Staying here indefinitely would be far, far worse!" I threw my hands in the air. This was insane. We couldn't keep them like pets.

"You cannot know how much worse it could be. Best-case scenario, they think it was a terrible nightmare. But it's far more likely to cause critical damage, and you cannot tell me that does not concern you. As our primary Earth liaison, we need you to work with them and assess the situation. After that, we can discuss the details of sending them back to Earth."

I'd have tried slapping myself awake from this nightmare if the pain from the ampere wasn't still lingering. "You cannot be serious."

"Casheous, this is real! As real as the source inside your chest cavity. Focus on the task at hand. Influence is not working, and assimilation of this magnitude is just not possible. You know perfectly well they will die if they stay here for an extended period of time."

I took a breath. I had to admit he was right, and someone had to do something.

Zane continued, "While I do not care much for humans, killing thousands at this time would not bode well for my future plans. Can you see what type of predicament we are in? They now know we exist, they are on our planet, and we don't know what will happen if we send them back in this condition." He took a deep breath. "And even if we sent them now, we'd have to then destroy all the wormholes. And that we cannot do!"

The shock I was feeling dissipated, and I went into full crisis-management mode. "Lock the city down indefinitely. There are probably many more humans scattered across the planet, in and outside of the habitable zones. Send the guards out and find the ones we haven't picked up yet. And section them off by the wormhole location they fell through so we can at least make an attempt at keeping the families and acquaintances together."

Zane smiled and I knew without him saying it, this is exactly why we were arrested. He needed me. "Fine. You've got me. I'll do it," I agreed without having to read his thoughts or hear his words. "I'll lead the charge in figuring this out. How long do we have?"

"Past estimates have only seen humans survive a month at most, but with some dietary modifications our scientists think they can stretch that to two months before the iron-rich core will affect the heart's ability to circulate enough blood for their body's needs. After that, anyone not fully assimilated will go into congestive heart failure or have a stroke," Dock said crossing his arms over his chest. "You'll have to pretend you've been captured too. They can't know you are a Ferroean. They will never trust you. And as it stands, most of the humans already believe they have been abducted by aliens." Captain Dock rolled his eyes, revealing a Ferroean moment without regard for his position. "You'll have to live here with them and infiltrate from within."

I nodded. I already understood that when I offered up my services. "One condition." I held up my hand. "Ashton and Beatrice are to live in the Royal Home unharmed and unaware."

"Done. I'll have Samptin and Piteon do it tomorrow," Zane said, perhaps too easily. I'd worry about that later.

I pinched the arch of my nose, still trying to wrap my head around this. "How many wormholes?"

Blue illuminated words popped up in front of Dock and he swiped them. His jaw feathered as he answered, "332 wormholes, thirty-five destroyed by the blast, nineteen were in desolate areas where no humans slipped through, and the remaining 278 were all penetrated." He swiped two more times. "Out of the 278 wormholes, over 2,000 humans slipped through."

"Open up the training hall, Tali's banquet center, the first floor of the Observatory, and we will continue to use the rec area in the Holding Tank. Each place will get 500 humans. Captain Dock, you take the training hall and infiltrate. Try to be as human as possible—lighten up a bit." Dock's lips thinned but he remained silent. "Recruit Officer Samptim and put him in charge of the Banquet Center. I trust him. He cares about the humans, and he's extremely loyal to the King. Officer Piteon, one of the Royal Guards, will take the first floor of the Observatory. After they move Bea and Ashton tomorrow, they can join their groups. I'll stay here. Each week, a guard will escort us out and we will meet in this room to share what we have learned." I paused, rubbing my temples and concentrating on deep breaths. The screaming thoughts of the humans were so deafening, it was crushing my brain. "We have a little over seven weeks to figure out how to right this wrong, and that's banking on the hope no one dies before then."

Both Zane and Captain Dock nodded in agreement and led me down the hall to a changing room, a room typically used for preparation of source comas. Inside, there was Earth clothing that I was certain to burn the second I could rid myself of these threads. Hideous. Then they led me to the room with my new human compatriots. I spoke into my father's mind. *You and I have unfinished business. Our allegiance is only until we figure this out. After that, I know the war you are planning, and we will not be on the same side.*

I didn't have to see Zane's face to know he was smiling. *There's not a better opponent in this world or the next that I'd rather fight against, Captain Cash.*

Metal walls. Two thousand humans. Voices overloading my brain. A disaster.

I was impressed with the amount I was able to learn in only a few hours, let alone the following week. It seems that wormholes opened on every coast and every continent. We had to call in a few Ferroean linguists and even a handful of students for translation help in some cases, but we managed. Luckily, there is a Ferroean interested in every Earth culture, and our computerized translators came in handy to fill in the gaps. It appeared the majority of humans that "fell" into Ferro had been the outdoorsy type—they were in parks and other open areas, swimming, camping, hiking, skiing, etc. As far as we could tell, no wormholes opened up in people's homes or workplaces. It was a little comforting that no DOAA agents or Hive rebels had come through as well. The wormholes under those buildings must have been stabilized, either from how they were used or by the people working there during the disruptions. I did a lot of listening, learning their stories and their fears. I tried to keep my own sharing to a minimum but used my Earth cover when I needed to. The other three Guards had similar experiences with their refugee groups, but none of it made sense. We couldn't figure out why our Influence wouldn't work. Could it have something to do with how they fell through, or the power we'd used?

I was in the middle of a conversation with a blond woman in her late forties. She fell through near Cartwright's wormhole, which happened to be where my team and I had entered Earth for the first time. It was at that facility that we were assimilated to Earth all those years ago. I was interrupted by a Guard.

"Prisoner 14789, you are allotted your bath time. Move," the Guard said, kicking me in the side to get up. I'd remember that when I was out of here and he'd then remember me.

I stood and walked out and toward the containment room, confused as to why we were meeting here two days early. When I opened the door, my mother was seated at the table. Part of me wanted to turn back around and hear more of Peggy's story, but the other part of me was curious what my mother had to offer. "Tali," I groaned. "This is an unexpected visit."

"Casheous." She nodded to the seat across from her. I spun the chair, straddling the backrest in an attempt to look as nonchalant as possible. Luckily, she didn't bury the lead on me. "Your brother and girlfriend are doing well."

As relieved as I was, I didn't flinch. She didn't deserve to see my appreciation for their safety.

"I'll make this brief," she said, barely looking into my eyes. "I realize we have never had a close relationship and even if I explained why, I don't think it would really matter to you."

"Probably not." I had very little interest in her excuses. We all had a choice, and she clearly made hers a long time ago.

She nodded in understanding. "I do hope wherever life takes you, you know I have always loved you. And so does Zanith, regardless of his political crusade."

I pushed away from the table and stood up. I was done with this conversation. Tali stood with me and before I could react, she grabbed my hand. Like a thin pane of glass, my shields were shattered against the force of her telepathic powers. *When the war happens—and it will—know that we have always stood on the same side. Two worlds as one, this oath I take: to Ferro, to Earth, to the Rebellion.* My eyes widened as she continued. *Take care of my children, Casheous. Tell Tasha I love her. Remind Ashton he is a gift. And in the hours you question what you were to me, tell yourself—you are my champion.* Tears fell down her otherwise stoic face. Before I could process or respond she was gone. Out the door in a blink of an eye.

The next six weeks put Ferro's scientists to the test. Some of the human refugees were getting ill faster than others, and it felt like a race against time to save their lives. However, the weakened condition seemed to benefit us in some cases. Influence was finally starting to work on some of them, whether from the effects of the alien atmosphere on their bodies or just from Ferro regaining its strength from the asteroid's departure. It was finally working. I was about through a hundred of my unwell prison mates when a guard came and retrieved me. He walked me through the halls to the containment room, where the three officers were inside waiting to share their reports.

"I had one die today," Captain Dock said. No sadness coated his words, but I sensed he felt he was failing his mission due to the deep-set creases around his eyes. "There's a fine line from when they are ill to when they will die. We need to act faster. We need more Ferroean Guards in the holding areas."

"I lost three," Officer Piteon said. "The humans will notice new Guards. That's not an option. We'd have more work to do if we added new Ferroeans."

Samptim held his head low. "Two of mine died. I should have been able to stop it."

I placed my hand on his shoulder. "We are doing the best we can." I gave it a squeeze. "You are doing the best you can. And that's all anyone can ask of us."

I paced around the table while the others sat in quiet thought. After we'd each offered several ideas and logically broken them down as impossible, it came to me. "The biggest problem is humans noticing new refugees in their ranks, right? Well, what if we mix everyone up? They won't be able to tell the difference if we sprinkle a few Ferroeans into each group of humans. Gather the guards you trust the most and break things down into groups for the different holding areas. Start influencing them and sending them back to Earth as quickly as possible, before they even have a chance to wonder why they were moved. We have less than a week to get this done," I said, counting how many there were and how long it had taken me to Influence the ones I had and another Guard to take them and send them through the wormhole to arrive back on Earth.

With some help from Zane, Tali, and twenty-five other guards we trusted, we got the job done in five days. The humans were all sent through the wormholes with their minds intact and erased of our world and their jarring experiences. They would need serious medical attention and have lost some time, but they would be ok. We hoped.

It wasn't until I was watching the last family leaving the facility that I began to think about next steps. Certainly, Zane wouldn't just let me go back to Earth, so that meant we'd need to orchestrate some kind of escape. Just as I was about to start planning, Samptim opened my door in the Holding Tank. "Subaltern Tali has your ride out front. She wanted me to tell you, 'Go be where you belong and fight the good fight—the one she could only manage from the shadows.'" He bowed. "It's been an honor serving you, Captain."

"It's been an honor working with you, Tim," I replied. He didn't need to go to Earth to have his Earth name bestowed. He had shown more compassion for humans in the last two months than any assimilated Ferroean I'd known. He had earned his chosen name.

Tim's cheeks reddened as he bowed his head respectfully. "Thank you, Captain."

I stood outside, waiting for the needle to pull up. The stairs descended and I released a breath I had been holding since we were arrested two months ago. I slowly walked up them, exhausted from the last eight weeks of work. "Don't even ask." I held my hand up to Bea, Sera, and Jellybean. "It's been a wild two months and I am ready to leave this planet for good. Let's go get Ash."

Bea sprinted toward me and jumped into my arms. I wrapped myself around her and our mouths collided. It was brief kiss but also a promise for more and longer when we were out of here. I pulled away slightly and wrapped a loose hair around her ear, sending words through my mind to hers.

Jellybean interrupted our private moment and Bea found delight in the banter. I didn't care what either of them said; I was just happy to be with Bea and on our way home. So much had changed in the last year, so many things I would have never imagined, but my love for this Blood-Light was the one I was most proud of. When we got home, I would tell them all what happened in the last two months, but not here, and not now. Now I would make the most of us all being together—but we had one more to get.

Jellybean and I slipped into the Royal home undisturbed. I had assumed this was Tali's assistance. The halls were quiet and empty as we approached the door to Ashton's bedroom. I knocked, it opened, and Ashton's face said it all. A shower wasn't the only thing I needed. Worry flicked over his features as he raked his eyes down my body.

"Well you look good," I said, subtly acknowledging his unspoken expression. "Have a nice two-month stay at the Ritz-Carlton?" I remembered he enjoyed the Travel Channel and was hoping a little humor would lighten the mood.

He shook his head. "Two months? Where were you held?"

"The Holding Tank," I growled, hoping he wouldn't probe any further.

"For the whole two months?" he asked, his brow rising.

I nodded. I would tell Ashton too but, like Bea, not now, not here. It seemed to have appeased him for the moment as he looked at Jellybean. She gave him the shortened version as to where she had been as we fled through the halls and to the outside undetected. We boarded the needle and Bea immediately offered her story to Ashton as we soared through the city to the outskirts toward the wormhole leading back into the Hive. We hauled out of the vehicle and sprinted down the destroyed airstrip to our exit.

"I'm not going back," Sera said. She threw her arms around Bea and they hugged. The mutual affection clawed at my heart. I wasn't sure of the details, but I knew whatever peace they needed, they had gotten in the last two months. Sera released Bea and turned to Ashton. "Go on Ash, go home to Earth. Be the change Ferroeans need you to be."

Sera started to walk away, never meeting my gaze. Throwing words into my head, she said, *Saying good-bye to you would be too painful. I love you. I always will.* I grabbed her hand and gently pulled her back. I wouldn't let her leave this way. "Crede Mihi, Sera," I said out loud but finished in her mind. *The love I have for you in my source will be carried for the rest of my days. You will always be a part of me, and you will always have a place with us.* She turned and smiled. "Crede Mihi." And I knew that was her answer, that she believed me, and for now, that was enough.

I turned to my brother and waved him toward the wormhole. "Age before beauty!"

Ashton bowed and replied, "Oh no. I insist."

I grabbed Bea's hand and nodded to Jellybean to follow. Why not take her with us? It might get me some brownie points with Sammie, Mark, and Paul. And boy was I going to need them, especially with Sammie. I gazed into Beatrice's hazel eyes and said, "You ready to go home?"

Before she could answer, I pulled her through with me into the twirling array of light and motion. I closed my eyes, taking what felt like the first breath in two months, and embraced the darkness. A jolting feeling of tension slithered up my spine as the ethereal energy pulled and pushed my weightless body through space. The floor fell away, and the Ferroean world, the world I no longer recognized as home, was gone. I squeezed Bea's hand, reminding myself and her this was real. We were together and we could get through anything. She squeezed back, confirming my sentiments. Breathing intensified as we neared reentrance, as weight compressed my lungs. Within seconds, the wind died down, my feet found solid ground, and the heaviness lifted.

My eyes opened and I immediately growled.

"You are under arrest," a guard said, holding thermo daggers incorrectly across his chest.

"Who the hell are you?" My source amplified, sending shock waves under my skin, generating rippling veins along my forearms. We went from one false arrest to the next and I was exhausted. If I had to blow this house down with power, I would because I needed a good night's sleep and, as Bea mentioned, a shower.

"We are the Blood-Light Army. And we will use force if we have to. There is no clemency for what your people did to us and we will never forget."

Great. Even though we saved their asses, healed their lost humans, and came back to fight on their side, we were still the enemy.

Ashton appeared out of the wormhole. "What in hell's bells is going on here?"

"You will never believe this, brother," I growled.

I saw his blond hair and then his familiar blue eyes as the guards moved out of the way to let him through. My immediate reaction was the same as always, I wanted to take him by his collar and shove him up against a wall. But last time, Bea was mad at me for that, so I'd let him continue and see where this was headed. "Thanks to whatever you did in your world, you ruined ours," he spat.

"Chris, what did they do to you?" Bea moved forward to go to him, but I lugged her back, speaking into her mind. *Do not engage him. Something's not right.*

Chris smirked and started to speak but his voice was drowned out by my anger as I saw the pointed glare he threw in Bea's direction. It took all my self-control to not pummel him. She was shaking uncontrollably. *What's wrong? Why are you shaking? Talk to me!*

But before Bea could answer, Jellybean fell through the wormhole, rolling onto the cement floor, clinging to her chest. The pressure in the wormhole took some getting used to. Guess we should have told her about that and maybe added "feet first when landing." Beatrice lowered herself to the ground and helped Jellybean sit upright, coaching her to take in oxygen.

"Where are we?" Jellybean wheezed.

Chris's hands crossed over his chest, the hilts of his thermo daggers resting under his biceps. "Welcome to The Reprisal."

To be continued...

DANA CLAIRE'S

The Blood-Light Trilogy

The Connection

The Awakening

The Reprisal COMING SOON.....

Look for Dana Claire's new novel - Available Now!

The Reclaimed Kingdom

ACKNOWLEDGMENT

Acknowledgment

First, I'd like to thank my father. Ever since *The Connection* came out Thanksgiving of 2020, he's been hounding me for the sequel to *The Blood-Light Trilogy*. This book took me less than two months to write primarily because of my father's persistence. Dad, you are hands down my biggest inspiration. You've introduced me to a love of action and adventure and have been a major influence in my writing. A special thank you must ALWAYS go out to my cover designer, my co-pilot, and my younger but wiser cousin, Erin Foster. Does this cover rock or what? We crushed it! Over the years you have supported all my harebrained ideas, stayed up way passed our bedtimes to collaborate, and shared your honest opinions to make me a better writer and marketer. I am so lucky to have you in my life and get to work by your side. Kristen Roberts, my diamond, my rock, my writing soulmate, my everything editor. You're the best book friend a girl can have. Thank you for all the calls and emails helping me fix plot holes, background scenery, and telling me when I've gone astray. Your collaboration, wisdom, and advice are priceless. You make a lonely art, not lonely at all.

A BIG thank you to all the beta readers and ARC reviewers. Having your enthusiasm, motivating words, and kindness has made this book even more special. I am profoundly grateful for your encouragement, support, and love for Cash, Bea, Ashton, and the gang. They say thank you as well.

And lastly, the biggest thanks to my husband, Jason Michael. I know I shhh you more than you'd like when I'm in the writing zone but having you by my side while I type is the greatest gift as an author you could give me. I love looking over at you playing *Call of Duty* and smiling. Thank you for ignoring the light from my kindle when I'm reading at 2:00am while you sleep. Thank you for loving me for exactly who I am. Thank you for being my biggest cheerleader and number one fan. You and I will always be the best love story of all. Always and forever...

Author Dana Claire

Author Dana Claire believes that the beauty of reading is that one can live a hundred lives within the stories of books. A shared dream of hers and her mother's, she promised her dying mother that she would become a published author and that dream has been realized. For more information about Dana Claire, please visit her website danaclairebooks.com